For Your Love

A Blessings Novel

Beverly Jenkins

CENTER POINT LARGE PRINT
THORNDIKE, MAINE

This Center Point Large Print edition is published
in the year 2015 by arrangement with William Morrow,
an imprint of HarperCollins Publishers.

This book is a work of fiction. The characters, incidents, and dialogue are drawn from the author's imagination and are not to be construed as real. Any resemblance to actual events or persons, living or dead, is entirely coincidental.

The text of this Large Print edition is unabridged.
In other aspects, this book may vary
from the original edition.
Printed in the United States of America
on permanent paper.
Set in 16-point Times New Roman type.

ISBN: 978-1-62899-693-7

Library of Congress Cataloging-in-Publication Data

Jenkins, Beverly, 1951–
For your love : a blessings novel / Beverly Jenkins. —
Center Point Large Print edition.
pages cm
Summary: "Beverly Jenkins returns to Henry Adams, Kansas—an unforgettable place that anyone would want to call home—with a story of family, friends, and the powerful forces from our past that can irrevocably shape our future"—Provided by publisher.
ISBN 978-1-62899-693-7 (library binding : alk. paper)
1. City and town life—Kansas—Fiction.
2. African Americans—Fiction.
3. Large type books. 4. Domestic fiction.
I. Title.
PS3560.E4795F67 2015b
813′.54—dc23

2015020461

To all the mothers
and their sons

Bing & Clay Farm
PROPERTY CONDEMNED
Hotel
Clark Homestead
Riley & Genevieve
Main Street
Power Plant
Church
Studio
Henry Adams
B. Brown
Trent's Old Place

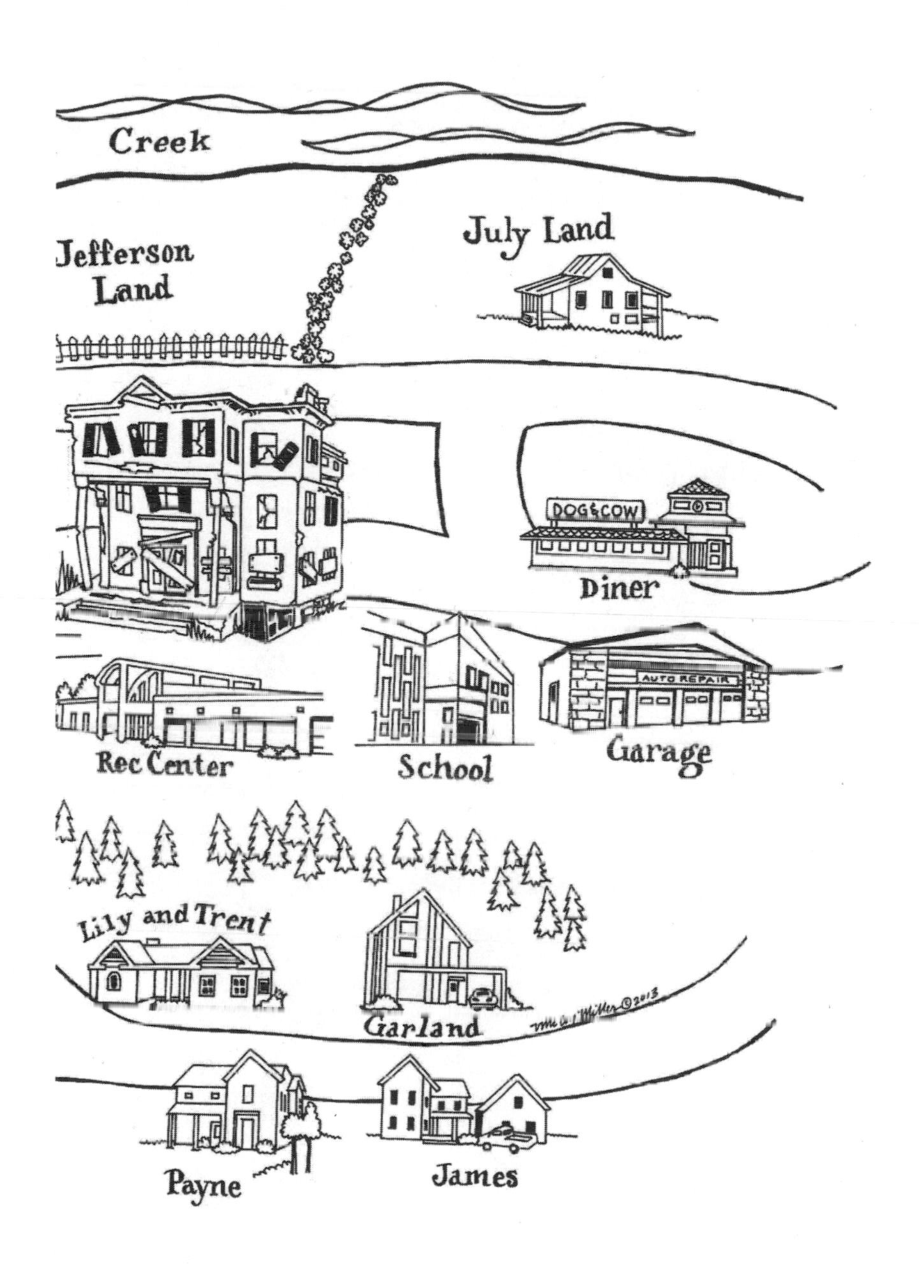
Creek
July Land
Jefferson Land
DOG&COW
Diner
AUTO REPAIR
Rec Center
School
Garage
Lily and Trent
Garland
Payne
James

Prologue

Rita Lynn Babcock had a good life. At the age of sixty-two she had no health issues; her husband, Paul, a cardiac surgeon, still loved her madly; and their daughter, Val, was founding partner of an eponymous law firm. Rita was thankful for her blessings, but at the moment her heart was heavy. Two days ago she'd buried her mother, Ida Merchant. Except for an indiscrction Rita had committed at the age of seventeen, they'd never had reason to share a cross word. Now Rita Lynn and Paul were meeting with their lawyer in his office to discuss Ida's will.

"Please, have a seat."

The lawyer, Dexter West, was an old college friend of Paul's. He took a moment to look through the stack of papers before him, as if to make sure all was in order. The estate wasn't large. Ida hadn't been wealthy by any means, but she'd been well loved and, until her stroke eighteen months ago, maintained her own home and finances.

With Dexter's guidance, Rita and Paul made the final arrangements for Ida's earthly possessions, from her house to the ten-year-old sky-blue Toyota she'd lovingly called Gladys. Her extensive cache of African-American history books was donated to the local library, and all the money left in her bank account after her bills were paid would be going to True Saints AME, the church she'd worshipped in and loved for over half a century. As executrix, Rita affixed her signature to each document Dexter slid her way, and when they were all done, she put her fingertips to the corners of her teary eyes to staunch the flow.

Paul gave her shoulder a tender squeeze and said softly, "It's okay, babe." Five years ago they'd buried his beloved mom, so he understood her grief.

"There's one more thing," Dexter said gently. He handed her a sealed envelope. "Your mother gave this to me a few years back. She asked me to hold on to it until her passing."

Rita paused. "What is it?"

"You should read it."

His face told her nothing, but she had a strong sense of foreboding. She looked to Paul and received a reassuring nod. The letter was one page and penned in her mother's strong handwriting. She read the beginning silently, but by the midpoint her eyes had widened. She whispered in a shocked and broken voice, "No!" The further she read, the louder her "No!" echoed, until she was screaming the denial again and again from the depths of her broken heart.

Chapter 1

Hearing the high-pitched peals of female laughter coming from inside the new addition he'd built for his wife, Lily, Trent July smiled. She and the ladies of the Henry Adams Ladies Auxiliary were celebrating the room's grand opening. He'd been promising that she'd have her own space for some time. Being the only female in the family, she needed someplace to escape all the testosterone generated by him and their sons— fourteen-year-old Amari and twelve-year old Devon. He was glad she was enjoying it.

"They're having way too much fun in there," Amari announced, entering the living room and dropping down onto the couch beside Trent, who was watching the NFL game between the Indianapolis Colts and the home team, the Kansas City Chiefs.

Trent chuckled softly. "Yes, they are."

Trent loved his oldest son. He'd come to him as an eleven-year-old foster child—a pint-size car thief extraordinaire, filled with swag, street smarts, and a talent for asking a million questions. Since finalizing his adoption two years ago, Trent had watched Amari grow into an exceptional young man. Yes, there'd been instances when Trent had to lay down the law, like the time

Amari and his friends were caught surfing the Internet in places they had no business being, but such was the life of a parent. All in all, Amari July was a good kid with a big heart. "What's your brother doing?" Trent asked.

Amari shrugged.

As if on cue, Devon entered. "Dad, can I go in and see what Mom's doing?"

"No, sorry."

"Why not?"

Trent loved Devon too, but the boy was at that trying stage between child and teen. "Because you weren't invited."

"It'll just be for a minute. I have something I want to ask her."

"No, Dev, but you're welcome to ask me. What's the question?" Trent assumed Devon wanted to be nosy, but he was willing to give his son the benefit of the doubt.

"Um, I wanted to know what we're having for dinner."

Amari sighed and shook his head at his brother's grasping-at-straws answer, but Trent kept his voice kind. "The three of us are going to the Dog for dinner." The Dog—real name, the Dog and Cow—was the local diner owned by Trent's father, Malachi July, and was the social hub of the community. "Do you want to watch the game with us until then?"

Devon quietly turned down the offer. "No,

thank you. I'll just go back to my room."

"Okay. I'll call you when we're ready to go."

Devon nodded and left.

Watching him exit, Amari drawled, "I still think we should trade him for a draft pick."

The two boys were sometimes like oil and water, but even when things got hairy, Amari put up with his younger brother because Amari was all about family. Before Trent and Lily married last year, Devon had been Lily's foster son. Back then, all Devon wanted in life was to be the town preacher. Reality made him reset that goal, and now he was having difficulty just being a kid. His new mission in life seemed to be getting on everyone's last nerve. Even Zoey Garland, Devon's former BFF, had grown so tired of his behavior that she'd given him two serious beatdowns recently just to make her point. Reverend Paula, the town's priest and certified child psychologist, was meeting with him a few days a week to help him work out his issues. Trent and Lily remained hopeful. Even though he'd been spoiled rotten by his maternal grandmother, Devon was loving, talented, and charismatic.

"Do you ever think about your mom, Dad?"

The question caught Trent off guard, but he answered truthfully, "Every now and then." Trent's parents were teens when he was conceived, and according to what he'd been told by Malachi, his mother's family had moved away once the pregnancy became known. After Trent's birth, his maternal grandmother brought him back to town, handed him over to his paternal grandmother, Tamar, like someone returning shoes to a store, and promptly drove away. The Julys hadn't heard a word from them since. "Have you been thinking about yours?"

"Yeah. After Brain's bio mom came for Thanksgiving, they've been e-mailing each other every day. Hard not to be jealous when mine wants nothing to do with me."

Preston "Brain" Payne was Amari's BFF and another of the adopted kids in the small town of Henry Adams, Kansas. Preston's biological mother, NASA scientist Dr. Margaret Winthrop, had visited him and his adoptive parents, Barrett and Sheila Payne, for the first time during the holidays. As a result, Brain was on cloud nine. By contrast, Amari's biological mother had made it clear that she wanted no contact with her son, and her adamant stance weighed heavily on the boy's gawky teenage shoulders. Considering Trent's own situation, it was a weight they shared. "Maybe she'll change her mind," Trent said, "but in the meantime, all you can do is go on with your life." Just as he'd done, even though to this day he wondered why his mother had never sent him so much as a postcard.

On the TV the Colts quarterback threw a fifty-yard pass to the end zone to score on the home-team Chiefs. The disappointment caused Trent and Amari to shake their heads sadly.

As the Colts celebrated, Amari said, “I know you’re right, Dad, but it’s really hard. I don’t want to make it sound like I don’t appreciate Ms. Lily as my mom. I mean, she’s the kind I used to dream about in foster care—but . . .”

“You’d like ties to your bio mom.”

“Yeah, I would.”

“Understandable. I feel the same way.”

“Deep down inside, I’m really happy for Brain, but it’s still rough.” Amari glanced over. “You’re an awesome dad, by the way.”

Trent smiled.

The Chiefs fumbled the kickoff, and Amari cracked, “Too bad we don’t have an awesome NFL team.”

“Keeping hope alive for the second half.”

“Yeah, right.”

It was the first week of December. Four inches of snow had fallen overnight, and according to the dashboard gauge on Trent’s truck, the temperature outside was a balmy fifteen degrees. As he drove down Henry Adams’s main street to the Dog with his sons, not even the winter weather kept him from marveling at the changes to the landscape brought about by the largesse of town owner Bernadine Brown. The open stretches of land that had once been strewn with the crumbling remains of the town’s nineteenth-century past now held a new recreation center, school, and church. The old dirt roads were paved. Asphalt parking lots had been added, along with cement sidewalks and towering solar streetlights. Other improvements were in the planning stages, and Trent couldn't be more pleased by the town's rebirth. His family, residents since the nineteenth century, had seen it rise over the years to become a model for African-American communities nationwide. But by the twenty-first century, Henry Adams had fallen so low that, as mayor, he was forced to offer it for sale on eBay. That's when Bernadine Brown, armed with a multimillion-dollar divorce settlement, rode to the rescue like a one-woman battalion of the famed Tenth Cavalry. She'd even footed the bill for rehabbing the Dog, turning what was once a well-loved but dilapidated eyesore into a glistening eatery complete with brand-new red leather booths, smooth-topped tables, a state-of-the-art kitchen, and Wi-Fi.

Inside, old-school music played on the fancy red jukebox, as always. The mounted flat-screen TVs were tuned to the day's football games, and the interior was filled with the familiar faces of those Trent had grown up with: Rochelle "Rocky" Dancer, the diner's manager and Henry Adams's resident bombshell; Clay Dobbs, his godfather and his dad's best friend; and Bing Shepard, the crusty old World War II vet now living with Clay after the death of his wife. Both men had played significant roles in Trent's life, growing up.

His dad, Malachi, walked over to greet them. "Well, if it isn't my favorite son and grandsons."

"We're your only son and grandsons," Trent countered, which made the boys grin. Father and son ribbed each other constantly, a testament to their strong bond.

"You overeducated engineers always have to point out the obvious," Mal groused. "Go on and get a seat. Your booth in the back's waiting on you."

After pausing a few times to speak to friends, Trent and his sons took seats in their favorite booth. Crystal Chambers-Brown, Bernadine's seventeen-year-old daughter and the resident big sister of the town's kids, came over to take their order. "Hey, guys. Your usual burgers and fries?"

"Yes, ma'am," Trent told her. While she wrote down the order, he asked, "When are your friends coming from Dallas?"

"Tomorrow morning. Mom's going to let me miss school so I can ride with her to the airport. I'm so excited."

"I'm looking forward to meeting them. Hope they'll like living here."

"What's not to like?" she asked. "We live in the middle of nowhere—no fast food, no clubs, no real music on the radio. It's paradise." She left them to go put their orders in.

Trent looked to Amari. "Was she being sarcastic?"

The boy shrugged. "Who knows? With her it's hard to tell, but I do know that after running away and having to come back to 'paradise' after only a few days, with her tail between her legs, she's figured out Dorothy got it right: there's no place like home."

Trent concurred. After earning his master's degree in engineering from Stanford, he'd taken a job with a multinational architectural firm in LA and for ten years immersed himself in big-city living. Eventually, wearied by the breakneck pace, the sometimes cutthroat nature of the people, and two failed marriages, he'd returned, never to leave again. He glanced Devon's way and saw him staring across the room at his former best friend Zoey, sitting with her dad, town pediatrician Reginald Garland, and eleven-year-old Wyatt Dahl. Wyatt and his grandmother Gemma were the town's newest residents, and he and Zoey had become inseparable in the short time since the Dahls' arrival. Everyone in town was well aware of Devon's long-running feud with Miss Miami, as Zoey was affectionately called, and although Devon wouldn't admit it, Trent knew he missed calling her friend. "You want to go over and say hi to Zoey and Wyatt?"

"No," Devon replied, as if Trent had just asked him to drink motor oil.

Amari shook his head but kept his opinion to himself.

Trent didn't press, but the irritation in Devon's eyes was mixed with unspoken longing and a deep sadness. Later in the week, they'd be meeting as a family with Reverend Paula. He hoped the rift with Zoey would be one of the topics on the agenda.

A short while later Crystal returned with their meals. Devon said grace, and they dug in.

When Trent and the boys returned home, all the ladies' vehicles were gone, and the interior was quiet. They found Lily in the kitchen, feeding the dishwasher.

"Hey, baby," he said affectionately. "Did you and your girls have a good time?"

Her smile said it all. "Yes, we did. No one wanted to go home. How was your afternoon?" Her eyes brushed over her sons.

"The Chiefs lost," Amari said.

"We saw Zoey and Wyatt," Devon said.

"Did you wave?" Lily asked.

He shook his head.

"Did you want to?" she pressed gently.

"She doesn't want to be friends with me, so I don't want to be friends with her."

"She might be waiting for you to make the first move, Devon."

But her son wasn't buying it. "She's the one

who started it, so she should make the first move."

Apparently Amari wasn't buying it, either. "No. You were the one who started it." Devon tensed, but Amari ignored him and asked, "Is it okay if I go hang out at Brain's for a little while and watch the Sunday night game?"

Devon's eyes shot daggers.

Trent asked, "What's wrong, Devon?"

"Nobody ever agrees with me."

"That's because you're always wrong," Amari pointed out.

"Amari," Trent cautioned.

"Well, he is." Under Trent's mild look of censure, Amari amended his answer. "Okay, maybe not all the time, but for sure ninety-nine point nine percent of the time. So, can I go?"

"The colonel's out of town, but if Mrs. Payne's okay with it, you can stay until halftime." Trent sent Amari a speaking look.

Amari sighed loudly before asking his brother, "Do you want to go?"

Trent and Lily had been encouraging Amari to include Devon in some of his activities, with the hope it might help Devon chill out. They knew Amari would rather walk to Topeka through the snow with bare feet, but he never overtly balked.

"No. I'm going up to my room to watch some videos."

"Okay. Be back at the half." Amari left to get his coat, and Devon headed for his bedroom upstairs.

Once both boys were gone and Trent was alone with his wife, he draped his arms around her waist and looked down into her dark eyes. To him she was still as beautiful as she'd been when they were in high school together. "This parenting business is more than a notion."

"No kidding."

"Have I kissed you today, Mrs. July?"

She made a point of thinking. "Hmm. I don't remember, so you should probably get busy."

Chuckling softly, he did as requested. When they finally came up for air, she whispered, "Very nice."

"Do you want help cleaning up?"

"Men who help with housework are considered very sexy."

"Really?"

"Yes, and later, after the knuckleheads are snuggled in their beds, I'll show you just how much."

"I like the sound of that."

She waggled her eyebrows. "Thought you might."

It took only a short while to remove all the spent plastic cups and plates and reposition the furniture. As they worked, Trent watched the way she moved, the flow of her walk, and savored the way his heart rate accelerated like a teenage boy's each time she glanced his way and smiled. Circumstances tore them apart after high school, but now after nearly two decades they'd settled their differences and were man and wife. He loved her as much as he did breathing. When his first two marriages crashed and burned, he'd thought his life would never hold happiness again, but his Lily Flower brought all that and more. He felt blessed.

When they had the space cleaned to their satisfaction, Lily walked over and circled her arms around his waist. "Have I thanked you for my beautiful room?"

Mimicking her, he paused for a moment to think. "Hmm. Not today, so tonight, I'll be looking for a little extra in my reward package."

"I think that can be arranged."

"You know that silky little black number you brought back from Spain?"

Mischief shone in her eyes. "Yes."

"I want my reward package wrapped in that."

Laughing, she nestled against him. "You got it."

Chapter 2

Trent's first love was cars. Were it left up to him, he'd spend his days and nights restoring them, sanding and painting the bodies and then stepping back to admire the finished product. Instead he spent his days doing something he didn't really care for—being mayor. Riley Curry used to be mayor of Henry Adams, but folks got so tired of his boasting and shenanigans that they wanted him out. When word got around about his plan to have Henry Adams annexed by the neighboring town of Franklin and that he was in line for a sizable kickback, clamors for his head rose high enough to be heard on the moon. There was one problem, though—no one wanted the job. Not Clay Dobbs or Bing Shepard or Malachi. Back in the nineteenth century, Olivia July, wife of the infamous train robber Neil July, had been mayor for many years, but even Trent's grandmother Tamar eschewed following in her ancestor's footsteps and running for the office. For the first time in living memory, she deemed herself too old. Trent didn't believe a word of it. As the deadline to be added to the ballot neared, people began approaching him about taking the job. Some touted his advanced degree as a positive factor, while others pointed to the years he'd lived in LA. Why that made a difference, he still didn't understand. His former teacher Marie Jefferson encouraged him to run, as did many of the local farmers and ranchers. Even Will Dalton, the county sheriff and an old friend, suggested he throw his hat in the ring. It got to the point where everywhere he went, someone was telling him what a great mayor he'd make, but it was Tamar who finally sealed the deal. She'd raised him, and he loved her with each beat of his heart. She was a tough, no-nonsense kind of woman and not above hitting below the belt to make a point. In this instance, she sat him down and together they looked at the old photo albums chronicling Henry Adams's historic past—from the ones dedicated to the August First parades to others holding tintypes of Olivia, her outlaw husband Neil, and other members of the family. Tamar talked to him about the Great Exodus of 1879, the migration that brought African Americans to Kansas, and all the Dusters, as they called themselves, endured to found the town and secure its future. He then got a lecture on legacy and honor and what the ancestral Julys like Mayor Olivia were owed by Julys like himself. The guilt was laid on so thickly and with such weight, all he could do was surrender because he knew she was right.

So, he ran, and won. Riley received only two votes—the one he'd cast for himself, and the other from his wife, Genevieve. Were the vote taken today, Genevieve would rather set her hair on fire than vote for her now ex-husband and by association his nasty pet hog, Cletus.

It was Trent's hope that when the next election came up in two years, he could turn the reins over to someone else and spend the majority of his time raising his sons and making love to his beautiful wife. But for the moment, he was still mayor. As he turned on the lights in his plush office and took a seat at his desk to begin his

Monday, he knew he could be in a far less cushy place of employment, working with people he hated instead of his wife and her generous boss, Bernadine, so with his blessings in mind, he booted up his laptop.

Twenty-four hours ago, Bobby Douglas had been eating dinner alone in the small kitchen of the Dallas apartment he shared with his girl, Kelly "Kiki" Page, and their eleven-month-old twins, Tiara and Bobby Jr. She and the kids were out with his mom, which gave him the opportunity to ponder their decision to move to Henry Adams, Kansas. The offer to relocate had come from a lady neither he nor Kiki had ever met, Ms. Bernadine Brown, the mother of Kiki's best friend, Crystal. It all began a few months ago, when Crystal unexpectedly showed up at their door, announcing she'd run away from her Kansas home and was moving back to Dallas to start over. The three of them had known each other since middle school, but he and Kiki hadn't seen Crystal in three years and had no idea she'd been adopted and was living in Kansas. Her plans for life in Dallas had quickly gone awry, however, and she wound up returning home. A few weeks later, she called to relay her mother's invitation.

The life he and Kiki shared was a paycheck-to-paycheck existence rooted in food stamps, state aid, and struggle. The idea of trading it in for what

Ms. Brown assured them over the phone would be a much better one seemed to be a no-brainer, especially since he'd been promised a job and housing too, but he was concerned.

He and Kiki had been together since middle school. She was from a single-parent home, and he'd grown up in foster care, aging out a year ago when he turned eighteen. He'd spent his high school years gang-affiliated and tatted up. The moment the twins were born, he took the intense beating required for getting out and turned his eyes to the future. Working two jobs and getting his GED on the side left him exhausted and still broke. Kiki never complained. They both wanted their babies to have more, but could that happen in a place he'd never seen, surrounded by people he knew nothing about and who, more importantly, knew nothing about him? Having been born, bred, and raised in Dallas, he knew how to deal there. He didn't know a thing about living in a small town, and what he'd seen on the television news programs left him with the impression that the people who lived in them seemed pretty rigid in their thinking. Would he be profiled and pulled over by the cops because of his color and tats? Would he be viewed with suspicion for being a former banger? Kiki had dropped out of high school after getting pregnant. Although she wanted to finish her education, she hadn't had time because of their children. Would that be held against her?

In truth, his worries were moot. He'd already given his notice to the owner of the car dealership where he was employed as a full-time valet, and to the supervisor at his weekend job parking cars at one of the downtown hotels. Ms. Brown would be sending her personal jet for them in the morning. The only option was to go forward. The deal was done.

So he had finished his meal and washed up his dishes. To keep himself busy while he waited for Kiki and the babies to come home, he packed the rest of his clothes into the beat-up old suitcase he'd borrowed from his mom and fought to convince himself that this whole Henry Adams thing would work out for the best.

Now Bobby and Kiki entered the small airport in Hays and spotted Crystal right off. She and Kiki screamed simultaneously and flew into a hug. A chuckling Bobby stood holding both babies in their carriers, looking into the kind brown eyes of a tall, curvy woman wearing a killer fur coat.

"Hi. I'm Bernadine, Crys's mom. Welcome."

"Thanks. I'm Bobby Douglas. This is Tiara and Bobby Jr."

She leaned down to get a better look at the babies staring up at her. "Aww. They're cuties. Hi, little ones. You've no idea how anxious everyone in town is to meet you. They're planning to spoil you rotten."

Seeing his bright-eyed children's responding smiles, Bobby replied, "Not too rotten, I hope?" He liked Ms. Brown. For a woman rolling in money, she had a nice easy way about her—not stuck up at all, even though he was still trying to wrap his brain around her owning a jet.

"How old are they?"

"They'll be a year in January. Thanks for sending us snowsuits for them."

The teary Kiki and Crystal finally parted. "Kiki, this is my mom, Bernadine Brown. Mom, this is Kelly Page, but everybody calls her Kiki."

"Pleased to meet you, Kiki. Welcome."

Kiki wiped her eyes. "Thank you. Same here, and thanks for the flight. Your jet is—there are no words."

"Glad you enjoyed it. I've heard lots of good things about both of you. Thanks for helping Crys out while she was in Dallas."

"No problem. It's what friends do. And thank you so much for this invitation. Right, Bobby?"

"Exactly. It means a lot."

"Let's head to the car."

The shiny black town car came with a driver—a White guy named Nathan Nelson. "Welcome to Kansas," he said with the same easy manner Ms. Brown exuded. The weather was freezing, and although Bobby was anxious to get out of the wind, he wasn't sure whether he was supposed to help the driver load their one suitcase into the trunk or not. Nathan solved the issue by gently placing his hand on the handle. "I'll take this. You go ahead and get in before you freeze. The babies and their seats should fit fine."

Riding in Ms. Brown's private jet had been a new experience for Bobby. Making himself comfortable in the back of a luxury vehicle was also new. As he shivered, wishing for a thicker coat, he hoped it didn't show.

Kiki asked, "Is it always this cold?"

Crystal laughed. "This isn't even real winter. Wait until January."

Once they were underway, Crys and Kiki chatted away while Bobby spent most of his time marveling at the snow-covered countryside and taking discreet glances at their benefactress. He caught her checking him out just as discreetly and wondered what she might be thinking. In an effort to make a good first impression, he'd worn his only suit—a black one usually reserved for funerals—and a tie. Beneath his inadequate jacket, his tats peeked above the collar of his threadbare blue dress shirt. He was certain Crystal had explained to her mom that he no longer did the banging, but he hoped she wasn't alarmed by the sight of his extensive ink.

"So, Bobby," Ms. Brown said. "Crys told me you enjoy working on cars."

"Yes, ma'am."

"Then you and Trent July, our mayor, should

get along well. He owns the local garage and restores old cars."

"Looking forward to meeting him." Bobby was thankful for the two years he'd worked at the car dealership. As a lowly valet, his interactions with the customers had been minimal, but he'd learned to speak properly and to handle chitchat. Before he was hired, his speech had been strictly street; he doubted the people in Crystal's town rolled that way.

Crystal was telling Kiki where they'd be living. "There's a trailer on Tamar's land that Mom is going to put you in. You'll love it, and Tamar. Although she can be tough sometimes."

"Who's Tamar?" Kiki asked.

"Our matriarch," Ms. Brown explained. "I may own the town, but she runs it. She's in her late eighties. Her family has been in Kansas since the 1800s. She's also Trent's grandmother."

Bobby wondered what this trailer looked like. All the ones he'd ever seen were broken-down, rusted hulks. He was also concerned about living near such an old lady. They hadn't come all this way to be personal-care aides, had they? "What kind of work's available, Ms. Brown?"

"Depends on what you'd like to do. If you want to work on cars, I'm sure Trent has some contacts in the area. Any other interests?"

"I'd eventually like to own my own detailing business."

"Trent will be the person to talk to about that, too."

The answer satisfied him. He hoped this Trent July wasn't the hassling type, though. If he was going to work someplace, Bobby wanted to get along with the man in charge. He also hoped that being mayor didn't mean July was a jerk. If that turned out to be the case, he'd just have to deal with it. To provide for his family, he needed a job, and at this stage of the game he couldn't afford to let a boss's messed-up personality interfere with that.

"Did you eat on the plane?" Ms. Brown asked.

Kiki shook her head. "No, ma'am. We were too excited. Bobby and I have never flown before."

"There's a bunch of food waiting at your new place," Crystal said.

Ms. Brown must've seen the confusion on Bobby's face. "Courtesy of the local women's group," she explained. "We thought you might want to just get here and relax. Everyone wants to meet you, but there's plenty of time for that after you get situated."

Bobby appreciated that. He wanted to check out where they were first before having to do a bunch of hand-shaking and smiling. The babies were getting fussy and starting to whimper. He figured they were tired of being strapped in the carriers. They didn't like them, and he couldn't blame them. "How much longer before we get there?"

"About thirty more minutes."

Kiki reached into her bag and took out two bottles. Both held water. The twins took the offerings in their chubby little hands, and as they began sucking on the nipples, they settled down.

Ms. Brown said, "Once they get out of those seats, they'll probably be a lot more comfortable."

Bobby noted her smile and the way she watched the twins. Maybe this would all work out after all—if they didn't freeze to death.

When they exited the highway onto a dirt road, Bobby saw more fenced, snow-covered fields. Some small houses were set back from the road, with a lone truck or two parked nearby, but there weren't any businesses in sight. None. Were it not for the houses, he'd think the area was totally unpopulated.

"Where are we?" Kiki asked, peering through her window. She sounded as confused as Bobby felt.

"Almost home," Crystal offered reassuringly.

"Your town's bigger, right?"

"Not really," Ms. Brown answered. "We have a subdivision and a few buildings on our main street, but the rest of the area's just like this."

Bobby sat back. *This* was where they'd be living? This desolate stretch of snow-covered nothingness? He and Kiki shared a look. He wished they were alone so they could talk, but for now, all they could do was wait and see what the rest of the day might bring.

A short while later they drove up a cleared driveway. Bobby saw an older home up ahead, but Nathan steered onto another dirt road. Bobby looked around. There were four trailers spread out over a large expanse of land. They stopped in front of one of the four.

"Here we are," Ms. Brown said.

Although the exterior was nicer than he'd been expecting, he worried about furniture and appliances and how he was going to afford them—all things he'd thought about when he and Kiki initially accepted Ms. Brown's invitation. He'd mentally buried the concerns beneath the excitement tied to moving. Now, the worries were back.

Nathan took their suitcase out of the trunk and handed it to Bobby with a smile. Shivering in the frosty air, they stood waiting while Ms. Brown unlocked the door, and then followed her inside.

Stunned, Bobby stared around. The interior was fully furnished. The walls were a creamy vanilla, the carpet a bit darker. The kitchen had what appeared to be all new stainless appliances.

"Oh, my goodness!" Kiki whispered. She looked both confused and amazed.

"Ms. Brown, I appreciate you bringing us out here," Bobby said. "But Kiki and I can't afford a place like this."

"Sure you can," she contradicted gently. "Rent's free for the first year, and my office will handle the utilities. So take off your coats, get the babies out of those seats and snowsuits, and let me give you the tour."

He met her eyes. He was sure she saw the emotion glistening in his, but she didn't call him out on it or belittle him. She simply said, "Welcome home."

After they'd left Bobby and Kiki at the trailer, Nathan drove Bernadine and Crystal back to town. Bernadine was admittedly impressed by the young couple. From what Crystal had initially told her about who they were and the struggles they were having, she'd been expecting less *polish,* for lack of a better word, but they were both well-mannered and polite. Kelly was about Crystal's size. Her skin was a few shades brighter and her face dusted with freckles. She'd been wearing a skirt, boots, and a red turtleneck faded by too many washings, but everything she had on was clean. Her hair was her own—no weave—and pulled back into a simple ponytail. Bobby had dark skin, and at his size could easily be playing linebacker for the Chiefs. She'd noted the suit. It wasn't new by any means, but the fact that he'd worn one at all said a lot about how he was approaching this new adventure. She found that pleasing. Going by what the foster kids experienced their first few months in town, the Dallas natives were in for some culture shock. She just hoped they didn't find it too overwhelming.

She glanced over at her daughter. "How do you think they'll do here?"

"I think they're going to do okay. They were really impressed with the trailer. It's a thousand times better than their old apartment back in Dallas."

While they were touring the fully furnished two-bedroom place, there'd been smiles and sheer awe on their faces. The Ladies Auxiliary had provided everything from new beds for the twins to a fully stocked pantry and refrigerator.

"Thanks so much for letting them come here."

"You're welcome. Giving them a helping hand was an easy decision."

"But you could've said no."

"True, but when you asked, I saw how serious you were, and how much it meant. I'm looking forward to getting to know them."

"Bobby seems a little uncomfortable, though. I don't think he's ever had anyone be nice to him like this."

"Possibly." She remembered how moved he'd appeared when he realized that the trailer was theirs rent-free. The emotion she'd seen in his eyes said a lot about him. "Considering what you told me about his past, I'm sure he hasn't, but he'll get used to it."

“I hope so. I don’t want them to go back without giving this place a chance.”

“Neither do I, so keep an eye on how they’re adjusting. They’ll probably be more comfortable confiding in you if they have a problem. If something comes up that you think I can help them with, let me know.”

“Okay.”

There was something else Bernadine had been wanting to talk with Crystal about, and she thought maybe now might be the time. Keeping her voice light, she asked, “So, how are you feeling about this whole college application process?”

She saw Nathan’s eyes catch hers in the mirror. She didn’t mind that he was listening. Like everyone else in town, he and his wife, Lou, and their baby, Ethan, were family.

Crystal shrugged. “Not being able to get into the places I want is kinda depressing.”

Crystal had come to Henry Adams as a streetwise, mouthy fourteen-year-old runaway, and Bernadine adopted her a year later. She’d be graduating in the spring, and because she was also an outstanding artist, she’d applied to some of the major East Coast art schools. They’d all sent letters of: *We regret to inform you . . .*

“My SAT scores suck.”

“Only because of all the school you missed when you lived in Dallas. Academically you have some catching up to do, but you can enroll in the community college, work your butt off for those two years, and go from there. Easily fixed."

"I guess," Crystal said gloomily. "When I was in Dallas, I didn't want to go to college. Now that I do, I can't get in."

"You'll get in—just maybe not right away. Is your triptych almost done?"

"Almost."

One of the museums in California was sponsoring a contest for high school artists, and Crystal had been working for over a year on the three-paneled project she planned to enter. First prize was scholarship money and the honor of having her work hung in the museum. When Crystal ran away from home this past fall, Bernadine had been afraid she'd turn her back on her art, along with everything else she'd gained since coming to Kansas. But now she was on track again in school, art, and life.

"Submissions begin in January, right?"

"Yes, and when I win, I can tell all the schools that turned me down to KMA."

Nathan's smile was caught by the mirror.

"Not sure that's the mature way to respond," Bernadine pointed out. "But winning might make those schools give you a second look."

"Maybe."

"Either way your future is bright, Crys. Real bright. Just keep doing your best."

“Thanks, Mom. I’m trying.”

“I know you are, and that’s all anyone can ask.”

Since it was only a little past noon, Nathan dropped Crystal off at school before driving Bernadine to the low-slung red architectural wonder called the Power Plant. It was named that not due to a connection to utilities but because Bernadine, Trent, and Lily, who was chief procurement officer and Bernadine’s right hand, ran the town’s operations from their offices inside.

“Thanks, Nathan,” Bernadine said as he opened the car door and gave her a guiding hand. “Have a great rest of the day.”

“You, too, Ms. Brown.”

She hurried to the door to escape the cold wind, and he drove away. She’d just hung up her fur inside when a knock on her open door made her turn. It was Trent July. “Hey, Mr. Mayor. Town still in one piece?”

“Far as I know. How’d it go?”

“It went well. Got them settled in, and they really liked the place. Bobby’s about the size of a Chiefs linebacker, and Kelly, or Kiki, as they call her, is a little bitty thing with freckles. Babies are precious. He says he likes working on cars. Wants to own a detailing shop down the road.”

“Good to have goals.”

“Yes, it is. They don’t have any wheels, though, so can you take them over to Anderson’s sometime tomorrow and see if he has something that’s reasonably priced? I'll pay." Anderson's was a used car dealership over in Franklin.

"Sure. I'd like to meet them. Do you think they'd mind if I swung by later?"

"Don't see why not. I'll check with them and see what's a good time."

"Good. Thanks. So what's your take on Bobby? Do you think he'll be okay here?"

"I do. He wore a suit, which impressed me." She told him about Bobby saying he couldn't afford the trailer, and his reaction when she explained the terms.

"So he's not here expecting a handout?"

"Crystal said he worked two jobs to take care of his family down in Dallas, so the answer is probably no. Former gang member notwithstanding, I think there's a fairly decent young man beneath all the ink."

"Ink? As in tats?"

"Yes. Not sure how extensive they are, but I could see them above the collar of his shirt." She watched him think on that.

"Interesting."

"I'm not sure how his background and the ink are going to play here, but he'll have my unconditional support until he shows me it's undeserved."

"Good thing Riley Curry's not around. I can just hear him screaming about the kid having been a gang member."

"Me, too." The former mayor was a narrow-minded, judgmental little twerp. When Bernadine first came to town, he was convinced her money came from ties to a drug cartel. "Crystal hasn't said anything about his family other than his mom, but I'm assuming he's not had a strong male presence in his life. Then again, I could be wrong."

"You, wrong? Never."

Trent's sense of humor was one of the many things Bernadine liked about him, along with his being the son of the man she loved.

"But even if you are, seeing how people live in small towns can be beneficial, and if you're not, there are enough men here to make up for that—at least for the future."

She agreed. The boys—Amari, Preston, Devon, and new arrival Wyatt—would go through life strengthened by lessons learned from men like Trent. Eli, the teenage son of the town's teacher, Jack James, had always had his dad, but he too would step into an adulthood made stronger by associating with Henry Adams's males. "So now your turn. What's going on in that engineer's head of yours? How do you feel about them moving here?"

"We did invite them, so I'm going into my first visit with an open mind."

Bernadine smiled. "That's all I ask."

Chapter 3

Once the twins were settled in their new cribs for their afternoon nap, Bobby and Kiki sat together on the couch.

"Been an amazing day so far," she said.

"I know."

"So how are you feeling? Still worried?"

He gave her a smile. "Who said I was worried?" Her insight always surprised him. She knew him better than he knew himself sometimes.

"Call it woman's intuition. You haven't said anything out loud, but I know you, Bobby."

Rather than deny the truth, he offered, "Not sure how I'm feeling. Never been in a situation like this. I keep thinking something's going to happen and make everything disappear."

"Same here. We didn't see a lot of city stuff on the way in. No movie theaters, no traffic, no buildings—no malls, no nothing. Now I get why Crystal ran away. I still think she was out of her damned mind, though." She glanced slowly around the room. "Do you think we would've ever been able to get such a nice place on our own?"

"Maybe in ten years, but definitely not overnight like this. The street in me keeps thinking there's a catch. This place looks like somewhere TV White people would live."

Amusement in her eyes, Kiki nodded. "But instead, it's us."

She scooted closer, and he draped an arm over her shoulder. Since they'd made the decision to move, he'd been worried about so many things, from food to rent to furniture, but the moment they walked in, all that slid away. In the kitchen were top-of-the-line appliances. The dark wood cabinetry and drawers held utensils and dishes and silverware, glasses, pots, and pans, even kitchen towels. The pantry was fully stocked with everything from trash bags to pasta and oatmeal for the babies. When he pulled open the fridge door, the sight of all the food inside made him turn to Ms. Brown in shock. What kind of place was this, where they stocked a fridge for people they didn't know? And then there was the bedroom for the twins. The walls were a pale yellow, the floor a nice clean carpet, a vivid contrast to the dirty, stained one back in Dallas, and there were nice drapes on the windows. He'd watched Kiki run her hands reverently over the wooden frames of the two new baby beds and, like him, take in the books and toys on the white wood built-ins. There was even a big upholstered rocker in the corner, where she'd sat down and rocked and wiped at the tears wetting her cheeks.

Her soft voice broke his reverie, pulling him back to the present. "Living here is going to be good for the twins and for us."

"I know, but I feel out of place—way out of place."

"I do too, but let's roll with it and see where it takes us. You're not thinking about us going back to Dallas already, are you?"

Her eyes were questioning, and he sought to reassure her. "I wouldn't do that to you, baby. I—I just don't know if this is right for us yet, that's all." He didn't know how to handle a life that didn't involve struggle.

"How about we give it some time, and if it's not working, we'll go back. Deal?"

"Deal." That she would agree to leave knowing how much moving here meant to her reminded him why she was the best thing that ever happened to him. He pulled her closer and placed a kiss on her forehead. "Thanks for hanging with me all these years."

"Who else was going to put up with your butt?" she laughed, then turned serious. "I love you, Robert Douglas Sr."

He slowly traced her cheek. "You're my world, girl. Believe it." And because it was the truth, he wanted to make this work.

A knock at the door grabbed their attention. Out of habit, Bobby went to the window and pulled the drape aside just enough to see. A large black pickup was parked out front, but the driver was nowhere to be seen. He walked to the door. "Who is it?"

"Trent July," a male voice called back.

He opened up. July was a few inches taller, lean and wearing a black cowboy hat and a partially zipped black parka, with a black turtleneck beneath. His legs showed worn jeans, and his feet were in well-seasoned tan work boots.

"I'm Bobby Douglas," Bobby said guardedly. "Nice to meet you." They shook hands as Trent entered, and Bobby closed the door behind him. "That's my girl, Kelly Page."

"Nice to meet you, Mr. July."

He removed the hat. "Same here, but call me Trent. Welcome to Kansas—both of you."

"Thanks." She rose from the sofa. "I'm going to check on the babies."

With her departure Bobby felt an awkward silence rise. "Have a seat," he invited, gesturing.

July removed his coat and complied. "Ms. Brown told me you said this would be a good time to stop by. I'm not interrupting, am I?"

"No. You're fine."

"Just wanted to come over for a minute to introduce myself and make sure you and the family are settling in."

"We are. Just trying to get used to the place."

"Bernadine show you the mechanicals?"

Bobby paused.

"The furnace. Hot water heater."

"Oh. Yes, she showed me all that. Just never heard them called that before." Out of habit,

Bobby sized him up. July wouldn't be somebody he'd've targeted back in his gang days. Even relaxed, the man exuded a quiet power that let you know he'd not be easy prey. The eyes meeting his were direct—frank. Bobby wondered how many people in July's past had been fooled by the seemingly easygoing exterior.

"Ms. Brown wants me to help you find a vehicle as soon as we can work out a time. Do you have time to go looking in the morning?"

"I—don't have money for a car."

"Understood, but it's part of your welcome package. None of us want you and your family cooped up in the house all winter."

Bobby paused and stared. "She's giving us a car, too?"

"Yeah."

"Where's she getting all this money?"

"Huge divorce settlement and wise investing. We were blown away when she bought our town a few years back, too."

"She owns the whole town?"

"Yes." July told the story of how Bernadine saved Henry Adams, and all that had transpired in the years since. "She's an incredible lady," he wound up. "She's got a huge heart."

"I guess."

"And so you'll know, turning down the car is not an option. Knowing her, she'll have it ordered and driven out here anyway, so save her the trouble, and let's go look at something. It won't be new, but it'll run and last you until you can get on your feet."

"I don't believe this."

"None of us believed she was for real at first, either. Even now, her generosity still throws us a curve sometimes. When she first arrived, we all walked around looking as stunned as you do now."

Bobby smiled. "This is damn crazy."

"Tell me about it. The lady is one of a kind."

"So where do we go to find a car?"

"There's a dealership in Franklin, the next town over."

Kiki came out of the back, and Bobby asked, "Still asleep?"

She nodded.

"Ms. Brown is giving us a car," he informed her.

"What?"

"Yeah, Trent and I are going to go look for one in the morning."

July told her, "You and the babies are welcome to come along, too, if you want."

"No, I think we'll just chill here. I don't want them going out in the cold too much at first—none of us are used to this weather. What kind of car?" She still seemed confused.

"Something suitable that runs well," Bobby said.

There was another knock on the door and he

wondered how this could be. As he'd done earlier, he went to the window. "Do you know who drives an old green truck?"

"My grandmother, Tamar."

"She's the one who owns the land?"

She knocked again. Harder.

"Yes, and you should probably open up. You don't want her mad at you from jump."

At the door Bobby was still cautious, though. "Who is it?"

"Tamar July."

Bobby opened up, and she walked in, bringing with her the cold air and a frank assessment from dark eyes that were a few inches above his own. She was dressed in a brown knee-length parka, jeans, and black boots. A large brown felt cowboy hat covered the gray hair that hung in a knot low on her neck. She peered down at him like one of those birds of prey from the nature shows Kiki liked to watch.

"Wanted to come over and introduce myself. Hi, grandson."

July nodded.

"I'm Bobby Douglas. That's Kiki." She seemed frozen in her tracks. "Would you like a seat?"

"Thank you, no. I'm not staying."

She was so not what Bobby had been expecting. He wouldn't've targeted her, either. A mugger would get his ass kicked fooling with her.

"Everything about the trailer okay?" she asked.

"Yes, ma'am."

"Manners. I like that. Is Kiki your real name, my dear?"

Kiki seemed to come out of her trance. "No, ma'am. It's Kelly."

"Then you'll be Kelly. Crystal spoke very highly of you both. Looking forward to knowing you better. We'll be having a town meeting tomorrow. I'll expect you to be there, so you can meet everyone."

Bobby noted that she hadn't given them a choice, but he instinctively knew to keep his mouth shut and go with it. "We'll be there."

July told her, "Bobby and I will be going to look at cars in the morning."

She nodded as if that were a good thing. "I'm in the house that you probably saw when you arrived. If you need anything, just let me know. Here, let me give you my number."

To his surprise she withdrew from her pocket a top-of-the-line smartphone. Seeing his surprise, she smiled for the first time and punched in her password. "I'm old, but I'm not dead. Yet."

Numbers were exchanged, and when that was done, she said, "Okay, I'm going home. Nice to meet you two. Welcome to Henry Adams." And with a parting nod to her grandson, she was gone.

Closing the door behind her, Bobby glanced at July questioningly.

"Her bark is worse than her bite—most of the time."

"When Ms. Brown said she was in her eighties, I expected—"

"Someone a little less forceful?"

"Yeah."

"Remember the Aaliyah song 'Age Ain't Nothing but a Number'?"

Bobby and Kelly smiled.

"That's my grandmother. Runs rings around all of us. We're hoping she lives forever." July rose to his feet. "I'm going to head back. Been great meeting you."

"Same here." Bobby didn't know why, but he was looking forward to knowing July better. The verdict on the grandmother was still out, though. "What time do you want me to be ready in the morning?"

"The dealership opens at nine. So make it nine. It's only a short ride. That okay?"

"That works." They shared a shake. "Thanks, Trent."

"You're welcome. Kelly, take it easy. Looking forward to meeting the twins."

"Remember you said that," she tossed back, smiling.

"See you folks in the morning."

Closing the door behind July, Bobby said, "I like him."

"I do, too. Ms. Tamar is off-the-chain scary, though."

"No shit."

And they laughed.

On his drive home, Trent thought the short visit had gone well. Nothing about the couple jumped out at him or raised red flags. Like Bernadine, he looked forward to knowing them better. Bobby's wariness at the door had been memorable. Living in a major urban area was sometimes full of danger, and with his gang-banger past, the young man had probably experienced more than his share. Henry Adams would be a safer environ-ment, which he was certain they'd figure out soon.

On another note, he would've loved to have been able to read Bobby's mind during Tamar's visit. She definitely was not your stereotypical senior citizen—nothing about the July matriarch said "feeble" or "old." In his heart, Trent did indeed want her to live forever; a far-fetched desire, but he couldn't imagine a world without her presence.

After school, Brain and Amari waved good-bye to Leah Clark and her little sister, the always pain-in-the-butt Tiffany Adele, and started the walk home. Amari also watched the new girl, Kyra Jones, drive off with her dad. She lived in Franklin; she and her family went to Reverend Paula's church, and she and Amari were on the same acolyte team. A few weeks ago she'd transferred to their school, the Marie Jefferson Academy, because life in Franklin was going down the tubes, thanks to their crazy mayor, Astrid Wiggins.

"Is it just me or does Kyra look different?"

"Kyra Jones?"

"Yeah."

"Different how?"

"It's like she's cute."

"Kyra?"

"Yeah. Weird, huh. Maybe I'm coming down with the flu or something."

Brain stared. "Maybe. She and her braces look the same to me. Jaws from James Bond."

Amari wanted to defend her, but Brain was his best friend, so he let it go. "Maybe it's just my imagination."

Brain grinned. "You developing a thing for Jaws, man?"

"Stop calling her that."

Brain studied him for a few moments. "Wow. You are."

"No, I'm not. Just wanted to know if she looked different to you. That's all."

"Whatever."

He and Brain rarely argued. Their shared foster-care pasts and experiences in Henry Adams had bonded them close as blood. They supported each other, and knew that if one needed to talk, the other would listen without judging. Yes, Amari was jealous of Brain having his mom in his life, but he was still his BFF. “So, how’s your mom doing?”

Up in his room, Amari sat lounging in his gaming chair. He had his controller in his hand, but he couldn’t concentrate on the game on screen because Kyra’s face kept flitting across his mind’s eye. She was a mousy little thing, with features no one would ever compare to Beyoncé’s or Rihanna’s, but he swore something about her had changed. All day at school he’d done nothing but stare at her face, her hair, the pink sweater she had on, and the way her jeans fit. He even liked the quick whiff of her perfume that teased his nose when she passed him on the way to her seat. Amari knew he had an over-the-top personality, so how could he possibly like a girl who rarely even spoke? The more he thought about it, the more certain he was that Brain was right. Amari “Flash” Steele July was liking Jaws aka Kyra Jones, and he didn’t have a clue what to do with it or what it meant. He thought maybe he should talk to his mom or better yet his dad about it, but then again, maybe if he waited a couple of days, the weird way she had him feeling inside would miracu-lously go away, and he’d return to fantasizing about having a really hot babe as his girlfriend. Deciding to roll with that, he hit start on the game and resumed saving the world with Spider-Man.

Chapter 4

That morning in Henry Adams, after having breakfast with Lily and the boys, Trent drove out to pick up Bobby. In spite of his laid-back ways, Trent was anal about being on time, and finding Bobby dressed and ready to go pleased him. He glanced at the thin fake leather jacket the kid was wearing. It was totally inadequate for a Kansas winter, and by mid-January, newspaper might be warmer. But rather than begin the day by suggesting they go and look for something better and maybe upset the younger man, he talked football and cars as they drove out to the main road.

"It might be nice to cheer for a team that at least made the playoffs last year," Bobby said referencing the Kansas City Chiefs. "Cowboys sucked big-time."

"Yeah, well, the Chiefs blew a twenty-eight-point lead to the Colts and wound up losing forty-five to forty-four in last year's Wild Card game. Might've been better if they hadn't made the playoffs."

"True."

"You ever play?"

"I did. One game my freshman year in high school. Coach got on me about missing a tackle, and I quit."

Trent glanced over.

"I wasn't about him being all in up in my face screaming."

"Ah."

"Did you play?"

"Yes. Quarterback. All-State, three of my four years."

"Nice. Jocks thought they were the shit, though."

"Couldn't tell me different."

Bobby smiled.

"So you want to own a detailing business?"

"Yeah, I do. This guy I worked with had one. He'd let me help with the sprayers and stuff sometimes."

"Did he do repairs, too?"

"No."

"Do you know anything about engines, stuff like that?"

"No. No interest."

"Ah."

The car dealership had a few good selections on the lot, and due to all the business the owner had been getting from Henry Adams, he offered Trent and Bobby a good deal on a three-year-old crossover SUV with only fifteen thousand miles.

"Owned by an elderly man who only drove it to church and the grocery store," the dealer explained.

Trent and Bobby both looked it over. "Can you drive a manual?" Trent asked.

"Yes."

"Good. Will this one work for you and Kelly, you think?"

"Yeah."

Their decision made, they agreed to the offer and started the paperwork.

When everything was in order, the dealer said, "Give me about an hour to get it prepped and gassed up, and you can drive it home."

The two men nodded and walked back to Trent's truck, Bobby visibly shivering in the twenty-degree air. "Let's go find you a coat while we wait."

"I'm good."

"No, you aren't."

Bobby stopped. "Look, man. You already bought me a car. I don't need you buying me a coat, too."

"I'm not trying to hurt your pride. Just offering a hand until you get on your feet."

"You've helped enough."

"Okay. Suit yourself, but I promise you, if my grandmother sees you shivering like that, she's not going to want to hear your no, and neither will Ms. Brown."

"You all let the women run you like that?" Bobby tossed back with a hint of belligerence.

Trent let the dig roll off his back and chuckled. "When they make sense, yes."

"I'm good. No coat."

"Up to you. I need to make a run. Do you want to come, or stay here?"

"I'll ride."

But when Trent pulled up to the county sheriff's office, he sensed Bobby stiffen.

"Why are you stopping here?"

"Someone I want you to meet."

"Who?"

"Will Dalton. He's the county sheriff, and a friend."

"Why do I need to meet him?"

Trent didn't sugarcoat it. "Because you're a big Black guy covered with tats, and I don't want you profiled and pulled over every time you leave your house. That plain enough?" The rebellion in Bobby's face was plain, but Trent ignored it. "You decide."

Bobby's eyes flared angrily for a moment longer, but without a word, he opened his door and stepped out.

They found Will seated at his desk in his office. He was in his mid-fifties, and his bulk was a testament to his years of playing linebacker at Kansas U. The face was weathered, the hair graying, and the blue eyes keen. He smiled at Trent's entrance. Any surprise he may have felt upon seeing Bobby never showed. "Morning, Trent. How are you?" He rose and came around the desk to shake Trent's hand.

"Doing good. Want you to meet Bobby Douglas.

He and his wife and twin babies moved into town yesterday."

"Good meeting you," Will said, extending his hand. "Welcome to Kansas."

"Thanks, and I don't have any outstanding warrants."

Will looked at Trent, who kept his face bland. He understood Bobby's response was undoubtedly rooted in his past dealings with law enforcement, but that didn't mean he liked it.

Will crossed his arms. "Did I ask if you had any warrants? Trent's a pretty smart guy. I doubt he'd bring you here to meet me if he thought you'd be arrested."

Bobby had the decency to appear embarrassed.

"So, let's start over. I'm Will Dalton."

"Bobby Douglas. Nice to meet you."

"Same here. Welcome to Kansas."

"Thanks."

Will added, "You couldn't ask for a better group of people to live with than the folks in Henry Adams. In fact, the wife and I are thinking about asking Ms. Brown if we can move there sometime down the road."

Trent was pleased to hear that. "Really?"

He nodded. "After thirty years and all the kids, that old house of ours has seen better days. I don't have the time or the inclination to fix everything that needs fixing."

"You know you'd be welcome."

"I do." He directed his next words Bobby's way. "I'll be putting the word out on you to the agencies in the area, so you don't get disrespected. That okay with you?"

For a moment the two eyed each. Bobby finally said, "Yeah. I'd appreciate that."

"Here's my card. If you run into a situation where you think you need my help, call me, and I mean that. If I can't come right then, I'll send my son Kyle. He's with the FBI field office here."

Trent saw that Bobby was blown back by that generous offer. He smiled inwardly. How many gang members, former or otherwise, were given such courtesy? He hoped Bobby had a better view of Will now.

The three of them spent a few more minutes talking about Bobby's move and Kelly and the twins before Trent and Bobby shook hands with Will and took their leave.

Back in Trent's truck, Bobby looked his way and said, "Thank you."

"No problem. We take care of our own. Will's a good man."

"Not used to dealing with the police on a personal level."

"Understood."

"Sorry for being a jerk."

"No apology needed. You were dealing from the only place you know. Nobody's faulting you for that."

Trent could see him thinking. Again, he wished he could read Bobby's mind.

"Do we still have time to get that coat?"

Trent smiled. "Sure do."

An hour later, after the purchase of a coat made to withstand the Kansas winter, a pair of boots to replace Bobby's Nikes, gloves, and outerwear for Kelly, they were on their way back to the dealership when Trent's phone rang, and Lily's voice came over the sync. "Hey, handsome."

"Hey, Lil. What's up?"

"Is Bobby with you?"

"Yes."

"Then I guess we can't talk about how you rocked my boat last night."

"Lily!"

Bobby grinned.

"What do you want, crazy woman?"

"Seabiscuit wants you to swing by her office. Says she has something she needs to discuss."

"I suppose it can't wait."

"Not according to her."

"Okay, let me pick up Bobby's car, and I'll go see what Her Horsiness wants."

"Okay. Love you."

"You'd better."

As the call ended, Bobby asked, "Who's Seabiscuit?"

"Astrid Wiggins. The mayor of Franklin, and a pain in the ass."

"That was your wife on the call?"

"Yeah."

"How long have you been married?"

"A little over a year. We were high school sweethearts but broke up after she went off to college."

"But you hooked up again."

"Yes. Twenty-five years later. When she moved back here we had a pretty rough time getting the knots untied, but we did, and it gave me new life."

"What do you mean?"

"I'd moved back here after living in LA for ten years. I have an engineering degree, two failed marriages, and was living here doing mostly nothing. Then Ms. Brown came to town, and a few weeks later, Lily. Nothing's been the same since. Owe them both a lot." Trent looked over at Bobby. "There's an old saying that a man is only as strong as the woman who holds him. I'm strong. Real strong."

The car had gone through its prep and was gassed up and ready when they returned to the dealership. After Bobby got in, Trent leaned down to speak through the rolled-down driver's-side window. "Mayor Wiggins's office is just a few minutes away. How about you just follow me there, and we'll go back to town when I'm done? I doubt the meeting will take long. She hates my guts, and the feeling's mutual. I'll tell her you're my new assistant."

Bobby appeared wary. "You sure it'll be okay for me to be there?"

"It'll be okay with me. I don't care if it's okay with her or not."

"Then I'll follow you."

When they arrived at the mayor's office, her secretary, after eyeing Bobby with wide, fright-filled eyes, sent them right in.

"Well, hello, Mayor July. I—" The sight of Trent's companion seemed to freeze her in midspeech.

Trent did the introductions. "Mayor Wiggins. My new assistant, Bobby Douglas."

"Pleased to meet you," said Bobby.

Astrid appeared to be too busy staring to respond. Then, as if she didn't feel the need to, she gave him a dismissive look and turned to Trent. "Thanks for coming. Have a seat, please. This won't take long. Oh"—she turned to Bobby—"you can sit, too."

Bobby replied tersely, "I'll stand."

Trent held on to his temper. Astrid Franklin Wiggins was a piece of work. Her family had founded Franklin back in the early 1900s. Up until a few weeks ago, the two neighboring communities had gotten along fairly well. But Bernadine's rebuilding of Henry Adams, adding services and perks for the town that Franklin didn't have, was giving Astrid fits of jealousy. Right before Thanksgiving she'd hired a young knucklehead to set loose cockroaches in the aisles of the new Henry Adams grocery store, which led to the Health Department shutting it down. She'd also incited a crazed bunch of gold seekers to riot, causing a lot of destruction in town. Astrid was Trent's age. In high school she'd been the epitome of a mean girl. Twenty-five years later, she still wore the crown.

"I wanted to let you know that Franklin will no longer be able to make town services available to your people," she began.

Trent chose to overlook the "your people" remark. She knew it was offensive and was trying to push his buttons. He refused to play. "Meaning?"

"Due to budget constraints, we'll no longer be able to offer you any assistance from our fire department."

She waited for his reaction. He didn't give her one. "What else?"

"Our library's going private as well, and will only lend books to our residents. Your people are no longer welcome in our continuing education classes or GED program. Effective immediately." She gave him a smug little smile.

"Anything else?"

"No."

He stood. "Have a nice day."

He and Bobby exited.

Once they were outside, Bobby said, "Wow. What a bitch."

"No kidding."

"So what's your town going to do?"

"Once Ms. Brown gets done cursing, she'll probably open the vault and declare war."

On the drive back to Henry Adams, Trent pushed his anger at Astrid aside. He knew Bobby was going to need employment. His original plan to put him to work in the garage was no longer feasible now that he'd learned the young man knew nothing about working on engines or anything else mechanical tied to repairing cars. Not even Bernadine was going to pay him for doing nothing, and from what Trent knew of him, Bobby wouldn't accept that kind of arrangement even if it was offered, so Trent had another job in mind. He'd make the announcement during the town meeting.

Bernadine looked up to see Genevieve Curry peeking around the frame of her opened office door.

"Are you busy?"

"Never too busy for you. Come on in and have a seat. How are you this morning? Do you want coffee?" Bernadine was on her second cup.

"No, thank you. I'm on my way to help out at the rec. I just stopped by to let you know that I've officially gone back to my maiden name, Gibbs."

After having her home razed as a result of the antics of her husband—Riley, the town's former mayor—and his eight-hundred-pound hog, Cletus, she'd divorced them both. Getting all the paperwork sorted out had taken some time, especially after she found out Riley had been embezzling the money she'd inherited from her parents.

"I assume your lawyer's handled the name changes on all your documents and accounts?" Bernadine asked.

"Yes, from Social Security to bank accounts."

"Good. No word from Riley, I hope?"

Her face soured. "He called collect the other day, but I refused to accept the charges. I'm guessing he and that hog aren't taking Hollywood by storm the way he'd envisioned."

Bernadine agreed. He'd taken the hog to Hollywood hoping to make him a star like Arnold of *Green Acres* fame. The only reason he'd call was if he needed something, like maybe a bus ticket home. She wasn't planning on accepting any collect calls, either.

"I'm hoping you aren't going to take his calls."

"You just read my mind."

Genevieve smiled. "Good. Now, when do we ladies get to meet the babies?"

"I'm hoping Kelly and Bobby will be at tonight's town meeting. If they come, I'm sure they'll bring the twins."

"I can't wait." Genevieve had no children, and she considered that fact one of the biggest disappointments of her marriage. Since being told the young family would be moving to town, she'd been chomping at the bit to meet them.

"Anything else on your mind?" asked Bernadine.

"Not really, but I think the next time Marie and I go to Vegas, I'm going to get a makeover. Nothing drastic, but getting rid of Riley has made me think about all the things I might have done or could've been had I not been his glorified maid my whole life." She leaned forward and whispered. "Maybe I'll be a cougar."

Bernadine choked on her coffee.

Gen added, "Crystal suggested I listen to Beyoncé or Mary J. She said they're very inspiring for the young women of today."

Bernadine was pretty sure Genevieve had no business taking life advice from her seventeen-year-old daughter, but kept the thought to herself. "I like Mary J.'s music."

"I do too. Amari's going to help me pick out a new phone so I can put music on it, and a speaker to play it through when I don't want to use the earbuds."

"You certainly have the vernacular down, Ms. Gibbs," Bernadine said sassily.

"I want to enjoy my golden years, so I'm reinventing myself."

"You go, girl."

Smiling, Genevieve got to her feet and zipped up her claret-red down coat. "I'm planning to do just that. See you at tonight's meeting."

"Bye."

After Genevieve took her leave, Bernadine thought back on the cougar remark and laughed. While married, Gen had been a model of decorum, but after the divorce she'd turned into quite the feisty woman—to the point of treating Riley to a mean right hook at the Dog last year that left the former mayor knocked out cold on the floor. She was presently in a relationship with Mal's best friend, Clay Dobbs, but it didn't seem to be going anywhere. Ideally, Gen would find someone to love her as fiercely as she longed to be loved.

Bernadine's phone sounded with the opening notes of Sade's "Smooth Operator," and she smiled. Speaking of love . . . "Hey, Mal."

"Hey, sweet thing. How's turning the world going this morning?"

His voice always made her melt inside. "So far, so good. How're you?"

"Wishing I was there with you instead of here working on the books."

"Aww. How about we have lunch?"

"You really going to show up?"

She chuckled. "You're not going to let that go, are you?" Twice last week, due to the weight of her workload, she'd had to cry off from their daily lunch date, and he'd been rubbing her nose in it since.

"No, I'm not. Fine older gentleman like myself

is not used to being stood up by the woman he loves."

"You're a mess."

"But I'm your mess."

"Yes, you are, and I'm glad about it. I won't stand you up. Promise."

"Then that's good enough for me. You have a good rest of the morning, and I'll see you later. Love you, girl."

"Love you more."

Disconnecting, Bernadine sat back and smiled.

Lily stuck her head in the door. "My hubba-hubba hubby back yet?"

"No."

"You looked awfully happy there. You must've been talking to the former gigolo of Graham County."

Mal's reputation as a lady's man had been the stuff of legends. "Operative word is *former*."

"And that's a good thing. It takes a real woman to make an old player turn in his card." Lily grew serious. "You're exactly what's he's been needing all his life."

"He's a good guy."

"Yes, he is. His son's not too shabby, either."

Bernadine agreed. In many ways Mal and Trent were as different as night and day, in others, alike as two peas in the pod. She and Lily were both blessed by the love of the July men.

Lily asked, "Any idea what Seabiscuit wants?"

"Only the devil knows."

"True. Let me know when he gets in, if you see him first."

"Will do."

Turning to her e-mail, she opened a message from Gary Clark, the manager of the town's grocery store. He wanted to know what was going on with Bernadine's baby sister, Diane Willis. She'd moved in with Bernadine and Crystal this past fall after being served with divorce papers by her long-suffering husband because she was spoiled, demanding, and not a very nice person. She'd left town right after Thanksgiving to spend time with her son Marlon and his partner, Anthony, at their home in Maui. That was almost ten days ago. Bernadine hadn't heard a peep from Diane since, and neither had Gary, her boss. He'd be looking to hire her replacement if she didn't touch base soon, and Bernadine couldn't blame him. She hoped that Diane had found employment in Maui and would thus be out of Bernadine's hair, but she doubted she'd be that lucky. Although her sister had reconciled with her children and with Bernadine, she had a ways to go to completely shed her sometimes selfish attitude. There was no telling what her intentions were concerning her job or the future. Bernadine would put in a call to Maui later.

The next e-mail was from Sheriff Dalton. After reading the content, Bernadine sighed with irritation. Local law enforcement still hadn't located Tommy Stewart, the skinny, smelly young man who'd showed up in her office a few days before Thanksgiving threatening to sue Henry Adams because he'd supposedly found a cockroach in a sandwich he purchased at the town's new grocery store. When a review of the security camera showed him spreading roaches through the aisles like a perverted Johnny Appleseed, he disappeared before he could be arrested. Bernadine and her people were pretty sure Astrid Wiggins had put him up to the nasty stunt—he'd come within a hairbreadth of admitting as much. They were also convinced that Astrid had helped him fly the coop so she wouldn't be implicated, but until he was found, the prosecutor could do nothing further with the case. Astrid—aka Seabiscuit, aka Secretariat—was determined to put Henry Adams in its place, and although Bernadine hated to admit it, she'd won that round. When local hermit Cephas Patterson left a bag of gold to Roni and Reg's daughter Zoey this past summer, Astrid spread word of the boon, and every gold-seeking crazy in the state had descended on Henry Adams like one of the plagues of Egypt. A riot ensued, and the town was left to pick up the pieces of their nearly destroyed recreation center. Astrid had won that round, as well.

The only bright spot for Bernadine in this

mini-war was a Thanksgiving Day newspaper article penned by Austin Wiggins, Franklin's former mayor and Astrid's soon-to-be-ex-husband. To get back at Astrid for booting him from office, Austin had confirmed in print that her family had paid him to marry her. He then left town with his girlfriend Lindy, a pretty, baby-voiced blonde who'd been runner-up in the county fair's Ms. Heifer contest. Bernadine was sure Astrid was in the market for a hit man to put him away, but in the meantime, the mayor of Franklin had been turned into a laughingstock.

Still, Astrid was a formidable opponent. Though Bernadine had no desire to go toe-to-toe with her again, she didn't want to lose any more rounds. Astrid's earlier call about wanting to meet with Trent made her wonder what ol' Horse Face had up her sleeve this time.

It didn't take her long to find out.

"She's cutting all ties to Henry Adams," Trent reported to her and Lily after he and Bobby had arrived and taken seats in Bernadine's office, and Bobby and Lily had been introduced.

"What does that mean?" asked Bernadine.

Trent explained, and when he was done, Bernadine and Lily stared, stunned. "But we have a signed contract for their fire department's aid," Bernadine stormed.

"I know, but now that she's mayor, she's decided she doesn't have to honor it."

"That's unconscionable," Lily snapped. "Two of her citizens died in that fire last spring."

Trent shrugged. "Guess she doesn't care about that either, or the other folks in the county working on their GEDs, or our kids using the library, or the people enrolled in the continuing education classes. None of that."

"Unbelievable." Bernadine thought for a moment. "We'll have to take up the slack. Let's put this on the agenda for the meeting tonight and figure out a way to work around her."

"Agreed," Trent said. "I'll be calling the Board of Regents to see if she can summarily exclude people from the GED program."

"Good idea. Maybe they'll slap her with a big fat fine." She turned her attention to Bobby. "Did you get your car?"

"Yes, ma'am. Thank you. Met Sheriff Dalton, too. He gave me his card."

"Good for Will. Were you with Trent at the meeting with Mayor Wiggins?"

He nodded.

"And your assessment?"

"She's a bitch."

"Give the young man a prize," she said solemnly. "The monthly town meeting is at the Dog this evening. You and Kelly might want to attend so you can meet everyone."

"I know. Tamar already said she wanted us there."

"Sounds good."

Trent stood. "I'm going to let Bob follow me back to his place just to make sure he knows the way. When I get back, we can talk more."

She nodded, and the men left.

Once they were gone, Lily turned to Bernadine. "I say we go over to Franklin and set her hair on fire."

"I'll get the matches."

Chapter 5

Bobby turned left out of the Power Plant's parking lot onto Henry Adams's main street and followed Trent's black pickup past the school, the recreation center, and the lone church. Ms. Brown hadn't lied about how small the place was. Less than a minute later they came up on a newish-looking building with a large glass front and a low roof with a sign reading *Dog and Cow*. He assumed that was the diner, but wondered what was up with the name. Figuring he'd get the lowdown on it sometime soon, he stayed with Trent as they hooked another left and headed north and east onto July Road. Less than five minutes later they were driving up the gravel road that led to the trailers.

Bobby parked. Trent rolled down his window to call out, "I'll see you tonight," and he roared away in the big truck. Turning off the engine, Bobby got out and stood a moment to admire their new ride. Still smiling, he popped the trunk to grab the bags holding Kiki's new coat and all the other gear Trent purchased before heading up the steps and putting his key in the door. He was anxious to show Kiki their new wheels and tell her about his morning, but he found her sitting and talking with a woman he didn't know.

"Hey, Bobby," Kiki said cheerily.

"Hey."

The twins were crawling around on the carpet. Bobby Jr. had a cloth block in his mouth. Picking them up in turn, Bobby planted kisses on their cheeks. Their little smiles lit up his heart.

The visitor smiled.

"This is Reverend Paula Grant," Kiki said. "She's the priest here, and lives in one of the other trailers."

Reverend Paula stood and extended her hand for a shake. "It's a pleasure to meet you—welcome to Henry Adams. You have a lovely family."

"Thank you. Pleasure to meet you, too." He and Kiki had never been much on churchgoing. He hoped the reverend hadn't come over to bug them about attending.

Kiki said, "Reverend Paula and I were talking about having the twins baptized."

He froze. He looked at his girl and then at the priest. "Really?"

Kiki nodded. “I know it’s not something we’ve talked about, but it’s something I’ve always wanted to do.”

“Okay.” He knew he sounded doubtful, but couldn’t help it. This was news to him.

“I only stopped by to introduce myself and to welcome you,” Reverend Paula said, “so let me get going. I hope to see you at the town meeting this evening. Bobby, again, pleasure meeting you.”

“Same here.”

The reverend slipped on her parka and departed.

“Did she put you up to this?”

“No,” Kelly replied with an attitude. “I do have a mind of my own, you know.”

“Then why this talk of baptizing all of a sudden?”

“It’s not all of a sudden. I grew up Catholic. I’ve missed being in church.”

“Since when?”

“Since my mama said sinners like me and you shouldn’t be in church.”

He studied the hurt and anger on her face. “She said that to you?”

She nodded tightly.

He walked over and gently pulled her in against him and held her close. He kissed the top of her head. “You never told me that before.”

She shrugged. “That’s because I believed her. But when I talked to Reverend Paula, she basically said if I wanted to come, I’d be welcomed.”

Bobby felt like his world was on a roller coaster, and it was all he could do to hang on. He was in a new state, wearing a new coat, driving a new car, and had the business card of the county sheriff in his pocket. Now his girl wanted to attend church. What other changes would this new life bring? "If you want to go to church, you should go."

"You mean that?" Kiki asked, looking up at him.

"What am I going to say, no?"

She smiled and snuggled back into his chest. Tiara began pulling herself up on his leg. She was getting good at it, but her brother seemed content to simply watch for now. Bobby reached down and picked her up. "Do you want to go to church with your mama, Ti? Daddy's not going, but you and your brother can. That okay with you?"

She clapped happily, as she did for everything these days, and he grinned. "I think that's a yes."

"New coat," Kiki said, assessing him.

"Yes, and one for you in the bag."

Her eyes widened. He looked on, pleased, as she tried it on. "It fits."

"Of course it does. You think I don't know what size you wear?"

Bobby told her about the conversation he and Trent had about the coats, adding. "I have to admit, the one I have on now is way warmer than the leather."

"So how'd the rest of the morning go?" Kiki asked, still admiring her new coat.

"Kind of crazy, but I got the car."

"Oooh. I want to see!" She ran to the window. "God, it looks new."

"Three years old, the dealer said. And unlike that piece-of-shit van we had in Dallas, it has heat and a working radio—not that's there any music here, but folks won't hear us coming a mile away because this one has a muffler that works."

"Can we go for a ride?" Kiki asked excitedly.

"Sure. Roads are cleared, so we won't have to worry about sliding into somebody's fence. We're going to have to learn to drive in the snow, but not today."

"Let me grab their snowsuits."

She returned and tossed him one. While they got the babies bundled up, Bobby said, "I went to a meeting with Trent. This little place has a lot of drama going on."

"Really?"

"Yeah, there's this lady mayor in the next town over everybody calls Seabiscuit . . ."

Tommy Stewart wondered how long Mayor Wiggins was going to keep him locked up. The night after he put the cockroaches in the Henry Adams grocery store, he'd driven to her house to pick up the money he'd been promised for doing the job. After letting him in, she told him the store had been shut down, and how happy and proud of him she was, and would he like some champagne to celebrate? He'd never had champagne before and was feeling pretty good about himself, so he said, "Sure!" She left the room for a few minutes and returned with two of those tall, skinny glasses that rich people drank champagne out of on TV. She handed him one. They clinked glasses, she said, "Cheers!" and he drank it down. A few seconds later, he didn't feel so good. His head had begun to spin. He looked around for a chair to sit in, but fell to the floor instead. The last thing he remembered was the smug smile on her face as she lifted her glass to him in a toast.

When he came to, he was lying on a dirt floor. Above his head, a low-watt bulb gave off just enough light for him to make out the confines of the small, shadowy room he was in. He had no idea where he was, or how much time had passed. He struggled to his feet and instantly puked. After a few more rounds, he felt a little better. The memory of the meeting with Mayor Wiggins came back, along with the certainty that she must've put something in the champagne. On rubbery legs, he wove his way to the door and pulled on the knob. Locked. He puked again, his head throbbing like he'd been slamming it against the trunk of his mother's old Buick. Whatever he'd been given also had his mind so muddy he couldn't think straight, but he knew he needed to get out of there. He reached for his phone, but the pocket of his jeans was empty. Thinking maybe it was on the floor, he looked around. Nothing. His car keys were gone, too. Panic set in. He pounded on the door and frantically yelled for help.

His voice was raw and his hand ached by the time the door finally opened. The mayor walked in, carrying a big shotgun. The sight of it coupled with the cold glitter in her eyes made his heart race. He swallowed hard and took a step back.

"I'm real sorry about this," she'd said, "but it'll only be for a few days. The store had cameras, and you and the roaches are on them." That scared him almost as much as the shotgun.

"Once the stink dies down, I'll get you a ticket to anywhere in the county, but you can't come back here. Ever."

He'd swallowed harder.

"Be grateful I'm keeping you out of jail."

That said, she left, locking him in again. And that's when he knew hooking up with her had to be the worst mistake he'd ever made in his life.

Trent sat at a long table at the front of the Dog as the residents filed in for the meeting. Smooth jazz floated from the sound-system speakers. He knew his neighbors weren't going to be happy about Astrid's news. He also knew they'd rally on behalf of themselves and the town, just as they'd done after last spring's devastating fire and the destruction the rioters had caused a few weeks before. Her mean-spirited decision about the GED program and the library in no way equaled those incidents, but it would still be viewed as an attack on Henry Adams and what it stood for. A more serious issue was the dissolution of the fire pact. Lives could be affected if his town no longer had access to Franklin's fire department—but that too would be taken care of, hopefully with all due haste.

The kids trooped in en masse and took their usual seats in the back booths. He noticed that Zoey made a point of not sitting beside Devon, prefer-ring to sit and laugh with Wyatt instead. A reconciliation between her and Devon would go a long way toward getting his youngest son on track again, but apparently Zoey wasn't having any—and in truth, Trent couldn't blame her. Devon had been a pain in the butt to everyone who knew and loved him.

Bernadine and Lily joined him at the table. Lily functioned as meeting secretary, so she immediately opened up her laptop in preparation.

Most of the residents were now inside, filling their plates from the buffet provided by diner manager Rocky and her head chef, Siz. Bobby and Kelly hadn't arrived yet, though. Wondering if they'd encountered some kind of difficulty, Trent took out his phone. Before he could begin a text to them, they walked in.

"Sorry we're late," Bobby gushed. "Had a time

getting the twins' carriers locked into the backseat." Seeing Lily, he took a moment to introduce her to Kelly and the twins, and she and the smiling Bernadine leaned down to give the babies a welcome.

"Hold on a moment before you sit down," Trent said to the couple, looking for his dad. As he and Mal had arranged previously, when Trent nodded, Mal paused the music. Everyone stopped and looked Trent's way.

"Folks. Want you all to meet Bobby Douglas, his lady, Kelly Page, and their twins. They're our newest citizens. Let's give them a big Henry Adams welcome."

Roof-shaking applause and yells followed the announcement. As wave after wave rolled over the young residents, the applauding Trent watched Bobby swallow emotionally and do his best to remain stoic and unmoved. He failed miserably. Everyone was on their feet. Kiki had tears in her eyes. The still-applauding Trent saw her and Bobby share a look that turned into a smile. The welcome continued, as did the cheering. Even the kids joined in. Finally Trent said into the mic, "Okay. Thanks everybody. Give them a few minutes to find a seat, and we'll get the meeting started. You can welcome them personally after we're done."

Genevieve and school superintendent Marie Jefferson had the young couple sit with them at a table in the center of the room. A very pleased Gen was helping the babies out of their snowsuits when Trent announced, "I had a meeting with Mayor Wiggins over in Franklin this morning."

Booing and hissing followed that. He used his gavel to quiet the room. "Hold on. You'll get your chance to express yourselves once you hear what she's done."

When he finished telling them, the place erupted with angry denunciations, boos, and lots of hissing.

"Has she lost her mind?" schoolteacher Jack James barked. "Can we sue her for backing out of the fire department agreement?"

Bing Shepard yelled, "I vote we ship Her Horsiness to France and let them turn her into a roast!"

That was met with a chorus of sarcastic amens, laughter, and applause.

Trent used his gavel again. "Since the fire last spring, we've been talking about starting our own department, and now we'll have to stop talking and get it done. We'll need to get someone in to train us. I should have someone lined up soon. Being trained on hoses and the like in the middle of winter isn't going to be a picnic, but it's necessary."

Trent turned to Bernadine. She took the floor. "Jack, I'll need you to open up two unused rooms in the school that we can turn into a library, then get with Lily ASAP and let her know what we need to purchase so we can have it up and running. Marie?"

"Yes, ma'am."

"Can you work with Jack on the GED program? I'm not letting Astrid wreck the students' futures. Need you to find out who's enrolled, what hoops we need to jump through to start our own program, and if we can do something to salvage the present term for the folks being impacted."

"Gotcha!"

Tamar raised her hand. Trent gave her a nod, and she stood. "Don't tell Astrid this, but her mean-spiritedness is a good thing. It's forcing us to make lemonade out of her lemons. If we want this town to grow, we need our own services, and this will be the start."

The applause shook the walls. Trent was pleased. She was right—their dream of Henry Adams expanding and thriving was now being jump-started. He just prayed there wouldn't be any fires before they'd worked out the logistics of establishing their own fire department. He glanced at Bernadine. "Anything else you want to say?"

"No. It's all been said, I think."

Trent focused his attention back on the crowd. "On a side note, as soon as the weather breaks, the Henry Adams Hotel rehab will be up and running, which means spending the winter commis-sioning and reviewing blueprints, setting up construction schedules, hiring contractors, and the like. Bernadine wants new houses added to the sub-division so we can house new residents, and the rec center still needs work. It also looks like we'll be building a new library and firehouse. I'm up to my hips coordinating all this, so I'm appointing an assistant. Bobby Douglas, you're it."

In the midst of the applause, Bobby shouted, *"What?"*

"Now, that's all the new business. Anyone have anything else they want to talk about?" Trent chose to overlook Bobby's stunned face. Kelly raised her hand. Thinking she had something negative to say about her husband's surprising appointment, he acknowledged her warily. "Go ahead, Kelly."

"Is there someplace in town I can start doing hair, so the ladies don't have to leave town the way they do now?"

Before he could reply, Bernadine shouted happily, "Yes!" The women in the room hooted and applauded. "See me after the meeting."

A shy smile crossed Kelly's face, and she retook her seat.

"Anything else before we close?"

No one stepped up, so Trent gaveled the meeting closed.

Bobby was furious, but held it inside as he told Kiki, "I need to talk to Trent. Be right back."

"What're you so mad about?"

He didn't reply. Instead he made his way through the crowd to where Trent stood talking with his wife. When he reached him, he said through his teeth, "Can I talk to you for a minute? Privately?"

Trent eyed him calmly. "Sure. Let's use my dad's office. I'm sure he won't mind."

Bobby had no idea who Trent's dad was, but didn't care.

Trent led the way to a small room at the back of the diner and leaned against the desk. "What's up?"

"Why did you say I was going to be your assistant?"

"Because you are."

"No, I'm not. You think it's funny, playing me in front of all those people?"

"I'm not playing you. Don't you need a job?"

"Yeah, I do, but I need one I can do."

"How do you know you can't do this one?"

Bobby's jaw tightened. He didn't know what the hell was up with Trent, but there had to be some kind of a catch. "Look, let me ask you up front. You gay? Are you trying to hit on me? Is that what all this is about?"

Trent stared, and then laughed, hard. When he finally recovered, he said, "Oh, that's funny. No, Bob. Not gay. I have all I can handle with Lily, and besides, you're not that cute."

Bobby stared off angrily. "Then tell me what it is, so I can understand."

"It's called H-E-L-P. Nothing more, nothing less. This is what we do here. Other places do it as well. We—meaning the people who live here—want you and Kelly to be all you can be. That's it. Not trying to play you or get you in bed. I understand this is all new, but it's the real deal."

Bobby sighed. He was so out of his element, he was having difficulty determining up from down and front from back. "But all I want to do is start a detailing business."

"Great goal, but you're going to need workers. Can you set up a payroll system so they can get paid? You're going to need suppliers. Do you know anything about inventory or invoices? What about small business taxes?"

Bobby's lips tightened. Admittedly he knew nothing about any of those things.

"If you want that business of yours to be successful, you'll need to know all of that and more. You're what, nineteen?"

Bobby nodded.

"Perfect age to begin setting up for your dreams, and you start by learning all the things you need to bring to the table. Let us help you."

Bobby met Trent's gaze. Since the age of thirteen, he'd been in charge of his own life because he'd never had anyone in his corner—

not parents, teachers, or social workers. Kiki had always been supportive, of course, but aside from her, the closest he'd ever had to someone having his back was during his gang years. The members functioned as the family he'd never had. But now Trent was proposing something totally new and foreign, and the way he broke it down made Bobby consider a different path and a different way of tackling his life. He wanted better—had he not, he wouldn't have moved his family to this place in the middle of damn nowhere. Could he really achieve his dreams here? Trent was making him realize all the things he didn't even know he didn't know.

"Well?" Trent asked.

"What if I can't do it?"

"What if you can?"

Bobby smiled and looked down at his feet for a moment. When his gaze rose, Trent was smiling, too. "You're something. You know that?"

"My sons think I'm an okay guy." Trent's voice took on a serious tone. "I need you to try this, Bob. It can't hurt. If you don't want to, I suppose we can find something else. The school and the Dog are always in need of custodial help. It's honorable work, but it won't set you on the path you say you want to be on."

"Can I think about it?" Bobby asked. He could tell by Trent's posture that it was not the answer he wanted, but Bobby never liked being pressured.

Trent relented. “Sure. If the answer is yes, I need you at my office in the morning, eight sharp.”
“Thank you.”
“You’re welcome.”

On the drive back to their trailer, Bobby was silent.
“I’m really excited about being able to do hair again,” Kiki said happily.
Bobby, lost in thoughts about Trent’s offer, replied distractedly, “Yeah, baby. That’s great.”
“What’s up with you? Was Trent serious about making you his assistant?”
“Yes. Not sure I want to do it, though.”
“Why not?”
“I don’t know anything about being a mayor’s assistant.”
“He’s going to teach you, though, right?”
“He said he would.”
“Then what’s the problem?”
“Still trying to deal with how they roll here. Never had anybody want to do something for me with no agenda attached.”
“It’s different, but it’s a good different, don’t you think?”
“I suppose.”
“So if you don’t take the job, what’re you going to do?”
He turned onto July Road. “Custodial work for the diner and the school.”

She looked away, shaking her head in what appeared to be either disbelief or disgust, he wasn't sure. "What?"

"Did we come here to get a better life or not?"

"Well—"

"Yes or no?"

"Yeah, but—"

"But, my ass. Come on, Bobby. Either we're in, or we go back to Dallas. I'm just as scared as you. This seems way too good to be true to me, too, but what if it isn't? What if you actually can get that business you've been dreaming about? What if we can really have a life that's not paycheck-to-paycheck, and have a few dollars left over at the end of the month instead of having to borrow from your mom to buy diapers?"

He pulled in to the drive that led to the trailers, and when they reached their own, they sat with the engine running while the twins slept in the backseat. Bobby spoke earnestly. "All my life, people told me I'd never be nothing, and I've always wanted to prove them wrong, which is why I had that dream of owning a business and got my GED. So now I get here, I got some people who want to help me out, and I guess I'm scared, like you said."

"When the babies were born, you took a beat-down to leave the gang that put you in the hospital for three days. You had four broken ribs, a busted collarbone, and your face looked like something out of Halloween. You're the strongest, baddest man I know."

That made him feel good. "I guess I'm so used to hustling and having that golden ticket just out of my reach, and now that I have the ticket in my hand . . . This is the next step, isn't it? Why I took that beating and worked two jobs, and tried to do the right thing."

"Yes, it is," she agreed softly. "And you've made me incredibly proud."

Her words filled his heart. "Then let's do this. Let's take this second step. Trent wants me there at eight sharp."

"Then I'll cook you a big breakfast and give you a kiss out the door like the women on TV do their men."

He chuckled, and his voice turned serious. "You're amazing."

"Yes, I am," she replied shamelessly. "And I have an amazing man. So let's go in and put these kids to bed, and then you can give me some loving and get a good night's sleep. You have to see a man about a job in the morning."

Leaning over, he kissed her with all the love he felt. After turning off the engine, he gently picked up the sleeping Tiara, Kiki did the same with Bobby Jr., and they went inside.

After Trent and his family got home, he went up to talk to his sons, as he did each night before they turned out their lights. Devon was in his pajamas and in bed. "Hey, Dad."

He sat down on the edge of the mattress. "Hey, son. Homework done?"

"Yes."

"Saw Zoey sitting with Wyatt at the meeting. You two still haven't worked things out."

"No. She still doesn't like me. I don't like her, either."

Trent sighed inwardly. "You haven't been very nice lately, Dev."

"No one's been nice to me."

"Why?"

He turned his eyes away. "I don't know."

"I think you do, and if you take a real look at how you've been treating people, you might see your way out of this corner you've boxed yourself into. Growing up is tough. It was tough for me, your mom—for everybody we know—but being nice helps a lot."

Devon looked chastened, but Trent wasn't sure if it was a true reflection of remorse.

"Give me a hug, and you get some sleep." Trent hugged him tight. He loved this little boy so much. "Love you a lot, buckaroo."

"Love you too, Dad."

As Trent exited, Devon turned out his light.

Trent stuck his head into Amari's room. He too was in sleepwear, lying beneath his blankets, staring at the ceiling. "You okay?"

"Not sure."

"Something you want to talk about?"

"Not sure about that, either."

Trent walked in. "Should I press?"

"What makes you like girls?"

Trent paused and eyed him for a moment. "Science says it's a biological need to propagate."

"As in kids?"

Trent nodded.

"God!" said Amari, sounding anguished.

"Having girl issues?"

"Not sure. Hoping it's just the flu, or maybe something Dr. Reg can give me a shot for."

Trent held on to his smile. "Well, if and when you're ready to talk about it, I'm your guy."

"Okay. Thanks, Dad."

"You're welcome. Homework done?"

"Yeah," he said, but Trent could tell he was distracted.

"I'll see you in the morning. Good night."

"Night, Dad."

Downstairs, Lily was watching the news. "Our sons good?"

He sat beside her on the couch. "Devon is still in denial about why Zoey's treating him like persona non grata, and I think Amari's in love."

"I know he is."

Trent stared. "With who?"

"I think it's Kyra Jones."

"From church? The one with the six-five dad

who looks like he eats tractors for dinner?"

"Yeah. She and Amari are on the same acolyte team, and the past two Sundays I noticed him peeking at her, a lot, and her peeking back, a lot."

"How come I didn't notice?"

"Because you're not his mama. Mamas always know who's trying to get next to their sons."

"She seems nice."

"Yes. Way quiet, though. I don't think I've ever heard her say more than two or three words, but then Amari talks enough for everybody in town. Going to be interesting to see how this plays out."

Trent thought so too, but wondered how the six-five tractor eater would react.

Lily's voice broke into his thoughts. "What did Bobby want to talk to you about? He looked pretty upset."

He told her about the conversation in Mal's office.

"He thought you were hitting on him?" she asked, laughing.

"Told him he wasn't that cute."

"Definitely not as cute as your wife."

He put his arm across her shoulders and pulled her close, and then related the rest of the talk they'd had. When he'd finished, Lily asked seriously, "Do you think he'll show up in the morning?"

"What do you think?"

She shrugged her shoulders. “I don’t know him well enough to even speculate, but I hope he does.”

“So do I.”

Chapter 6

Sitting on the bed in her motel room, Rita Lynn knew if she wanted to get past the hurt brought on by the letter, forgiving her parents was paramount. But it was difficult. They’d loved her and did what they felt was best for her future, but that future was impacting the present with a heartache so consuming she was finding it hard to sleep. Because of their decision, so much was owed, but after the passage of forty years, did it matter? Had she been written off—forgotten? Worrying about how she’d be received couldn’t be a factor. That she’d played no part in her parents’ actions couldn’t be a factor either—it didn’t banish the guilt plaguing her, nor salve her overwhelming sense of loss.

The loss, more than anything, brought forth such a tremendous rage that her fists balled, and she shook with the urge to scream, but that wouldn’t change anything. The past was done. She had only the future, which meant returning to the place where it all began. There was no other choice.

She put on her coat, locked the door of the

motel room, and, pulling her roller bag after her, headed down the open walk to the rental car she'd picked up yesterday evening at the airport. Having lived in California most of her adult life, she'd forgotten how cold the Kansas plains could be in early December, especially at dawn. She blew on her freezing hands and shivered as she waited for the heat to cut the chill in the car's interior.

She hadn't slept well last night. She hadn't expected to. Worries about how she'd be received kept resurfacing, but she fought them down, reminding herself this was the only way.

The rental car was fairly new, so it didn't take long for the warmth to rise or the defrosters to take care of the iced-over front and back windshields. Once she could see clearly, she activated the GPS on her phone and let the electronic voice guide her out of the parking lot and onto Highway 183. Heading north, she swallowed her fears. "Dear God," she said aloud, "Please see me through this day. Amen." Hoping the small prayer would be answered, she settled in for the drive to Henry Adams.

An hour later, she pulled up in front of the house and studied it. The big porch looked the same, but the outside had undergone some renovations. The old shutters were no longer on the upstairs windows, and the roof looked new. She had no way of knowing if the person she sought was still the owner. Common sense said she should've called before leaving California and traveling all this way, but after her mother's letter, her determination to come back to Henry Adams and share the truth had overridden rational thinking.

The drapes on the front windows moved. Someone inside was checking out the car, so she gathered her nerves, picked up her purse, and walked to the porch. Climbing the steps brought back memories of how many times she'd done this before. Girding herself, she knocked.

The door opened, and there she stood. Older, of course. The passage of time had turned her hair silver, but the dark eyes were still keen and the bearing just as proud. "Ms. July. I'm—"

"Rita Lynn. I know. We've been waiting for you a long time. Come in."

Tears filled Rita's eyes.

"Come on," Tamar invited softly. "You're here. Nothing else matters."

Inside, Rita wiped at her tears and noted that the home's interior had undergone some changes as well. It was larger, more airy. The old furniture she remembered had been replaced with modern pieces.

"Have you eaten?"

"No."

"Then join me. We'll talk while we eat."

Rita opened her purse and took out the letter.

"I need you to read this first. My mother died two weeks ago. She left it for me."

Tamar viewed her curiously, but took it and began to read. Shock claimed her face, and she stared at Rita. "Oh, my lord," she whispered. "I need to sit down." She sat on the sofa and resumed reading.

When she looked up at Rita again, Tamar's voice shook with rage. "Ida told you he was dead?"

Too overcome to speak, Rita nodded.

"That bitch! She brought him to me like he was something she'd found in a sewer. Her only words were 'Here's your grandson.' And she drove off. All these years I thought . . ."

"I'd abandoned him, or didn't care?"

"Both."

"No," Rita assured her softly. "They told me he'd died a few hours after birth."

"My god," Tamar whispered.

"Is my son still here? I don't even know his name." That lack pierced her heart.

"Yes, he's here. In fact, he's the mayor. Name's Trenton. We named him for my father. Mal's still here, too."

"Ms. July, I am so sorry." Rita broke down.

Tears rolled unchecked down Tamar's cheeks as she stood and gathered her close. "You've nothing to apologize for, Rita Lynn. Nothing."

And for the next few moments the two women connected to Trent since birth cried out the pain and loss caused by a terrible lie kept secret for forty-five years.

"Let's call Mal," Tamar said softly.

Over at the Power Plant, Trent stuck his head in Bernadine's office door. As always, she'd beaten him in to work and was seated at her desk drinking coffee. "Morning, Bernadine."

She looked up. "Good morning."

"Came to grab some coffee."

"Help yourself."

He never bothered making coffee in his own office because hers was always available. As he picked up the carafe and poured the dark brew into his mug that read "My Dad Rocks!"—a gift from Devon for Father's Day—she said, "I was surprised by your announcement last night about Bobby."

He shrugged. "Need to get him a job doing something. Figured why not?"

"Do you think he can handle it?"

"No idea." He took a sip. "May take him a while to get up to speed, but I do need the help, and he's the only one in town not already wearing six hats."

"True."

"He's supposed to let me know this morning whether he's going to take me up on the offer." He checked his watch. "Told him to be here at eight sharp." It was seven thirty.

"I'll keep my fingers crossed."

"Lil's over at the school with Jack, trying to find a room for the library. Said to tell you she'd be in as soon as they were done."

"Okay."

They spent a few more minutes talking about their individual agendas for the day. Just as Trent was preparing to head down the hall to his own office, Bobby appeared.

"Morning," he said.

"Good morning," Trent replied, pleased.

Bernadine echoed his greeting. She looked pleased as well.

"I'm ready to go to work," Bobby said.

"Then grab some coffee if you want, and let's get going."

It turned out that the young man wasn't a coffee drinker, so with a departing nod to Bernadine, he followed Trent out to begin his first day.

"Glad you decided to take the offer," Trent said, watching him over his cup as he hung his coat on the free-standing rack.

"Didn't make sense not to. This is why Kiki and I moved here."

"Ever read a blueprint?"

"No."

"Then we'll start with that."

Trent was explaining the basics when Mal walked in. His face was somber, and Trent could have sworn he'd been crying. "Dad? You okay?"

"Yeah."

Trent's first thought was Tamar. Had something happened? Was she hurt? He willed himself to remain calm. "Tamar okay?"

"Yeah, she's fine. Need to talk to you." Mal nodded at Bobby. They'd met last night after the meeting. "Morning, Bobby."

"Morning, Mr. July."

"Trent, can you come out into the hall for a minute?"

"Sure." His confusion was high. Excusing himself, he followed his dad.

Out in the hallway, Mal asked, "Is there someplace private where we can talk?"

"Dad, what's going on?"

"Your mother's here."

Trent froze, studying his father's face for signs of joking. "Not funny."

"No, it isn't. She's out at Tamar's. I just talked with Rita. Came to get you."

A million questions screamed in his head. He drew in a deep breath, hoping it would slow his racing heart. "Let me send Bobby home." Stunned, he walked back into the office.

Bobby took one look at his face and asked, "You okay, man?"

Trent's brain was stuck on *Your mother's here.* "No. I mean yeah, but I need to talk to my dad. Take the day off. I'll probably be tied up most of the day."

"Everybody okay? Your wife, kids, Tamar?"

Trent nodded. "Yeah. Just something needing my attention. I'll pay you for the full day. Go on home. I'll give you a call later."

Still viewing him with concern, Bobby put on his coat. "If you need anything, let me know."

"I will."

After Bobby had gone, Mal stepped back in and closed the door.

"So why is she here after all this time?" Trent asked. The bitterness of being abandoned crept up even as he fought to keep it from claiming him. "Does she want forgiveness? Money? A kidney?" The sadness in Mal's eyes was something he'd rarely seen, and it made him pause. "What? Tell me."

"Up until recently, she thought you'd died at birth."

Trent's heart stopped.

Mal nodded. "Her mother told her you were stillborn."

Trent's eyes widened. Horror overrode bitterness.

"It's in a letter her mother left for her to read after she died a few weeks back. She has it with her."

Trent's knees were so watery he thought he might fall. He dropped into a chair. All these years, he'd never imagined anything close to this. "Why would her mother have done that?"

"Shame, I guess. Rita Lynn was seventeen. Out-of-wedlock babies were the ultimate disgrace back then. Her parents thought they were doing the right thing."

"God, Dad, look at my hands. I'm shaking."

"It almost put me on the floor when she told me, too. Tamar wanted me to come and get you because she wasn't sure you'd be able to drive safely."

He wanted to say he was fine and could manage on his own, but it was a lie. *Your mother's here.*

"She's waiting to meet you, Trent. Do you want to see her?"

Focusing was difficult, so he drew in another deep breath. "Yes."

"Okay. I'm going to let Bernadine know what's going on, if that's all right with you."

"That's fine."

"I'll meet you in the parking lot."

Like a man entranced, Trent stood alone for a moment in the silent office, not knowing what to say, think, or do. His world had been turned upside down. Nothing in life had prepared him for this. She thought you'd died at birth.

Minutes later he was in the passenger seat of Mal's souped-up red Ford truck being driven to Tamar's. He had so many questions. "Did she come alone?"

"Yes. She's married, but came by herself."

"Where's she live?"

Mal looked his way. "California. Parents moved there after they left here. I guess they wanted to get as far away from the scene of the crime as possible."

"All this time, I thought . . ." He stopped, not wanting the angst tied to forty-five years of being without her to rise again.

"I know what you thought. Me, I was damn mad that she never reached out. I know I wasn't ready for prime time back then, but you were a baby. Hers and mine."

"Tamar raised me well."

"Yes, she did. But a kid needs his mother. I cursed her every day for turning her back on you the way I thought she did."

"But she didn't."

"No. You two have a lot to catch up on."

"So it's okay with you—she and I connecting?"

"Yes, but even if it wasn't, you're her son, too."

He noted the tears shining in his father's eyes. They mirrored his own.

Mal stopped the truck in front of Tamar's house.

"Are you coming in?" Trent asked.

"No. She and I visited a little earlier, and we will again later. It's your turn now."

Trent looked up at the house, wondering what his mother might be thinking as she waited. He opened the door.

"Trent?"

He looked back. "Yeah, Dad?"

"A man couldn't ask for a better son. I'm so proud of you. Even prouder of the way you're raising your sons. You're much better at it than I ever was. Rita's going to be proud of you, too."

In spite of Mal's faults of the past—the years of drinking, the womanizing, and all the worrying he'd caused family and friends—Trent had loved him, and he loved this new and improved version even more. "We'll talk later."

"Okay."

As he climbed the steps to the porch, Mal drove away.

Tamar met him at the door. "She's in the kitchen. I'll look in on you two later."

He looked into his grandmother's familiar eyes and suddenly, there were so many things he wanted to say to her. He wanted to thank her for raising him and being the strong rudder he'd often needed to keep him on course in life. She, who drove her ancient truck Olivia as if they were qualifying for the pole at Indy, who'd taught him to catch fish and ice skate and made him paint the Jefferson fence *twice* one summer for what she called "stupid boy tricks," was the main reason he was standing there today. She meant so much, he'd love her until night turned into day.

"I'll see you in a little while." He walked into the kitchen.

She was wearing a soft gray sweater and matching gray slacks. “Trenton?”

“Yes,” he replied softly.

Her eyes welled up, and the tears spilled down her brown cheeks. Her hand covered her mouth as if she were too overwhelmed to speak.

“Please don’t cry,” he whispered, even as his own eyes filled up. He’d had no idea what he’d planned to say to her, but realized there was no script, only emotion. He went to her, she stood, he took her in his arms and held her like the treasure he’d been searching for his entire life while she held him like she never wanted to let him go. They rocked. She sobbed brokenly. He cried silently.

She whispered, “I’m so sorry.”

“You’ve nothing to apologize for.”

“What you must’ve thought of me,” she countered. “Oh, my son. My son . . . All the years I’ve missed, but I didn’t know.”

“You’re here now. That’s all that matters.” And for him it was. It must have taken great courage for her to come back, not knowing whether she’d be embraced or stoned, even though none of it had been her fault. But she’d come anyway, and that told him all he needed to know. He eased back a bit and met her watery gaze. “The past is the past. I’m so glad to see you.”

“I’m glad to see you, too.”

“Let’s go forward. Okay? You and me.”

She placed her hand against his cheek. "So wise. That must've come from your grandmother, because you certainly didn't get it from me or Mal."

The sarcasm caught him off guard.

Her wet eyes glowed with twinkling mischief, and he threw back his head and laughed.

From that moment on, things went well. After making liberal use of the box of tissues on the table, she had a thousand and one questions about him and his life. And he had just as many for her. He told her about Lily and the boys and their adoptions.

"I have two grandsons?" she replied eagerly.

"Yes, Devon is twelve, and Amari is fourteen."

"You and your Lily are very special people to open your hearts and home that way. I can't wait to meet them all." She quieted for a moment as if thinking on that, then echoed in a proud voice, "Two grandsons. Paul is going to be ecstatic."

Trent knew from what she'd told him that Paul was her husband. He also knew that she and Paul had a daughter named Val, who was ten years younger than Trent and a high-powered criminal attorney.

"She graduated top of her class from Harvard Law. Worked Wall Street for a year or two, then moved to LA. Represents the rich and infamous in everything from embezzlement to murder to baby-mama lawsuits." Her still-damp eyes sparked humorously. "Has a wall in her office I call her Wall of Shame, covered with pictures of her posed up with her clients: actors, rappers, politicians, Silicon Valley high-ups. She makes a very good living. And she's happy. Which is all that matters."

"Can't wait to meet her."

"She's anxious to meet you, too."

They talked about everything and nothing, but mostly they drank each other in with their eyes. Trent feasted on the way she moved, spoke, and laughed. At one point she said, "Lord, you look so much like Mal."

"That a compliment?"

She cracked up. "When I was seventeen, it definitely was. He's still a good-looking man, though, as are you."

"Thanks. You're not so bad yourself."

"I think I'm still pretty hot for sixty-plus. Not sure if the world agrees, but I don't much care."

He liked her feistiness. "So what do you do? Are you a teacher? A doctor like your husband?"

"I'm an artist. Own a small gallery in Monterey, not too far from where we live."

He found that surprising, though he didn't know why. An artist. He noted the many silver bracelets on her wrists and the striking silver earrings dangling from her lobes. Very old-school, but she wore them with the style and attitude he'd often seen in women her age.

Tamar entered the kitchen, carrying a couple of battered shoe boxes and a photo album. "Since it sounded like all the crying's stopped, I figured it was safe to come in." She set the items on the table. "Remember that old TV show, *This Is Your Life*?"

They nodded.

She gestured.

Confused, Trent removed the lids from the boxes and saw his track medals lying neatly on top of a stack of report cards held together with an aging rubber band. Beneath them were football game flyers from his high school days and programs from his band concerts. He saw his Boy Scout handbooks and all the badges he'd earned, and many other items from his formative years he'd forgotten about over time. The photo album held faded Polaroids of him as a toddler and other photos of him all spruced up for school picture day, ranging from kindergarten to graduation. There was even a shot of him and Lily on their way to the senior prom. The memorabilia filled him with such wonder, all he could do was stare.

Tamar smiled. "Enjoy. Mal will be here with lunch in a bit," she said, and then exited.

They dove in and lost track of time as Trent explained the items in the shoe boxes. His mother read over one of the band programs from high school. "You played the flute?"

"Yes, but after high school I let it go. Picked

it up again recently when I was courting Lily."

"Really? How romantic."

"Amari thought I was nuts, but I got the girl."

His college diplomas were in the album too, and when she saw them, she raised her eyes to his and her voice echoed with surprise. "You went to Stanford?"

He nodded.

"Gosh, you were just up the road from us. So close, and yet so far . . ." Tears shone in her eyes. She pulled a tissue from the nearly depleted box. "Sorry."

"You're fine," he said reassuringly. "We're fine."

About thirty minutes later, Mal entered the kitchen carrying a huge bag. "Is all the crying done? I brought lunch."

Rita and Trent replied with contented nods.

"Good. Then, Rita Lynn, would you mind having lunch with your baby-daddy?"

She laughed. "Lord, forty-five years, and you have not changed."

Trent shook his head and moved the photo albums and the shoe box contents aside. Mal set the bag in the newly cleared spot. "I have, but I try and keep that under wraps. Do you mind, son?"

"No, Dad. Just hand me my food, and I'll be out of your hair."

Mal passed him a sandwich wrapped in white paper that had his name written on it in Rocky's handwriting and a Styrofoam container of smoking-hot fries. Trent grabbed a can of cola from Tamar's fridge and told Rita, "If he gets too outrageous, just yell."

Once he'd gone, Rita said seriously, "He's a fine man, Mal. You raised him well."

Mal extracted two more sandwiches from the bag. "Not me. Had very little to do with his raising. You still like pastrami?"

Her smile answered.

They unwrapped their sandwiches, doctored their fries, and dug in. Rita groaned pleasurably at the taste of the pastrami. "Oh, this is damn good."

"From my diner."

"Your diner?"

"Yes, the Dog and Cow," he said proudly.

She choked on the cola she was sipping. "The Dog and what?"

"Cow. As in moo."

"Why in hell did you name it that?"

"Drinking."

"I guess," she said, still amused.

He turned serious. "No, Rita Lynn. Really, drinking."

She paused and studied the serious set of his features.

"Which is why I had nothing to do with how he's turned out. Tamar did it all."

And as if to answer all the questions competing

in her head to be asked, he gave a one-word answer. " 'Nam."

She understood, or at least she thought she did. Many of the men of their generation went into the jungles of Southeast Asia and were irrevocably changed by the death and horror. There were incredible stories of courage and sacrifice too, but when they returned home, they were vilified, spit upon, and marginalized for having served their country in a war like no other the world had ever seen.

"Out of the twelve men I signed up with, only two of us came back—me and Clay Dobbs. Remember Clay?"

"I do."

"He still lives here. 'Nam changed him from the happy-go-lucky joker we used to hang with into somebody so quiet and rigid you wouldn't even know he was the same person."

She was saddened by that. Clay had always been such a joy to be around.

"Me, I thought I'd come home fairly whole, but about a year later I started having nightmares."

She listened as he talked about using the liquor initially to help him sleep, but as his tolerance to alcohol increased, drinking more and more to escape the nightly demons.

"Five years in, I was a full-fledged drunk, and of course I didn't think I needed help. I'd managed to get my degree in veterinary medicine on Uncle

Sam's dime and start my practice. I was what they now call a functional alcoholic. In my mind I was controlling the drink, it wasn't controlling me. And during all this, Tamar raised our boy."

"How did he handle your drinking?"

"I don't know. I was too drunk to know, most of the time."

"Oh, Mal." She ached for their son. An absentee mother and an alcoholic father. She thanked God for Tamar.

For a few silent moments he stared off into the distance, as if viewing the memories. "If I could go back and change things . . . But of course I can't."

Her heart broke.

"If it hadn't been for Trent, though, I'd probably be dead or serving time."

"What do you mean?"

He told her about the teenage Trent hunting him down and pulling him out of bars. "He and Lily riding around in Black Beauty every weekend, dragging my sorry ass home when they should've been going to dances and the drive-in."

"Black Beauty? The New Yorker you used to have?"

"Yep. Gave it to him when he turned sixteen. He still has it."

If she remembered correctly, the backseat of that car was where Trent had been conceived, but she saw no need to bring that up. "How long have you been sober?"

"Eleven years and counting."

"Very proud of you."

"Proud of myself."

When she made the decision to return, she'd envisioned Mal's life being as full yet as uneventful as her own, not fraught with challenge. "Married?"

"No. Alcohol was my woman, and when I divorced her, I discovered PYTs."

She knew the acronym from the old Michael Jackson song. "Pretty young things?"

He grinned over his sandwich.

"Oh god." She groaned.

"Those little blue pills will make a man lose his mind."

She laughed.

"Then a few years back I met the love of my life. Her name's Bernadine Brown, and I'm hoping to live happily ever after."

That was good to hear. She wanted him to be happy. "Does she live around here?"

"Owns the place."

"Owns what place?"

"Henry Adams."

"What do you mean, she owns Henry Adams?"

So he told her about Henry Adams going broke, and Bernadine buying the town off eBay.

"Stop lying."

He held up his hand like he was taking the oath in court. "Truth. Hopefully, you'll get a chance to meet her. We've been good for each other."

"I'm glad you're happy, Mal."

"I am, too. She's amazing. So enough about me. Tell me about you and your cardiac surgeon guy."

In the living room, Trent heard the occasional laughter coming from the kitchen. "Sounds like they're having a good time catching up."

"Yes, it does," Tamar said.

They were watching *SportsCenter*. It was now the top of the hour, so she changed the channel. "Time for *All My Children*."

He laughed. "*All My Children* is still on?" She'd been an *AMC* fan for as long as he could remember. As the episode began, he was startled by the sight of two familiar characters from his youth. "Angie and Jesse are still on, too? Didn't he die way back when?"

"He did. Died of a gunshot wound in the hospital. Then he was a ghost."

He chuckled. "Wait. A ghost?"

"Don't judge. Now he's back as a real person, but a different character."

"But he's Jesse."

"No, he's not." She picked up the remote and turned back to *SportsCenter*. "I'll watch it later. Won't be able to enjoy it with you commenting the whole time."

"Sorry."

"Finish your lunch."

He grinned. "Yes, ma'am."

• • •

After lunch, it was decided that Rita would stay with Tamar. She'd originally planned on flying back to California the next day, but she thought she might hang around a few days longer. She especially wanted to meet her grandchildren. "Can I meet them and Lily tomorrow?" she asked Trent, who was in the kitchen with her. Mal had already said good-bye. "Today's been so emotional, I'm not sure I can take much more."

"I understand. Go ahead and rest up. I'll come get you tomorrow, show you around the new and improved Henry Adams, and you can have dinner with us."

"I'd like that."

They shared a long parting hug, "Thank you for today," she said.

"You're welcome. Thank you for your courage."

"Thank you for your grace."

He went out to her rental car, brought her suitcase in, and watched as she climbed the stairs to the second floor. He'd called Lily, who was on her way to pick him up and drive him back to his truck, still parked in the lot at the Power Plant. He stayed a few moments longer to talk with Tamar.

"Do you like her?" asked Tamar.

"I do." He couldn't wait for Lily and the boys to meet her.

"I wasn't a big fan of her parents. Both were

way too stuck-up and class-conscious for me, but Rita Lynn, I liked. When Mal told me she was pregnant, I wanted to slap both of them into next week for being so careless, but out of that mess came you."

"Yes." He'd seen a picture of the young Rita and Mal. They were seated on Tamar's steps, relaxed and smiling, both sporting the huge Afros that were so popular then.

"Now everything has come full circle, and the hole in your heart has been filled."

He never remembered talking with Tamar about it, but the kindness in her eyes stoked his emotions.

"Trenton, I know better than anyone how much it hurt you, not having her in your life. When you were little, it hurt me every time you asked where she might be, and why she didn't love you like the mothers of your friends loved them. When you got to be around eight or nine, you stopped asking altogether, and that hurt me as well."

Trent had fought hard to be stoic growing up, so that no one would see his pain. "You were my port in the storm. Thank you for raising me."

"I wasn't going to let Mal do it," she tossed back in her frank way. "As much as I love him, I knew he didn't have the maturity, plus there was the alcohol, so—it was you and me." She quieted for a moment, as if thinking back on those years. "You favor her a lot, you know."

"Do I?"

"Yes. You look like a typical July, but I could always see her in your face, too. Still can."

That made him smile.

A horn sounded outside. Lily. It was time to go. She opened her arms, and he stepped into her hug to be buoyed by her love. "You are one amazing old lady."

She hugged him tighter. "Most of this gray hair is from you, mister, but for your love it's been worth it."

He kissed her cheek. "Thank for your love, too."

"You're welcome."

On the walk to the car, Tamar's words resonated within like a heartbeat: *The hole in your heart has been filled.* And that's how he felt.

Lily got out of the car and walked into his arms. They held each other tightly. "I'm so happy for you," she whispered.

Indeed, he felt like the happiest man in the world. He was married to a beautiful force of nature, father to a pair of awesome sons, and he'd just spent the afternoon getting to know the mother he'd been longing for his entire life. "Thanks for loving me."

"No problem. You ready to talk about it?"

"How about we wait until we get home. That okay?"

"You bet."

On the drive back to town, he didn't know if

he was overreacting or being a wimp, but he wanted to think about this privately for a while longer. Finally he too had a mother. Growing up, he'd wondered more times than he cared to acknowledge whether there'd been something wrong with him, whether it was his fault that she never came to see him. Of course, he never lacked for love or guidance, but Mother's Day was always hard. He'd wanted to be able to buy cards for his mother the way Gary Clark and his other friends did for theirs. He'd wanted to see her smile, give her presents for her birthday and for Christmas, and sit beside her at church on Easter morning. Over the years he'd convinced himself that the hole in his life didn't matter; so what if he had no mom cheering for him in the stands at his sporting events, or to talk with on the porch on starry summer nights or take pictures of him and Lily on their way to the prom? Tamar had done all those things and more. But in the hidden recesses of himself, he'd always wanted Rita Lynn Merchant to suddenly appear and tell him how much he meant and how much she loved him. Being with her today was like being given a cool drink of water after crossing a desert. Lily and the boys filled his world with purpose, love, and joy, but his life had felt incomplete because of one small missing piece. Now that piece was in place, and he couldn't be happier.

They reached the Power Plant parking lot, and

he said, "Thanks. I'll see you in a few minutes."

When he got home, Lily was in the living room and, true to her word, silent, waiting until he was ready. He went into the powder room off the kitchen, splashed water on his face, and paused for a moment to view his reflection in the mirror. *What a day.* He flashed himself a smile, dried his hands, and went to talk with his wife.

Chapter 7

After lunch, Amari sat at his desk. He was supposed to be checking out the slide show of Jacob Lawrence paintings Mr. James was showing on the screen, but instead he was sneaking peeks at Kyra and trying to figure out why he found her so fascinating. By a fourteen-year-old boy's standards she wasn't hot at all, but she had the cutest little nose, and her eyelashes . . .

"Ground control to Amari July." He was startled by Mr. James's voice. "Are you with us, my friend?"

"Um." Amari heard the snickers from his classmates. "Sorry. What did you ask?"

"The name of this painting?"

Amari liked the Lawrence paintings, and with the test coming up on Friday, he'd spent some time over the weekend looking at a bunch of them on the Internet. He knew the title. "*The*

March. It's from Mr. Lawrence's Toussaint L'Ouverture series. Painted in 1995."

"Excellent. Thank you."

"You're welcome."

Brain gave him a thumbs-up. Kyra looked impressed, which made his heart speed up and feel stupid.

After the art unit, they took a break. He and Brain were in the hallway when Kyra and Leah walked by, and he had to force himself not to stare her way.

Smiling, Brain asked, "How's that flu thing coming along? You cured yet?"

Grinning and embarrassed, all he had for his BFF was "Shut up."

"Maybe Dr. Reg can give you something."

"KMA, Brain. KMA."

Brain laughed, but then turned serious. "You should ask her to sit with you at the movies Friday night."

"And have her say no? I don't think so."

"Hey, she might say yes."

"No. Not taking that chance."

"Well, whatever you do, before you can be any kind of official with her, you have to talk to her dad first. Remember me having to do that with Leah?"

He did. Brain had to speak with Mr. Clark before he and Leah could do stuff like sit together at the movies. Everybody liked Leah's dad, but

Mr. Jones was a thousand feet tall and looked like Megatron. "Oh god. Now I know I need to find a cure. Quick."

Mr. James called the class back to order, and Amari settled in for the rest of the day's work. He hazarded a look Kyra's way and found her watching him. He quickly averted his eyes and returned to his assignment.

After school, he was up in his room when a text appeared on his phone. It was from Leah. *FYI. She likes you too.* ☺

After reading it, twice, he didn't know whether to laugh or cry.

Trent was still on a high after his awesome connection with his mother as he sat in the kitchen, watching Lily get dinner ready. They traded off the cooking chores, and it was her turn this week.

"I'm so happy for you, baby, but I'm still trying to get over what her parents did."

"I know, but I guess they thought they were doing the right thing."

"But for whom?"

He couldn't answer that. He kept seeing his mother in his mind's eye and smiling.

"But at least the mystery's finally solved. I know you were hurting, not knowing."

"Yeah, I was. Not sure how Amari's going to take the news, though. He's working through his own abandonment issues, and we were sort of in it together."

"I can't see him not being happy for you."

On the surface Trent didn't either, but underneath, he wasn't so sure. Sharing the issue seemed to have helped Amari manage his feelings. "Wish there was something we could do about his situation. I hate having him going through life like I have, wondering and not knowing, doubting his worth."

"Me too, but we can't unless she changes her mind, and there's no indication that she will."

"Do you think this will affect Devon in any way?"

She shrugged. "Hard to tell with him. He knows where his mom is. Now, whether he's old enough to understand the circumstances surrounding his birth, I've no idea. But I'm sure he'll be happy for you, too."

Devon's mom, Rosalie, was in a beautiful, well-run facility for the mentally impaired. His birth was the result of a sexual assault. They'd all met her for the first time during an emotion-packed trip to Mississippi a few summers ago.

Thoughts of Rosalie sent his mind back to his own mother, and he wondered what she might be doing. He wanted to call her and talk some more, but he and Lily made a point of spending the evenings with their sons, and for him that would always be a priority. He'd call her later.

"If your mom's coming to dinner tomorrow, you might want to talk to Amari before she comes, but I'm sure he'll be fine."

He hoped so. "And I have a half sister now, too. I always wanted sibs." Both he and Lily were only children.

"Me too—which is why I'm glad Amari and Devon have each other. If they can work out the kinks, I think they'll be closer as they get older. Amari isn't the problem. It's Devon."

"He'll be okay. Just needs to grow up. Think I'll take them camping in the spring. Devon mentioned going fishing with his grandmother. He might enjoy that."

Lily looked so doubtful, he chuckled. "We'll see."

After dinner, the boys cleaned up the kitchen, then headed upstairs to tackle homework. Trent let them work for an hour, then went up to speak with Amari. He found him in his room, looking at artwork on his laptop. "How's the homework going?"

"Good. We're studying great American artists, and this week it's Jacob Lawrence. I like this stuff."

Trent glanced down at the paintings. "Do you have a favorite?"

"Yeah, this one. It's called *The March*. It's based on General Toussaint L'Ouverture and the people of Haiti fighting against France. When I get old enough to have my own place, I think I might buy some of his prints."

Trent eyed the painting, with its vivid red and black brushstrokes, and thought about how far his son had come. The Amari who'd initially arrived in Henry Adams knew everything there was about stealing cars, but had no idea who Jacob Lawrence even was. The idea of that Amari buying prints one day would've been ludicrous. "It is nice." Trent paused before saying, "Something I need to talk to you about."

"What is it?"

"My mother came to town today."

Amari's eyes widened, and his jaw dropped. "Get out!"

"No. In fact, she's over at Tamar's right now."

"Where's she been?"

He explained the story, and when he was done, Amari shook his head sadly. "Wow. She thought you were dead? That was some cold stuff her parents did. Man."

"I know."

"Are you happy?"

"Very."

"Then I am, too. Do you think she's going to mind that you have two adopted kids?"

"No. I already told her about you and Devon, and she can't wait to meet you. She'll be coming to dinner tomorrow."

Amari searched his face. "I think this is awesome, Dad. Really, really awesome."

"Do you?"

"I do. You came in here because you were worried about how I'd take it, right?"

Trent nodded at his remarkable oldest child.

"No worries, Dad. None. I'm getting another grandmother. What kid wouldn't want that? As for my mom?" He shrugged. "It hurts, but not so much that I'd be mad at you or not want you to connect with your mom. You're a great dad, and great dads deserve great things."

"Had to come up and make sure you were okay. You mean a lot to me, son."

Amari offered up that beaming smile of his. "Do you know where she lives?"

"California."

"Sweet! You think she'll let us come visit?" he asked excitedly.

"You can ask, and I'm sure she'll say yes." Love for his son filled him from the top of his head to the soles of his feet. "You rock, son."

"Like no other, but that's because my dad rocks."

Trent offered him a hand, and they went through a slow ritual handshake. "Thanks, Amari."

"Are you going to tell Devon?"

"I am, but I wanted to talk with you first."

"I appreciate that," Amari replied quietly.

"I'll let you finish up your homework."

Trent left the room, but before clearing the

threshold he looked back and saw Amari staring off at something only he could see.

When Trent shared his news with Devon, the boy smiled. "I need a new grandma. Is she coming here?"

"Tomorrow for dinner."

"Good. Can I ask you something?"

"Sure."

"Why do people put those ugly tattoos on their arms and necks?"

For a minute, Trent was confused, and then it came to him. Devon must have seen Bobby's tattoos at the meeting. "For a lot of reasons, I guess. Some people like to think of their bodies as a canvas and put artwork on it, like Crystal does with her paintings."

"I think it's stupid and nasty."

"Why?"

"I just do. I'd never do something dumb like that."

"Then don't, but you don't get to decide what other people do or want. I take it we're talking about Crystal's friend Bobby?"

"Yes."

"Are you planning on telling him you think his art is stupid and nasty?"

Devon's eyes went wide. "No. He's really big. He might beat me up."

"Bobby's a nice guy. I don't think he'd beat up a little kid."

"He used to be in a gang."

"But he's not anymore." Trent sighed. Now Devon had a new target for his disdain. Great. "Regardless of how you feel about his having been in a gang or his tattoos, I want you to keep it to yourself. Tattoos don't automatically make a person bad. Besides, you need to be more concerned about making Devon the best person he can be instead of judging others."

Devon seemed to think that over.

"Also, Bobby's a grown-up. I'm pretty sure the opinion of a little kid doesn't matter to him one way or the other."

"Oh."

Sometimes he and Lily had to be blunt with Devon, and this was one of those times. "Luke, chapter six, verse thirty-seven, says what?"

Devon squirmed.

Trent waited.

"Judge not, and you shall not be judged," came the small-voiced reply.

Trent nodded and gave Devon's shoulder a fatherly squeeze. "Get your homework done." And he left the room.

In the house next door, Bernadine sat with Mal in her kitchen. The two of them had just finished dinner, along with Crystal, who was now upstairs working on her homework. Mal had spent the past few minutes bringing Bernadine up to speed on Rita Lynn's visit, and she was glad to finally have all the details. "Trent has to be ecstatic," she said.

"He is. Rita Lynn's pretty happy, too."

"Having to spend most of his life not knowing if his mother is alive, dead, or just not interested has to have been hard for him."

"Yes, but now they've finally connected. There were lots of tears."

"I'm sure there were."

They were interrupted by the sound of the doorbell. Bernadine stood. "I wonder who that could be?"

She opened the door to find Franklin's fire chief, Luis Acosta, illuminated under the porch light. "Chief Acosta?"

"Evening, Ms. Brown. Sorry to disturb you, but can I talk to you for a few minutes?"

"Sure. Come on in and have a seat. Can I get you something?"

"No, thanks."

She ushered him into the living room, and they sat. She liked Luis Acosta, and not just because he was a tall, good-looking man of Mexican-American extraction. He'd initiated the aid compact after the Stillwell fire last spring, and she'd always be thankful for his big heart. "What brings you by?"

"Bottom line, my family and I need a place to stay. Astrid Wiggins has fired me because I disagreed with her about leaving you all high and dry, and we've been evicted. Effective tomorrow at noon. Is there anywhere in town here where my family and I might stay temporarily?"

Mal walked into the room.

"Hey, Mr. July."

"Hey, Chief."

Bernadine sighed. Astrid was tearing through people's lives like a rogue elephant rampaging through the bush. "So sorry to hear that. Mal, can you give Tamar a quick call about that last vacant trailer?"

Mal took out his phone and walked back into the kitchen.

Bernadine realized she knew nothing about Luis's family life. "The trailer has two bedrooms. Will that work?"

"Yes. There is just me, my mother-in-law, and my two kids. My son can bunk with me, and my daughter can share the other room with her grandmother. Lost my wife a few years ago."

"My condolences."

"Thanks."

"I wish we had a larger place for you."

"It's a place. More than we had an hour ago. The trailer will be fine until I can find a new department to work for."

"So Astrid was your landlord?"

He nodded. "Her family owns probably ninety-five percent of the housing over there, so everybody rents. Step on her toes or look at her sideways and she evicts you."

"Wow."

"Since taking over as mayor, she's been grabbing power like an Eastern European dictator, voiding contracts, firing teachers. Everybody in town is walking on eggshells. In a lot of ways I'm glad I'm out."

Mal came back. "She says she'll get it ready."

"Thanks, Mal." Something else occurred to Bernadine. "Henry Adams could use an experienced fire chief. How about a job once you get settled in?"

Luis went still. "Really?"

"That's a damn good idea," said Mal.

Luis looked from one to the other.

"Well?" Bernadine prodded gently.

"Are you serious?" he asked.

"Very. We'll be starting the department from scratch, so you'll get to put your own stamp on things. Job's yours if you want it."

"I do," he said enthusiastically. "Thank you!"

Mal asked, "Do you need help moving tomorrow?"

"Yes."

"We can help out with that, too. Give me your number and send me a text in the morning."

Luis looked floored. "This is so not what I expected. My mother-in-law is going to be thrilled."

"Can't wait to meet her," Bernadine said.

He stood. "I need to get back and help her and

the kids finish packing up. You're a godsend, Ms. Brown."

"Feeling the same way about you, Chief."

He and Mal exchanged phone numbers, and with one last thank-you to them both, Luis Acosta went back out into the December night.

Bernadine looked at Mal. "I love it when a plan comes together," she said, quoting Hannibal Smith of *The A-Team*.

He laughed. "Let the church say amen!"

Mal left for home a short while later. Bernadine turned out the lights and went up to check on Crystal. Upon finding her asleep, a fond smile curved her lips. She remembered when Crystal first designed the bright orange room, but wouldn't sleep in the bed because she didn't want to mess it up. Henry Adams's reigning teen queen had come so far, and God willing, she would go even farther. Bernadine moved on down the hall to her own room.

She was in her pajamas, just about to turn off her laptop and climb into bed with a book, when her Skype app activated. She opened it and, upon seeing her sister Diane's face on the screen, sighed.

"Hey, Bernie!"

Bernadine hated being called Bernie. Her sister knew it but didn't seem to care. "Hey there, Di. How are you?"

"Loving Maui and this warm weather."

Diane was outdoors, and the backdrop of the mountains and beautiful blue sky made Bernadine, dealing with yet another winter on the plains of Kansas, quite envious. "Good seeing you. I was starting to worry."

"Sorry. I'm having so much fun, I forgot to check in."

"Gary wants you to call him."

"Why?"

Bernadine did her best to keep the frustration out of her voice. "He wants to know when you're coming back to work. You were only supposed to be gone a week."

"I've changed my mind—I'm going to stay for Christmas. Be back after New Year's Day."

"Then you have another job lined up?"

"No."

As she'd noted earlier, Diane still had a ways to go on a lot of levels. The earlier version of herself had been estranged from all three of her grown children for being intolerant of who they'd chosen to love, and from Bernadine for refusing to assist with caring for their dying mother. "He can't just hold your job forever. The man's running a business."

"You own the town, Bernie. Just tell him I'll see him in January."

"No. *You* call Gary, and make arrangements. By tomorrow."

Diane made a face. "Okay. Gotta go. Anthony's

teaching me to surf. Talk to you later. Bye!"

And she was gone.

Bernadine blew out a breath and sent an e-mail to Gary. He was still awake, and sent back that if Diane didn't call him by the end of business tomorrow, he'd be posting her job. Bernadine didn't argue. Either Diane was going to act like a responsible adult and handle her business, or she wasn't. Bernadine's job as sister didn't include saving Diane's bacon. She powered off the laptop and crawled into bed.

Chapter 8

Bobby entered the mayor's office for his second day of work and found Trent having coffee with two men he'd not met before—one Black, the other White. The Black guy had a no-nonsense bearing that was either military or law enforcement. He gave the tats peeking above Bobby's collar a silent once-over before sticking out his hand. "Barrett Payne."

Bobby didn't react to the extra-firm handshake. When you grow up on the streets, you don't broadcast weakness. "Military or law enforcement?"

Payne gave him a ghost of a smile. "Military. Marine colonel. Retired."

"Pleased to meet you."

"Same here."

The two took each other's measure.

Payne said, "Welcome to Henry Adams. Trent speaks very highly of you. When you moved in on Monday, I was in DC at the celebration honoring the Montford Point Marines. First Marines to break the color line in WW2. Do you know about them?"

"No."

"Look them up when you can."

"I will," Bobby lied.

"Barrett is the town's equivalent of Homeland Security," Trent put in.

Uncertain how to reply to that, Bobby simply said, "Ah."

The White guy introduced himself as the town's lead contractor. "Warren Kelly. Nice to meet you, Bobby."

"Thanks. Nice to meet you, too."

There was a large map of Henry Adams rolled open on a table. Bobby asked, "What're you doing?"

"Trying to figure out where to put the new library and firehouse that'll be built in the spring," Trent explained.

For the next hour, the three men went back and forth over the best place to build, how much it might cost, and how long it might take. He'd never been party to such a discussion before and was therefore surprised to learn how many things had to be considered and decided upon during a construction project, like the proper size and gauge of sewage pipes and drains, the slope a building needed for the ice-and-thaw cycle in winter, and, because they were in Kansas, the best design for an area prone to tornadoes. Bobby began the discussion feigning interest but half-way into it, his interest became genuine. There were things he wanted to ask about, but kept quiet for fear of being thought dumb.

Trent seemed to have considered that. "Bobby, if there's anything you don't understand or you need explained, just ask, okay?"

"Okay." Buoyed by that, he asked them to explain zoning restrictions, what went into an environmental evaluation, and the reason to use solar panels instead of plain old electricity. Each question was answered thoroughly and patiently.

As the meeting progressed, Bobby noticed the colonel checking him out every now and then, and he wondered what the marine might be thinking. Yesterday afternoon Crystal had stopped by for a visit and given them a rundown on the people they'd met so far, as well as some they hadn't, like Payne. According to her, he'd been a hardass when he first moved to town, but had mellowed a lot since then. She attributed that to his wife leaving him for a while because of an old extramarital affair he'd had, and his parenting of the teen everyone called Brain. Bobby had no idea how he and the marine might get along, but he planned to keep an open mind.

"You ever work a construction site, Bob?" Warren Kelly asked.

"No."

"Then you'll get your chance in the spring. During construction season it's all hands on deck. We have a skilled trades crew, but everybody winds up helping out here and there. We'll train you."

"Okay," he said doubtfully.

"Don't worry, you'll do fine," Barrett put in. "If you're going to be Trent's assistant, you'll need to be a Bob of all trades."

The play on words made Bobby smile.

Barrett patted him on the shoulder. "We won't let you fail or fall. Promise."

Bobby could count on one hand the number of people in his past who'd offered him such a quiet gesture of assurance and support. The jobs he'd had in Dallas were bottom-rung, and he might as well have been invisible to those higher up the chain as he vacuumed interiors at the dealership and parked cars at the hotel on the weekends. For the most part he hadn't cared; the paycheck he took home every Friday was the only recognition he'd needed. But these three men were coming at him differently. It was almost as if he was the son or nephew they were grooming to take over the business. The thought surprised him. Hazarding a look Trent's way, he found the mayor watching him with a knowing smile. It was as if he were silently acknowledging the conclusion. Bobby didn't know what to do with that, so rather than attempt to figure it out, he turned his attention back to what Payne was saying about a high-tech motion detector he wanted to add to the new buildings.

Around ten o'clock, Trent rolled up the map. Kelly had a meeting with some suppliers, and as he prepared to leave, he shook Bobby's hand. "Pleasure meeting you, young man. Looking forward to getting to know you and working with you."

"Same here, thanks."

With a nod, Kelly put on his coat and departed.

"So what else is on the mayor's agenda today?" Payne asked.

"Promised Bernadine and Mal I'd help the Acostas move. Astrid has evicted them because Luis didn't agree with her trashing the fire department contract. She's probably standing on their front porch right now, screaming at them to hurry the hell up and get out."

Payne shook his head. "Her loss is our gain. I'm clear until after lunch. Do you want some help?"

"That would be great. The more muscle and vehicles we have, the faster they can leave."

Bobby hadn't met Acosta yesterday, but he *had* met Seabiscuit. "I'd like to help, too."

"Thanks," said Trent.

Bobby followed Trent and Barrett the short distance from Henry Adams to Franklin. Mal and his buddy Clay Dobbs would be meeting them there. It snowed last night and Bobby worried about spinning out or sliding off the snow-covered road, but he gripped the wheel tightly and drove as fearlessly as he could.

The house they pulled up to was small and reminded him of the homes in his part of Dallas—one story, with a porch and a postage-stamp front yard. The interior was a sea of boxes, stacked bed frames, and dresser drawers still holding clothes. There were short, squat laundry hampers holding pots, pans, shoes, and toys. Luis Acosta side-stepped his way through the mayhem and shook their hands. "Thanks, guys. Really appreciate this."

From behind him appeared a statuesque older woman and two children. The little girl, in jeans and a Hello Kitty sweatshirt, appeared to be seven or eight, and the dark-haired boy, who sported owlish black-framed Harry Potter glasses, might've been twelve. Luis made the introductions. "My mother-in-law, Mrs. Anna Ruiz, and my kids, Maria and Alfonso."

Bobby wondered why no wife, but decided to ask Trent about that at a more appropriate time.

Mrs. Ruiz's dark eyes looked angry. "Thank you for your assistance. I can't wait to leave this place."

Standing beside her, Maria looked on shyly.

Alfonso, on the other hand, appeared as angry as his grandmother and nodded a terse, silent greeting.

"Then let's get started," Trent announced.

For the next hour they loaded the big, heavy items—bed frames, dressers, a piano, a dining room table, its chairs, and as many boxes as would fit—into the beds of the big pickups belonging to Trent, Barrett, and Luis. More fragile belongings—boxed dishes and glasses, along with Maria's pink-and-white dollhouse and a trash bag holding her collection of stuffed animals, went into the back of Mrs. Ruiz's and Bobby's SUVs.

Once none of the vehicles could hold even one spoon more, it was decided that Luis and his son would return later to load up the last few items inside.

They were standing on the porch, about to roll out, when Astrid drove up in her big, fancy gold Cadillac SUV. She stepped out wearing a big fur coat and approached them with a smile on her face that was as cold as the snow.

"What do you want?" Mrs. Ruiz asked, her voice just as chilly.

"I expect you to clean this place thoroughly before you leave. I won't be able to rent it again if it reeks of beans."

In response to the nasty remark, Anna looked her up and down and in a withering tone scoffed, "And you profess to be a Christian. Jesus must be very proud of you." She stepped off the porch and ushered her grandchildren to her car.

Astrid's face was beet red. She turned on Luis. "If you want that security deposit back—"

He cut her off. "Keep it. Buy yourself a new husband. Let's go, guys."

Behind them, Astrid screeched, "Luis Acosta, I'll make sure you never work in a firehouse anywhere in this country ever again."

"Too late," he called back. "Ms. Brown already hired me. Last night."

Bobby saw Astrid's eyes bulge and her jaw drop. Chuckling, he started up his vehicle and joined the small caravan ferrying the Acostas to their new life in Henry Adams.

Tommy had no idea how many days had gone by. Luckily there was a small flush toilet and a sink in the corner of the room. She'd given him an old sleeping bag and a couple of blankets, but there was no heat, and the room was like a freezer. She showed up once a day to toss him a bag of burgers and fries. And she always carried the shotgun. When he asked about the room, she said it used to house migrant workers. He thought he might be in her basement, but there were no windows and he was never allowed to leave, so he had no way of knowing for sure.

What he did know was that the only person who might care that he was missing was his mother. He was her only child, but he'd taken off so many times in the past, she probably figured he'd show up again eventually and wouldn't start worrying for a while. He also knew that if he really was on the Henry Adams surveillance tapes, the cops were looking for him—but for how long was anyone's guess. It wasn't like he'd committed murder. He'd only dumped some vials of roaches on the store's shelves, so they probably wouldn't look very long. Besides, they wouldn't really put him in jail for that. Would they? Either way, he couldn't count on the police for a rescue. Since it looked like ol' Horse Face would be keeping him hidden until she came up with a way to get out of this mess without implicating herself, he needed a plan to get away on his own.

Driving out to Tamar's to pick up Rita Lynn, Trent willed himself to relax. The Acostas were all moved in. Bobby was spending the rest of the day with Barrett, and Trent was off the clock, so he could spend the rest of the day with his mother. He planned to give her the grand tour of the new and improved Henry Adams before stopping in at the Dog for lunch. After that, he had no set plans in mind, so maybe they'd head over to his place and sit and talk until the rest of the family got home. In truth, it didn't really matter. All he wanted was for the two of them to continue building their relationship as mother and son.

The voice sync on his dash opened. “Hey, Trent?” It was Will Dalton.

“Hey there, Will. What’s up?”

“Just got a call from Luis Acosta. You helped him move this morning?”

“Yes. He okay?”

“Yes, but when he went back to pick up the last load, he found everything in a pile of ash smoldering on the front lawn. Said there was a strong smell of kerosene in the air.”

“Shit. Astrid.”

“That’s what he said when he called me just now, but with no witnesses, nothing I can do.”

Luis said he’d be going back for a box of his kids’ books, the family Christmas tree, and a few other odds and ends. “What are we going to do with her?”

“Not my monkey, not my circus, unless the monkey breaks the law.”

Trent blew out a breath of disgust. “Okay.”

“I hear you hired him as your chief last night.”

“Yes.”

“He’s a good man.”

“Don’t know him real well, but that’s the impression I get. Since we can’t throw the monkey in a cage, anything else?”

“Yes. Two things. First, Tommy Stewart’s mother has filed a missing persons report on him. It’s going on three weeks since she last saw him. Apparently he’s taken off before, but never for this long. Second, Nebraska law enforcement found his vehicle abandoned on a back road just on their side of the state line. Torched."

"He wasn't in it, was he?"

"No."

"Good. I wouldn't want anyone dying like that. Do they think he set the fire himself?"

"They're still investigating."

"Okay, thanks for the update and for your patience with Bobby the other day. Much appreciated."

"No problem. Later." And the sync went silent.

In Trent's mind, this entire mess was on Astrid. Once it was proven, the law firm the town retained to represent its interests would be slapping her with a civil suit for the damages and lost revenue incurred from the store's closure mandated by the Health Department. With any luck she'd end up in the poorhouse, hopefully in a country far, far away. But they had to find Tommy Stewart first.

His next sync call was from Lily, informing him that Reverend Paula had to leave town because of a family emergency back home in Oklahoma, and would reschedule their family therapy session when she returned. Hoping everything with their spiritual leader would be okay, and that somehow, some way, Devon would find the peace he needed, Trent drove on.

As he put the truck in park in front of the house he'd grown up in, he pushed all the drama aside.

Inside, two women, the one who'd given him birth and the one who'd raised him, were waiting.

"So where are we going first?" his mother asked while locking her seat belt across her lap. "Nice truck." She sounded impressed as she glanced around the black and gray interior, with its spaceship-like dash. "I haven't ridden in a pickup since high school, and never in one this fancy."

"Thought I'd show you the town, then go grab something to eat at the Dog."

"The Dog and Cow," she said, chuckling.

"The Dog and Cow."

"That's insane."

"Nice place, though."

"All right, forward!"

He steered onto the main road. Still not quite believing she was there, he kept stealing looks at her which she met with a smile.

"Still can't believe this is real," she said.

"Same here. Trying not to stare at you."

She reached up and squeezed his hand. "It's okay, stare all you like."

It was one of those bright December days when the sun glistened off the snow-crusted fields.

"Haven't seen this much snow since we moved away," she said, glancing out her window. "Or been this cold." She was wearing a red parka and a black knit hat. "This jacket is almost doing the job. Almost."

"When I lived in California I enjoyed the

weather, but after a while I got tired of the sameness. Wanted to see the leaves change and the trees budding in the spring."

"Understandable, but I'll take sameness over freezing any day of the week. Do your boys like winter—do they ice skate and ski cross country, like Mal and I and our friends used to do?"

"Yes. In fact, we'll be setting up the town ice rink this weekend. Should be cold enough for it to stay frozen. Do you still skate?"

"I do. Taught Val when she was little. The lessons came in handy when she was in New York. She loved skating at Rockefeller Center."

He was taking the long way into town, past Clay and Bing's place.

"Clay's place, right?" she asked.

"Yes."

"Your dad said he was still here. His folks still living?"

"No, they passed away when I was in LA."

"Sorry to hear that. They were nice folks. I wonder what ever happened to Genny Gibbs? Clayton worshipped the ground she walked on, but she wouldn't give him the time of day. You probably wouldn't know—before your time."

He laughed. "She's still in town."

"Get out!"

"Yep. Still here."

"Oh, my goodness. I figured she'd be living in Paris or someplace. She so wanted to leave this little country town. Do you think we'll see her?"

"We'll hunt her down if you like. She stays with Marie and Tamar."

"Marie Jefferson?"

The skeptical tone made him turn. "Yes."

She had a slightly sour look on her face.

"You and Marie didn't get along?"

"I got along with her fine. She didn't get along with me."

He found this fascinating. "Why not?"

"She had a thing for Mal."

His eyes went so large, he almost drove off the road. "Marie Jefferson?"

"Yes, Miss My Family Helped Found This Town Marie Jefferson. Had a thing for him, just like Clay had for Genny. She couldn't stand me. I thought it was funny. As the kids say today, it wasn't like she was taking my man. Her and those stupid cat-eye glasses she used to wear."

He didn't know whether to be appalled or laugh.

"What?" she asked.

"Marie's still here, too." *And,* he almost added, *wearing her cat-eye glasses*. "In fact, the new school is named for her. The Marie Jefferson Academy."

"Oh, hell."

"And she's my Lily's godmother."

"Shit."

His eyes grew even larger.

"Sorry. I'm supposed to be trying to make a good impression. How am I doing?"

The mischief in her eyes made him laugh again. "Is this the real you coming out?"

"Possibly. I talked to my daughter last night, and the last thing she said to me was 'Mom, now that you and Trent have found each other and you're cool, please don't be out there acting like a hot mess.' "

"She know you pretty well?"

"You reach a certain age, and your children think they're the parent. Which is fine, especially when I need her to bail me out of jail."

He almost wrecked the truck again.

"Too much sharing?"

"Let me park before you make us hit a snowbank." He pulled into the Power Plant's lot and parked.

"What a beautiful building. What's something this cutting-edge doing here?"

Before he could respond, she undid her belt and got out. He watched her shade her eyes against the low-hanging winter sun and study the red architectural wonder. He supposed her interest was rooted in her being an artist. Its lines and structure had always appealed to his inner engineer as well. He cut the engine and got out, too.

She was still taking in the building appreciatively. "How long has it been here?"

"Almost four years now."

"My goodness, it's beautiful. Who was the architect?"

"I'd have to go in and ask. My office is inside."

"If I had to work a nine-to-five, I wouldn't mind doing it in such a great place. Can we go in?"

He made a grand gesture of offering his arm.

Inside, she found the atrium entranceway just as intriguing. She took in the lush plants lining the floor and then raised her eyes to the skylight overhead. "How do you keep the snow off the glass?"

"There are solar fibers threaded through it."

"Really?"

"Top-of-the-line tech in all the new buildings. Come on, let's see if Lily and Bernadine are here."

"Mal's Bernadine?"

He nodded, and noted her hesitation. "Don't worry. Bernadine's a very classy lady. She doesn't do drama. Promise."

Chapter 9

The sun was still shining when he and Rita walked back out to the truck. Just as he'd promised, she'd had nothing to fear from Bernadine. The Boss Lady had been warm and welcoming.

Fastening her seat belt, Rita cracked, “What in the world is a regal woman like her doing with a country jester like Mal?”

Trent chuckled and turned the key to start the engine.

“She’s what, five-eight and about a size eighteen?” she went on. “Built like a damn goddess, and drop-dead gorgeous. And you were right. Very nice.”

He remembered Bernadine’s first year and the hoops she’d forced Mal to jump through before even thinking about entertaining his company. “She gave Dad a real run for his money, believe me.”

“I’ll bet she did. And your Lily. Beautiful as the flowers she’s named for.”

“Thanks.”

“Easy to see she loves you madly.”

“I love her even more.”

“Have you been married since high school? I remember the prom picture in the photo album.”

“No, only a little over a year. She’s wife number three for me.”

Her surprise showed in her voice. “You’re kidding. We didn’t talk about this yesterday, did we?”

“No.” He told her about his failed marriages—first to Felicia, the high-powered lawyer he’d helped put through law school. “I wanted kids. She said she did too, and we agreed that once she passed the bar, we'd figure out how to balance children and our jobs."

"Didn't work out?"

"No. Told me she'd changed her mind about the whole child thing, and that she'd gotten a tubal during law school."

Her jaw dropped.

"Got married again two years later. Mia. Owned a bookstore. Lasted six months. She was sleeping with one of my business partners."

"Oh, Trenton."

"Decided the big city had kicked my ass long enough, and for the last time, so I came home."

"I'm sorry."

"Thanks, but I got Lily eventually, so I won in the end."

"Yes, you did."

He was about to pull out of the lot when he remembered something. "You never did finish telling me why you had to be bailed out of jail."

She laughed. "I'm sorry. Didn't mean to leave you hanging. Protesting. I'm a child of the sixties and seventies, and after we moved to California, I went to Berkeley."

"Oh, okay," he replied.

"Then you know all about what it stood for back then?"

"Yes. American history class in undergrad."

"Ah. I spent my four years at Berkeley protesting against everything from Nixon to the war to the police shootings of Black Panthers. Then I went to the Sorbonne in Paris to finish my art studies and protested there. Two years later I came back to the States, and I've been marching for or against issues since. Women's rights. Civil rights. Rights of the poor. Last month it was for a sound immigration policy, and two weeks before that against the navy's deep-water testing, which endangers our whales. Paul says Val grew up to be a lawyer because the two of them spent so much time in courtrooms watching my lawyers trying to convince judges why I shouldn't be locked up."

"But all great causes. She had to be proud of you."

"Oh, she is—they both are. And she's done her share of marching as well."

He pulled out of the Power Plant parking lot and tooled slowly down the street so Rita could see the new church, recreation center, and school.

Again she was impressed by the architecture. "Such great buildings—even the one named for Old Cat Eyes."

Trent smiled inwardly. He hoped there wouldn't be fireworks if the two met during Rita's visit.

"I was supposed to ask Ms. Brown the architect's name," she added, "but I was too busy being impressed by her fabulousness. And she's responsible for all this?"

"Every brick, paved road, and light pole.

There's a small subdivision, too. You'll see that when we go home for dinner."

The leveled lot holding the listing remnants of the Henry Adams Hotel, which had served as a movie theater in her day, caught her attention. "What happened?"

"Tornado in 2005. Took the school, too."

"That's so sad. A lot of necking went on in that balcony."

He chuckled. "Bernadine's trying to restore it."

"I like that idea. I hope it happens—that old building represents so much of what this town was about."

He agreed.

As Trent would tell Lily later, when they walked into the Dog and heard Stevie Wonder on the juke box singing "Skeletons in Your Closet," he should've taken it as a sign and walked right back out. Instead, he watched his mother look around in amazement.

"This is a nice place, Trent."

"We're real proud of it. It used to be a well-loved dump before Bernadine waved her magic wand."

Since it was a bit after the lunch rush, the place wasn't real crowded. Mal came up and was about to speak when Rita asked excitedly, "Is that Genevieve?"

Trent grinned. "Yes, it is."

"Mal, do you think she'll remember me?"

"I think she just might."

And at that moment Genevieve, seated at a table with Marie, glanced up. When she saw Rita, her eyes widened. She said something to Marie, who looked over as well, and Marie's eyes flashed icily.

But Genevieve was on her feet, hurrying over to where they stood. "Rita!"

They met and hugged and rocked and laughed, while Marie watched distantly.

"My god, girl," Genevieve gushed. "I didn't know you were here. You look so good!"

"California living. It's all about the bean sprouts and the yoga. You look damn good yourself."

"My goodness! When did you get in?"

"Yesterday."

Trent interrupted. "Let's find a seat, ladies. We're blocking the entrance."

They got a booth, and Mal brought Rita a menu. "You want something to drink, Rita?"

"Just water for now, Mal, thanks." She couldn't seem to take her eyes off Gen.

"So you're living in California?"

"Yes. I told Trent I expected you to be living in Paris."

"I wish. Glad to have you back."

"Hello, Rita." It was Marie.

"Hey, Marie."

"I heard you were here."

The air in the room changed. Genevieve looked tense.

Mal returned with Rita's water. "Good to have her back, isn't it, Marie?"

"Not really."

"Marie!" Genevieve gasped.

Mal was staring at Marie as if he'd never seen her before. Trent was pretty floored, too. He'd seen her angry before, but usually it was a classroom setting, when one of the students had gotten out of line.

Rita Lynn picked up her water and sipped slowly. She raised her eyes to Trent, and it was impossible to tell what she might be thinking. She set the glass down again. "Marie, I'm here to visit my son, not to rehash stupid shit from high school."

"Marie," Gen said quietly, "go back to the table."

"Shut up."

"What?"

"I said shut up, Genevieve." Marie glared at Rita Lynn.

Gen stood up and asked in an incredulous voice, "Who in the hell do you think you're talking to?"

By then all the other diners were staring.

Rita Lynn very calmly picked up her menu and began perusing the offerings.

Marie snapped, "Oh, what? Now you're going to ignore me?"

Rita didn't raise her eyes from the menu. "Yes, I am. Just like I did forty-five years ago. Mal, get your girl. The last time she and I got physical, it was two weeks before she stopped looking like Joe Frazier after being whipped by Ali."

Trent froze.

Mal shouted, "Time out! What's going on here?"

Marie looked like she wanted to jump across the table and snatch Rita up.

Gen asked him coldly, "Are you really that clueless, Malachi? Still?"

"Apparently. So fill me in."

"Shut up, Genevieve," Marie warned. "You just worry about the fact that she slept with Clay, too."

Genevieve paused, looked at Rita Lynn, who verified the disclosure with a tight nod. That fact rocked Trent, but he had to give it to Gen, who turned to Marie and yelled, "Earth to Marie! Forty-five years ago."

Mal blinked. "Wait. Rita, you had sex with Clay?"

"Just like you had sex with Lisa Green, Adele Pettiford, Constance Phillips, Bobby Jo Mitchell . . . shall I go on? At least I did it with Clay during one of the many times you and I broke up. You did those other girls on some of the same nights after we went out on dates."

Trent had never seen his dad look so small.

But his mother wasn't done. "And as for Ms. Cat Eyes here, the only reason she's got her panties in a twist is because you never asked her to take them off."

Trent jumped, and Mal did, too.

Marie screamed, "You bitch!"

Rita Lynn threw her water in Marie's face. "Go home."

Marie shook with fury. Trent thought she might be in tears, but she was so wet from the face down, it was hard to tell. Without a word, she hurried over to her table to retrieve her coat and purse and left.

There were shocked faces all over the diner, and you could hear a pin drop.

"Sorry, Gen," Rita said.

"She started it. You finished it. *Que sera sera*. How long will you be here?"

"After this, Trent may be taking me straight to the airport." She gave him a small smile, which he returned.

"Well, I need to go see about Marie, if she hasn't driven off and left me. Next time you're here, we need to get together and catch up. Good seeing you, Rita."

"Same here."

"Bye, Trent."

"Bye, Gen."

Genevieve walked past the silent Mal without a word.

Rita glanced up at Mal, who looked as if he wasn't sure how to react. Trent knew exactly how he felt. "Can I order now?"

"Uh, yeah, sure."

"I'll have your number six with the honey mustard on the side, please."

"Coming right up."

Later that night, as Trent and Lily lay in bed, he told her the story. When he'd finished, she said, "Wow. Sounds like that old show *Peyton Place*."

"I'd say it was more like *The Real Senior Citizens of Henry Adams*."

Beside him, she chuckled in the darkness.

Dinner with the family had gone well. Rita Lynn had been warm and showed great interest in her grandsons, but he'd noticed the hint of sadness behind the smiles. When he drove her back to Tamar's, she'd been quiet and subdued.

"So what was up with Marie, do you think?" Lily said now.

"No clue," Trent admitted. "I mean, she must be really hurting if she's holding a grudge after such a long time. And why be mad at Rita? Marie couldn't force Dad to like her."

"Maybe she thought she'd've had a chance with Mal had Rita not been there? I don't know."

"But she's been like his sister their whole lives. From his reaction, he didn't even know she had a thing for him." He replayed Gen's withering question: *Are you really that clueless, Malachi? Still?* "Have to admit, when they started talking about who was sleeping with who, and Rita rattled off that list of names, I was like, I am way too young to be hearing all this."

She chuckled once more. "Glad I missed it. Never known my godmother to pick a fight like that before, but sounds like she did."

"Definitely. Rita Lynn handled her business, though."

"Does Marie know the circumstances surrounding your birth?"

"I assumed Dad told her, but maybe not. She didn't bring any of that up." He wasn't sure who knew what about him being brought back to Henry Adams by Rita's mother or why Rita had never visited before now. "I'll have to ask him. Man, Rita really laid it on him, though. He looked like Inch High, Private Eye, when she finished."

"Her coming back has been very interesting, to say the least."

"True, but I'm still glad she's here."

"So am I." She turned her head on the pillow. "Just thought of something. I wonder if Marie's reaction had anything to do with her son and his adoption?" Marie found herself pregnant during her first year in college, and her out-of-wedlock son was taken immediately after birth and put up for adoption. Marie never even got to hold him. Two years ago, he'd called, asking to meet her.

She'd agreed, thinking he meant to establish a relationship, but she was wrong—he only wanted to see what she looked like and to learn whether there were any health problems in the gene pool. It broke her heart. "Do you think she resents Rita being in your life because she can't be in the life of her own child?"

Trent had no answer. He eased her into his side. "I don't know, but I hope she and Genevieve made up. I hadn't seen Gen that hot since the day she decked Riley."

"I've been wanting to have a high school reunion, but after this drama today, maybe I need to rethink that."

"Maybe."

"Rita should come back and spend Christmas with us. I know it's last-minute, but I assume you'd like that, and the boys certainly would."

"What about you? After all, Marie is your god-mother."

"We invite her too, and sell tickets."

He laughed so loud he was afraid he'd awakened the boys. Once he recovered, he asked, "Are you sure?"

"Certain. I want her to have a relationship with us. She's your mom. You two are owed that, after being apart for so long."

Trent didn't think his love for her could grow any higher. "You're a remarkable woman, Lily Fontaine July."

"Glad you figured that out."

"I'll ask her in the morning."

"Good. Now show me how remarkable I am."

Grinning, he pulled her closer and showed her that and more.

The following morning, Trent drove Rita Lynn back to the airport.

"Sorry again about the drama with Marie yesterday," she said as they sat in the truck outside the terminal. She hadn't had much to say on the ride there.

"No apologies needed."

"Did you tell Lily?"

"I did."

"She's probably furious, what with Marie being her godmother and all."

"No. Not a bit."

"You wouldn't lie to me, would you? I didn't come here to cause dissension in your marriage."

"I know that, and so does she. She's not mad at you in any way, shape, or form."

Rita seemed quietly grateful.

"We'd like to have you back for Christmas. I know it's last-minute."

"I can't. I chair a fund-raiser in Monterey every year the day after."

"Then what about after Christmas, and stay until New Year's?"

She looked surprised. "You mean that?"

"No. I'm just kidding. The family and I never want to see you again. Of course I mean it!"

"Lily won't mind?"

"Would you stop worrying about Lily? She was the one who asked me to ask you."

"She's remarkable."

Trent had nothing to say to that, but he did smile. "So can you come back? And bring Paul and Val, so we can meet them, too."

Tears filled her eyes. "Lord, I thought I was done with the waterworks." She fished around in her purse for a tissue. "Yes, I will come, and I'll see if Paul and Val can come, too."

"Good." Trent didn't want her to leave, because the little boy inside who'd missed her all his life was afraid he'd never see her again.

"I've so enjoyed this," she said.

"I have, too, and we'll be together from now on. Deal?"

"Deal," she whispered.

"Let's get your bag so you can go inside."

"I don't want to leave."

"Honestly, I don't want you to, either. Scared I'll never see you again."

She placed her hand against his cheek. "I'll be back. Promise."

He took her bag out of the back and held on to it as they walked to the doors. Inside, she hugged him tightly. He hugged her tighter. "You take care of yourself," she whispered.

"You, too. Make sure you text me when you land."

"Will do. Give my regards to Mal, even if he doesn't want them."

"I will."

She wiped her tears. "Now go on home, or I'll never stop crying. I'll call and let you know what day we're coming."

He leaned down and kissed her cheek. "Good. Tell Val you tried to behave, but it wasn't your fault."

"She's not going to believe a word. Bye, son."

"Bye, Mom."

Out in the truck, Trent drew his palms down his wet eyes and started the engine. Never in his life had he ever imagined he'd say the word *Mom*. But he had, and it felt good.

When the plane took off, Rita sat in her seat a tremendously happy woman. The memory of seeing her son walking through that kitchen door for the very first time gave her goose bumps. Not only had she regained him, but he'd come bearing gifts like the Magi. She now had a beautiful and gracious daughter-in-law and *two* grandsons. Seeing Mal after so many years had been emotional too—the drama aside. They'd had some great times growing up, and they'd made a child—a bond they'd carry to their graves. As she basked in the afterglow of the visit, she thought about her parents and chose to stop damning them for what they'd done. Her memories of them no longer had to be twisted by anger and betrayal. She had her son back, the balance in her life had been restored, and she could once again honor them with love. She was truly blessed.

Chapter 10

In the days following Rita's visit, Marie and Genevieve were still at such odds, Gen had Trent take her to the bus station so she could catch the Greyhound to Topeka and stay with her cousin for the weekend. Mal and Clay fell out over Marie's revelation, too. As Genevieve had tried to do, Clay pointed out that the incident happened during high school, but Mal wasn't buying. He started in on Clay about betrayal and loyalty until Clay shot back that had Mal been thinking above the shoulders and not below the waist back then, none of this would be happening. Mal took great umbrage with that truth and stormed off.

Clay, blindsided by the whole thing, drove over to Marie's and yelled at her for telling tales out of school, and because she couldn't defend the indefensible, she slammed the door in his face. Trent did his best to steer clear of all of it. He figured the Real Senior Citizens of Henry

Adams would come to their senses . . . eventually.

"So what do you think this is going to be about?" Bobby asked Kiki as they set out Monday evening for the short drive to Tamar's. Bobby parked. The area around the house was filled with vehicles.

"I don't know, but looks like everybody's here. Crystal said it's a welcoming ceremony."

"The last time we got welcomed, you'd've thought we were the president and the First Lady."

"But I thought it was nice, and you did, too. Admit it."

"Okay. It was kinda nice."

"Then let's go in."

They entered with the babies, and the sight of them set off a round of applause that they met with smiles. Genevieve, back from Topeka, rushed over to help get the babies out of their carriers. After hoisting one twin in each arm, she walked off to show them around. Bobby and Kiki handed their coats to Marie Jefferson, who was still mad at her housemate. The air was filled with the smells of good food wafting from the kitchen. Tamar, wearing an apron over a beautiful emerald-green-and-black caftan, stood before the blazing fireplace and called out, "Can I have your attention, please?"

Everyone quieted down.

"We're here this evening to officially welcome Bob and Kelly and the twins, the Acosta family, and Gemma and Wyatt as our new neighbors." Applause sounded in tandem with a chorus of welcomes. "We want to thank Crystal for bringing us Bob and Kelly."

Crystal got a round of applause. Grinning, she executed a curtsy.

"And we thank Astrid Wiggins for Luis and his family. Secretariat's loss is our gain. She was also the reason Gemma moved here, so we thank Her Horsiness for that, too."

Laughter filled the room. The Acostas smiled, Luis raised his cup of punch, and Gemma threw kisses.

"We'll have the ceremony after we eat, so for now, just have a good time. Food's almost ready."

Tamar, Mal, Rocky, Bernadine, and a few others returned to the kitchen, and everyone else went back to talking and visiting.

Bobby and Kiki knew everyone except Dr. Reggie Garland and his wife, Roni. They were pleased to learn the doctor was Henry Adams's resident pediatrician, and equally impressed that Roni was a multi–Grammy Award–winning singer. Neither of them were familiar with her music, but she had a great sense of humor and promised them one of her CDs.

Crystal took them into Tamar's den, where the kids were gathered. The young ones—Zoey, the daughter of Roni and Reggie; Wyatt, whose grandmother they'd met earlier; and the two

Acosta kids—were playing Angry Birds on the big flat-screen on the wall. The older ones—Amari, Brain, Eli, Leah, and Tiffany—sat at a small table, playing poker, of all things.

"OG and Mr. Bing taught us to play the first winter we were here," Crystal explained. "They said it would help with our math and concentration. But it was really to teach us humility, because they won all the time."

Trent's youngest son, Devon, was seated by himself. The kid curled his lip at Bobby as he glanced Devon's way. He'd done basically the same thing when they were first introduced at the town meeting. Having no idea what the little round-headed boy's problem was, Bobby ignored him and walked over to see who was winning.

"We're only allowed to play for pennies," Trent's older son, Amari, said, not taking his eyes off the cards being played by the others.

"Which is a good thing," Eli added, "because Leah is kicking our butts."

"Again," Brain groused, tossing down his cards.

The smiling Leah raked in her winnings. "Whose deal?"

Devon looked so put out that Crystal asked, "What's wrong with you, now?"

Zoey said, "He's mad because he wanted to play first and I told him to let Alfonso and Maria play first because they're our special guests."

Devon sneered. "You're always trying to run

stuff. I'm ready to eat and go home. It's always so boring over here."

Tamar walked in. "You're bored? Come with me. We need help in the kitchen."

Bobby thought the boy's eyes were going to pop out of his face.

Snickers were heard.

When he didn't immediately comply, Tamar said quietly, "Devon. Let's go."

He rose sluggishly, looking for all the world like someone on his way to an execution, and followed Tamar out.

Once they were gone, chuckling filled the room and Zoey drawled, "Dumbass."

The kids laughed.

Hearing a baby crying—Bobby Jr., to be specific—a smiling Bobby, Kiki, and Crystal exited, too.

Genevieve looked flustered. "I'm sorry. One minute he was fine, and the next . . ."

Kiki took him, and he pressed himself firmly against her. The wails diminished to whimpers. She gently rubbed his back. "You are such a mama's boy, aren't you? It's okay. GG Gen just wanted you to say hello to everyone."

Tiara seemed content in Genevieve's arms, but was handed off to Bobby anyway. "I don't want her getting upset too."

Genevieve leaned close to Bobby Jr. "I'm sorry, sweetie pie," she said, and he began wailing again.

"Okay, Baby Bob. I won't talk to you or even look at you for the rest of the night. I promise."

From behind them, Sheila Payne asked, "Genevieve, are you pinching those babies?"

Genevieve grinned. "Hush."

Sheila leaned close to Baby Bob and said softly, "Ms. Genevieve is really nice. You're going to love her just like we do one day." His crying started again.

"But apparently not today," Gen said, smiling. "I'll see you all later."

"He's just tired," Kiki said. "Hard work being a baby boy, isn't it, sweetheart?"

Sheila said, "If you need some quiet, I'm sure Tamar won't mind you slipping into her bedroom. Shall I ask her?"

"Would you? Before we all need earplugs."

People were turning toward the sound of the wails. Even though everyone looked sympathetic, Kiki said, "Lord, I'm so embarrassed."

"Don't be. Everyone knows this is what babies do—and those that don't? Now they do. Be right back."

When Sheila returned, Crystal grabbed the diaper bag and they went into Tamar's big, old-fashioned bedroom.

"Tamar said those cribs are here for them, if you want to lay the twins down," Sheila said.

Bobby and Kiki both stared. Two antique cribs stood side by side.

Tamar walked in. "That one was Trent's, and the other one Mal's. Dug them out and cleaned them up when Crystal got back from Dallas. Thought they might come in handy when you moved here."

Kiki shook her head. "You all are amazing."

Bobby met Tamar's dark eyes. The people of Henry Adams were so generous, he had no words. "Thanks."

"You're welcome."

Kiki extracted two bottles from the bag and laid the babies down in the cribs. After the first few sucks, they both fell asleep. Easing the nipples from their mouths, she covered them with the beautiful soft baby quilts in the cribs, and everyone tiptoed out.

Trent saw his dad sitting off by himself in a chair in a corner of the room. He'd noticed Bernadine with Mal earlier, and the two seemed to be having a quiet but serious conversation. "You okay?"

"No. Just stupid."

"Ah. You want to talk about it?"

"No."

"Okay, then how about I hang with you for a minute? Maybe the stupid will go away."

Mal smiled a bit. "You're a better son than I deserve."

"I'd heard that."

Mal raised his eyes. "I finally find the one

woman I want to spend the rest of my life with, and how do I prove it?"

"By being party to a semi-brawl over a woman you haven't seen in forty-plus years?"

"Bingo. And of course she heard about the whole thing."

"Who hasn't? I thought I was watching a reality show."

Mal sighed. "What a mess. Clay's mad at me. Gen's mad at Marie. How was I supposed to know Marie had a thing for me? She's like my sister—has been my whole life. But evidently everybody else knew."

Since Trent had nothing to say, he waited.

"So I tried to explain to Bernadine about a man's pride and Clay being my best friend, and how I couldn't believe he'd done such a thing. And you know what she said?"

Trent figured he did, but wanted to have it verified. "What?"

" 'It was forty-five years ago. Grow the hell up.' "

Bingo! "Sounds like pretty good advice."

"Yeah, well. Anyway, now she's mad at me, too."

"Then how about you take her advice and apologize? Rita Lynn's coming back after Christmas, and she'll be here until New Year's."

Mal hung his head. "Lord."

"So you need to get this cleared up between

you and Bernadine before then. Or do you still have a thing for Rita Lynn?"

"Of course not."

"Maybe you should start acting like it."

"I hate it when you're wise."

"Rita says it comes from Tamar, because I definitely didn't get it from my parents."

Mal laughed. "Good-bye."

"Love you, too."

A short while later, upon seeing his youngest laying down silverware at all the place settings around the large dining room table, Trent wondered what he'd done to deserve such a dubious honor. A few years ago, Devon would've happily volunteered for such a detail, but the pout ruling his face now told all. Trent walked over and asked easily, "So what did you do?"

Lily walked in, carrying a huge bowl of mashed potatoes. "Tell the truth, Devon." She set the bowl down in the center of the table, gave their son the universal mama glare, and left the room.

"Well?" Trent asked, and watched Devon debate with himself whether to tell the truth or not. In the end he confessed, "I said I was bored, and Tamar heard me."

"I see."

Tamar came in and set the ham down near the bowl of potatoes. "Devon, get the plates out of the sideboard."

"Yes, ma'am."

Having been in his shoes plenty of times growing up, Trent knew how he felt, and the urge to help was strong. Apparently Tamar could still read his mind because she said to Trent, "Don't even think about helping him."

And like Devon, he echoed, "Yes, ma'am."

Heading for the exit, Trent patted his son on the back. "Sorry, kiddo."

"It's okay, Dad."

Devon was opening the sideboard when Trent left the dining room.

After a dinner that left them all stuffed, they gathered in the living room for the ceremony. Bobby had no idea what was about to happen, but after checking on the still-sleeping twins, he and Kiki stood side by side and waited patiently while everyone formed a circle. Devon was passing out white candles. As he handed one to Bobby, he turned up his nose. Bobby ignored the slight, but Amari snapped, "Devon, I'm telling Dad. Quit it!"

Devon rolled his eyes and resumed his task.

"Sorry, man," Amari said. "He's an idiot."

"No problem," Bobby replied, but he was glad to hear that Amari agreed with his own opinion of the bratty little round-headed boy.

The lights were dimmed, leaving the blaze in the fireplace to illuminate the room. Tamar, her apron off and her wrists adorned with silver bracelets, lit her candle. "Would the original Henry Adams family step forward and light their candles from mine?"

Malachi, Clay, Marie, Bing, Genevieve, and Rocky stepped up, along with Lily and Trent.

"Now, Bernadine."

Following her were all the adoptive parents and their children.

The parents lit their candles from Bernadine's and passed the small flames on to their kids. Glancing Kiki's way, Bobby saw her watching intently as Bernadine and the adoptive families carried their lit candles back to the circle.

Tamar said, "Many years ago, our ancestors came to Kansas and founded this town with a lot of hard work, perseverance, and dreams. Now we open our hearts to new dreamers. Jack and Eli."

They stepped forward.

"Jack, you never received a formal welcome. All Henry Adams teachers are descendants of Cara Lee Jefferson, so light yours from Marie's."

Jack did so, and offered his flame to Eli. Once both were lit, they stepped back. Next came Gemma, crying silently, and her grandson Wyatt. They lit their candles from Bernadine's. Then came the Acostas.

"Luis and Anna, we welcome you and your family. We look forward to adding your rich history, culture, and traditions to our own." As the Acostas lit their candles from Bernadine's, unfettered tears streamed down Anna Ruiz's cheeks. Luis, looking moved, put an arm around her shoulder and eased her close. He then hugged his kids, and for the first time since their arrival, Alfonso smiled.

Bobby had never seen anything like this before. He was very moved.

"Last but not least, Bobby and Kelly. Crystal is your sponsor. Let her light be the light that brings you into the circle."

Bobby saw Kiki give her eyes a quick swipe. Her hands shook as they touched their wicks to Crystal's flame.

The circle of candles wavered in the darkness, and after a few moments of silence, Tamar said, "Any time there is doubt or worry or pain, call up the memory of this night to remind you that you are not alone. We are your family, you are ours, and we hold each other up. May the spirit of all our ancestors guide us and see that all our dreams come true."

She blew out her candle, and those gathered slowly did the same.

Bobby and Kiki shared a strong hug, and she whispered, "I love this place. I feel like I'm home."

He heartily agreed.

To cap off the ceremony, there was ice cream and cake, and once that was done, the residents of

Henry Adams, both old and new, gathered their families, put on their coats, and headed out into the lightly falling snow.

Devon had to stay behind with their mom to help with the cleanup. Amari was in his bedroom when he heard his younger brother come up the stairs. Amari sighed and shook his head. He hadn't tattled to their dad about Devon dissing Bobby, but he really wished Devon would get his act together.

After a few minutes, he walked down the hall to Devon's room. Looking in, he saw him in his pajamas, lying on the bed and studying the ceiling. Amari knew he was having a rough time. As his big brother, he wanted to help him find his way, even though he was a pain in the ass most of the time.

"How you doing, Devon?"

"I'm okay," he said softly.

Amari knew that was his cue to say adios and keep it moving, but the big brother in him made him stay. He walked in and sat on the edge of the bed. "Rough night."

"Yeah. There were like a thousand dishes I had to dry."

"You brought it on yourself. You know Tamar can see and hear through walls."

"I'm never saying that again." He studied Amari for a second. "Did you tell Dad on me?"

"About the way you dissed Bobby?"

"Yeah."

"No, but you need to get your act together. I'm your brother, Devon. If there's anything I can help with or you want to talk about, just let me know."

Devon seemed to think on that for a moment. "How do I get Zoey to like me again?"

"You want the truth?"

Devon nodded.

"Stop being such a butthead. Immediately. And you need to apologize to her."

"But I didn't do anything."

"Second truth. Stop lying to yourself about yourself. You've been tap-dancing on everybody's last nerve since the summer, and you know it."

Devon turned away.

"Don't ask for the truth if you don't want to hear it." Amari thought it was Devon's pitiful act that made him the maddest. Instead of feeling sorry for him, like he was certain Devon wanted everyone to do, Amari just wanted to grab him by his skinny little shoulders and shake some sense into his knuckle head. "Third truth. Your oh-I'm-so-pitiful, nobody-loves-me act is real old, too."

"But nobody does! Zoey doesn't."

"And why do you think that is?"

No response.

"You need to man up, Devon, and take responsibility for all the dumb stuff you've been doing. And you start by going to school tomorrow and apologizing to her. First thing."

"But what if she doesn't accept it?"

"That's on her, but you and everybody else will know you at least tried."

"Okay," he said quietly.

"And Jesus, will you stop with that I'm-still-eight-years-old voice? How old are you now?"

Devon's lips tightened.

"Not trying to be mean, Devon. I'm just trying to help."

Devon sat up. "I want to be you."

"You can't be me. I'm already taken. You can be yourself, though."

"But you've got swag."

"Yes, I do, because I'm from Detroit, and it's in the water. Not sure what's in the water in Mississippi, but you're a July, and all the Julys have swag. You'll get yours."

"You think so?"

"Have I ever lied to you?"

"No."

"You'll get your swag, promise."

"Okay. Thanks, Amari."

"You're welcome. I'll see you in the morning. And think about what I said, okay?"

He nodded. "I will."

Amari walked out, and there stood their dad. He froze.

"I heard what you told him."

Amari wondered if he was in trouble. "I wasn't trying to hurt his feelings. I—"

"You did fine, Amari."

He exhaled.

"I never had a big brother growing up. Devon's lucky to have you in his life."

"Just trying to help."

"Awesome job. See you in the morning."

"Thanks, Dad."

Trent stuck his head in Devon's door. "You good in here, son?"

"Yes. Do all Julys have swag?"

He paused. "I think we do. The OG and your brother certainly do."

"Tamar's got swag. Even if she did make me work at the ceremony."

"She definitely has swag."

"Do you think I'll get some too?"

"Yep."

"Amari thinks I should man up and apologize to Zoey."

"Do you think he's right?"

He nodded. "I do. Amari said if she doesn't accept my apology, then it's on her. Everybody will know I tried."

"Your brother's right, but you have to be sincere about it. You can't just say the words and not mean it."

That seemed to throw him. "Oh."

"And falling back on Bible verses might not be

the way to go about it, either. They have to be your words from your heart, Dev."

"Okay."

"I saw you rolling your eyes at Bobby."

"I don't like his tattoos."

"You said that, and I said I don't think your opinion matters to him, Devon."

He hung his head.

Trent gave him a fond smile. "See you in the morning. Get some sleep."

At school the next day, the weather was again too cold for the students of the Marie Jefferson Academy to take lunch outside, so they gathered in one of the vacant rooms, which Mr. James designated as the lunchroom. Devon spent all morning trying to work up the courage to approach Zoey and apologize, but the right moment never seemed to materialize. As he opened his lunchbox, he saw Amari giving him the eye, as if encouraging him to get it together. So when Zoey and the new boys, Wyatt and Alfonso, took seats at his table, Devon looked up and said sincerely, "Zoey, I'm sorry for being such a butthead."

She stopped, and everyone else did, too.

Devon didn't like the scrutiny, but he plunged ahead. "I really want us to be friends again. If you don't want to, that's okay, but I'm really, really sorry."

To his surprise, her lips curled up into a smile. "No more dumb stuff?"

"None."

"Promise and hope to die?"

"Promise and hope to die."

She extended her pinkie. "Pinkie swear, Devon."

They locked pinkies, and Devon felt happiness warm his insides.

Zoey said, "I'm glad we're friends again. I want to form a band. Are you in, Devon?"

"I'm in!"

Elated, he glanced over at Amari, who shot him a big smile and a thumbs-up.

After lunch, on the way back to the room, Amari and Brain were debating whether the Chiefs would win or lose Sunday's game against the Jets when Zoey came over. "Can I get some help after school from you two?"

"With what?"

"I'm putting a band together, and I need somebody to help with the sound and stuff."

Amari looked at Brain, who shrugged. "Sure. Who's in the band?"

"So far just me, Devon, and a boy named Reed from Franklin who plays the sax. I had Mr. James put a notice on our school FB page last week. I'm hoping some other kids will show up. Today's the auditions."

"How long will you need us?"

"Until five o clock. My mom said she'd give us a ride home."

"Okay."

"What kind of band is this going to be?" asked Brain.

"Hopefully a hard rock band like my bio dad Conor plays in."

Zoey left them to go back to her seat, and Amari shook his head. He couldn't wait to see how this band idea turned out. In the meantime, he sent their mom and dad a text to let them know he and Devon would be late getting home, and why. He went back into the classroom and looked over at Kyra. She smiled shyly and lowered her eyes back to her book. He sighed, wishing he knew what to do.

"So what kind of band do you think this is going to be?" Trent asked Lily as they sat together, waiting for the boys to get home after school.

She shrugged. "Your guess is as good as mine."

"Amari's text said both he and Devon were staying after. Do you think Devon and Zoey have finally made up?"

Before she could answer, the boys arrived.

"How'd the auditions go?" Trent asked.

Amari shook his head as he undid the buttons on his coat. "They're a long way from Coachella."

"We had fun," Devon countered as he dropped his backpack on a chair and removed his coat, too.

"So are you in the band, too, Devon?"

"Yes. I apologized at school, and Zoey said she wanted to be friends again."

"That's great."

"She said she was going to form a band like the one her bio dad Conor is in. And she asked me if I wanted to join," he crowed, grinning. "I'm going to be the singer. Thanks for helping me with the apology and stuff, Dad."

"You're welcome, but your brother is the one you should be thanking."

Devon looked over at Amari. "Thank you."

"You're welcome."

"So life is good again?" Trent asked.

"I hope so."

"Your mom and I are proud of you, Dev."

"Me, too," he said.

Lily smiled. "So tell us about the audition."

Amari shook his head. "Zoey is still learning to play lead guitar, which meant she was awful."

Devon shot him a censuring look, to which Amari responded, "She was, and you know it. The kid playing the sax was okay. One kid from Franklin tried to take over and tell everybody what to do, so of course, Zoey wanted to fight."

"He was a big kid, too," Devon added.

Amari said, "Zoey didn't care. Told him if he didn't get out of her face, she'd stick her guitar where the sun don't shine."

Trent held on to his smile, barely, while Lily

covered her laugh with a cough before asking, "Isn't she supposed to be taking anger management classes with Reverend Paula?"

"Yeah, but she's going to get an F. Brain and I should've had on referee shirts. It was a mess."

Devon said, "I want some rocker clothes."

Both parents paused and shared a speaking look.

Trent asked warily, "What kind of rocker clothes? Leather?"

"No. Something fresh and off the chain."

They all stared.

Devon explained, "Since I'm going to be the lead singer, I need to wear something with swag."

Trent wondered who this kid was and what he'd done with the Devon who'd left the house that morning. "Swag," he echoed, doubtfully.

"Yeah. Amari said I had to find my own, so I think I know how now."

"Don't put this on me," Amari warned.

Lily asked, "Where do you propose to get these swag clothes?"

"Amazon. They have everything on Amazon. Will you help me look after I get my homework done? I'll pay for the things out of my gold-coin money."

Trent and Lily shared another look. In truth, the boy had his parents by the short hairs. He wouldn't be cruising the net unsupervised, and he did have the money in his bank account. There was nothing about the plan they could honestly say no to. So Lily said, "Sure, honey. Let me know when you're ready to go shopping, and I'll come up and help."

He grinned and did a fist pump.

Amari rolled his eyes.

Trent wondered why he had a sinking feeling in his gut, but he was pleased with Zoey for accepting Devon's apology, and he made a mental note to let Reg and Roni know. She could've easily slapped the olive branch out of his hands and told him to kick rocks. That she hadn't was an indication of Miss Miami's solid gold heart. Maybe now Devon wouldn't have to suffer any more black eyes from her solid right hand.

Chapter 11

Bobby walked into the Dog that evening without knowing what to expect. He'd been invited by Trent to the monthly meeting of a group called Dads Inc. He really had no interest in attending and wanted to blow it off, but felt he owed Trent for being so cool with him all week. He had the rest of the month to come up with an excuse as to why he wouldn't be able to make the next meeting.

The diner's atmosphere was much more subdued now than during the day. There were only a few people inside and jazz was playing on the box. Bobby kind of liked the old-school tunes Malachi played during lunch, but he wondered if they ever played any Jay Z, T.I., or Pharrell—and not that sappy "Happy!" Although he admittedly felt better able to relate to the lyrics now than when he had been down in Dallas. He was starting to understand what true happiness was all about.

He spotted Trent and the men in a back booth. As he sat, Trent said, "Bobby, I think you know everybody here."

"I do." He nodded at Luis Acosta, who was sipping on a longneck. Luis nodded back.

"You want a beer?" Barrett asked.

"No. I'll take a Coke, though."

Mal raised his Pepsi on ice. "Man after my own heart. I'll get you one."

Bobby had no idea what Mal meant by that, but figured he'd find out sooner or later. He was finding that everybody in town was more complex than they appeared on the surface, and that was taking some getting used to, too. Back home, what you saw was who people were. There were very few subtleties.

Mal returned and set a cold can of Coke and a glass of ice in front of him.

"Thanks."

"I saw your look," Mal said. "I'm a recovering alcoholic. Only soft drinks for me."

Bobby was once again blown away.

"Been sober for a while now, though."

"And we're all real proud of him," Trent added.

Bobby didn't know what to say.

Mal saluted his son, and Trent acknowledged him before saying, "This meeting of Dads Inc. is now open. What's everybody got going on?"

Bobby settled in and listened.

Trent began by telling Reggie how pleased he was with Zoey for accepting Devon's apology.

"She told me," Reggie replied. "I think it's great, too."

Mal cracked, "Maybe now she can concentrate on something else besides kicking his little silly behind."

Trent gave Bobby the backstory.

Bobby was surprised. "Itty-bitty Zoey?"

"The Henry Adams heavyweight champion of the world," Jack pointed out. "Miss Miami does not play."

Bobby chuckled and wished he'd been around to see that.

"And Bobby," Trent added, "Devon and I had a talk about his rudeness to you. If it happens again, let me and Lily know."

"Will do, but he's just a kid."

"True, but he's a kid we're trying to raise right, and respecting others is a big part of that."

Bobby nodded.

Barrett shared how pleased his son Brain was to be reconnected with his birth mother, which led Trent to talk about his own reconnection.

“So when’s she coming?” Gary asked.

“A few days after Christmas, and she’s staying until the day after New Year’s. She thought it might be nice to start the new year off together, and I did, too.”

“That’s great,” Luis said, and added, “Thanks for the invitation tonight. Never been to anything like this before.”

Barrett explained, “We formed it after deciding we needed man time to survive all these forces of nature we’re married to.”

Jack tossed in, “Also gives us an excuse to knock back a few beers,” and everyone laughed.

Bobby felt awkward, but realized the gathering was no different from being with the members of his gang when they got together to shoot the shit. They inevitably wound up talking about their girls too, and how they were stressing the guys over whatever it might be, and who was beefing with who, and who they needed to take care of on the street after being dissed in some way, real or imagined. Of course there were no blunts being passed here, and no hard bass thumping on the box, but that was okay.

“So, Bob, are your kids’ shots up to date?” Reggie asked him.

The question caught him off guard, but he knew the answer. “Yes. Making sure stuff like that is good is one of the things Kiki and I keep on top of.”

"Great. When you get a free minute, bring them by the clinic. It's over in the school. I'd like to get their information and give them a quick checkup."

"Will do."

"Reggie, how are you and Roni doing?" Mal asked.

"Okay. Not back to where we were before I lost my damn mind, but we're slowly working our way. She and Cass are hunkered down in the studio, working on that tribute CD. Keeping my angst over missing her to myself."

Bobby wondered what that was about. Maybe he needed to be taking notes, so he could question Crystal later, especially if whatever the doc was referring to was common knowledge.

Jack said, "So you'll all know, Rocky and I are talking about moving in together after Eli goes off to school next fall. Not sure how I feel about living in sin." That drew a few laughs.

"I'd rather marry her, but you know Rock. I'm doing good just being with her."

"You got that right," Mal said, smiling.

"I'll keep you posted," Jack promised.

Bobby was once again surprised. Jack and Rocky?

Barrett turned his way. "So, Bob. You and Kelly thinking about tying the knot?"

That caught him off guard too, and this time he had no answer.

"How long have you two been together?" Luis asked.

"Middle school."

"Long time. I met my late wife in middle school, too."

"How long has she been gone?" Gary asked quietly.

"Be five years in February."

The men softly offered condolences.

"Thanks. Still miss her like crazy." He stared at the label of his beer. "She was my Aztec goddess. God, she was beautiful. Lost her in a fire at our home. The gods are cruel, my friends. Cruel." He took a small sip and set the bottle down. "Can you imagine answering an alarm in the middle of the night and realizing it's at your own place? When I jumped off the engine, the house was fully engulfed. Anna had the kids outside, but she said Lissa went back in to get the family cat. The place was so hot the windows were exploding, the roof was caving in, my men were holding me back, and I was screaming her name like my heart was being ripped out of my chest, because it was. We found her the next morning."

"So sorry," Mal whispered.

"Thanks. Of course the cat comes strolling up later. It had gotten out on its own. I almost took my ax to it, but Lissa was a surgical nurse, a person who saved lives. To her its life had value." He used the tip of his finger to slowly trace a circle in the condensation on the table from his beer. "Gave the damn thing to the humane society. The kids cried and begged me to change my mind. Had I waited a few more days, I might have agreed with them, but the pain was too raw. I couldn't stand the sight of it." He looked into the solemn faces surrounding him. "Is this what this group is for?"

A few of them nodded.

"Good. Damn glad to be here." He raised his beer.

The dads returned the salute. Bobby was so moved, all he could think was *Wow*.

Later that night, as he lay in bed beside the lightly snoring Kiki, Bobby replayed the meeting in his head. He'd never seen a man reveal himself the way Luis Acosta had, and the most shocking part was the aftermath. He hadn't been belittled, sneered at and called a bitch, or subjected to ridicule. Nobody he knew in Dallas would have opened up that way. It just wasn't done. Life on the streets was a dog-eat-dog, survival-of-the-fittest kind of existence. Although he was no longer in it, he still tended to live by those rules. Tonight had given him yet another experience to take in and weigh as it related to this new life.

He also hadn't answered the colonel's question about when he planned to marry Kiki. He glanced her way for a moment, and then back up at the ceiling. There was a lot to think about.

• • •

The next morning, Trent and his family were at the table, having breakfast. He noted how happy and relaxed Devon seemed and attributed that to him having Zoey as a friend again and from ordering his swag clothes. Lily refused to reveal what the clothes looked like. Devon wouldn't be allowed to wear them until he performed, she said, and she wanted Trent to be surprised. Frankly, that scared him to death.

"So how are the Acosta kids doing in school, Amari?" he asked.

"Okay, I guess. Alfonso doesn't talk very much. I think it's because he's new. Maria is real quiet, too."

"Is your crew helping them adjust?"

"Yeah," he said, taking a sip of his orange juice. "Best we can."

"Alfonso plays the violin," Devon added. "Zoey asked him to be in the band, but he said no."

"That was real nice of her," Lily said.

"Yeah," Devon agreed. "She said she's going to ask him again after he's been here longer. Maybe he'll say yes."

Trent watched with interest as Amari helped himself to more scrambled eggs and grits. He was beginning to eat them out of house and home, much in the same way Trent had done to Tamar at that age.

"Anybody going to eat those last two pieces of bacon?" Amari asked.

Lily chuckled. "Go right ahead, Mr. Hoover."

He seemed confused by that.

"Vacuum-cleaner company," she explained.

He looked embarrassed but added the bacon to his plate anyway. "I'm a growing kid."

And he was. By Trent's estimation, he'd grown at least two inches over the summer, but he still had a ways to go to equal Trent's six-foot-two or his bio dad Griffin's six-foot-four. Griffin was also Trent's cousin, but when Trent adopted Amari, his heritage had been unknown.

Trent hadn't heard from Griffin in a few weeks. He and his motorcycle could be anywhere in the country, but he always checked in eventually, so Trent expected he and Amari would be hearing from him soon.

They finished the meal, and the boys hurried off to get their coats and backpacks. Sheila Payne was running the carpool to school this week.

"Have a good day," Trent said, once they were ready to depart.

"You too, Dad. You too, Mom." And they were out the door.

As he and Lily cleaned up and fed the dishwasher, Trent asked, "What do you want for Christmas?"

She paused and then shrugged. "No idea. How about surprising me?"

"Come on. You must have something in mind."

"I don't, Santa, and since I've been a very good girl," she said saucily, "I expect my gift to reflect that."

He rolled his eyes.

"What do you want?" she asked.

"How about surprising me?"

"You copying off of me?" she asked, hand on her hip, sounding like one of the kids.

"Yes, ma'am." He walked over and draped his arms around her waist. "And since I've been a very good boy, I expect my gift to reflect that."

"You are a mess. You know that, right?"

"But you love me madly."

"Good thing I do. Kiss me, July. We need to get to work."

He followed orders, and when they reluctantly parted, she said, "You can wrap me up a couple dozen of those to put under the tree."

"Noted." He gave her another. "We need a play-hooky day."

She grinned. "I think so, too."

"How about today?" He waggled his eyebrows.

She gently pushed him away. "Get behind me, Satan." But then she took out her phone.

"What are you doing?"

"Texting Bernadine to tell her we're going to be two hours late."

He threw back his head and laughed.

When she was done, she raised her gaze, said,

"Race you!" and took off running for the stairs. He was right behind her.

When Bernadine received Lily's text, she smiled at their antics and headed out to her truck to pay a quick visit to Kelly. Bobby and Barrett were on their way to Topeka to look at a high-tech gizmo Barrett was considering buying, so everything on the business side of the town's life was being taken care of.

Which was more than she could say about her personal life. She still wanted to smack Mal. This whole mess revolving around Rita Lynn was so childish and uncalled-for. Who cared about who slept with whom forty-five years ago? Genevieve was so angry at Marie, she'd asked Bernadine to have an apartment building built so she could move in. Having had a slight verbal tussle with Marie herself a few years back, when her ex-husband Leo came to town, causing trouble, she knew Marie had a temper. What she didn't know was that her temper could nurse a grudge tied to an event that happened back when the earth was still cooling. So stupid. And when Mal tried to explain to her that this had nothing to do with his feelings for her or lack of feelings for Rita Lynn but with his manhood and how best friends don't sleep with another friend's girl, she was done. She planned to stay done until he woke up, smelled the coffee, and acted like he had some damn sense. Were they all still in high school, she'd be looking to lay this at Rita Lynn's door, but everyone involved was over fifty, most over sixty, and it wasn't Rita's fault. She'd come back to reunite with a son she thought dead, for heaven's sake, not to be blindsided by an ancient petty squabble that ended with her throwing a glass of ice water in Marie's face.

Bernadine was done.

Kelly answered her knock on the door. "So are you and the family all settled in?" Bernadine asked after settling herself on the sofa in the trailer's nicely furnished front room.

"We are, and thanks again, so much."

"You're welcome. Now that Bobby has a job, it's time to get you on your way, too."

The twins were in their jumper chairs watching a *Sesame Street* video while she and Kelly discussed the salon Kelly wanted to open. They discussed how many stations she might need, and what type of equipment. Bernadine was impressed with how clear and concise the young woman's ideas were on everything. It was apparent she'd been thinking of opening her own salon for some time. She was also licensed.

"You'll have to make some calls to see whether the license is transferable," Bernadine pointed out. "Lily can help you get with the right agencies if you get stuck."

"I should probably be able to do that on my own."

"Can you use a computer?"

"No."

"We'll get you some training. You have your high school degree?"

Another no, and an explanation. "I dropped out when I was sixteen, and after I had the babies, there was no time to go back and finish."

"I'm not judging, but you'll need to have your GED before I'll even think about giving you the opportunity to be the owner."

"I understand."

"You're going to need some business classes along the way, too. The community college has some great programs. Once you get your GED, I'll have you sit down with Jack James, and the two of you can come up with a plan."

"Thinking about going back to school is scary."

"No scarier than trying to run a business without the proper business skills."

"You're right."

Bernadine took in the twins responding happily to Big Bird singing. "We may need some day care for them, too."

"I know. I had a chance to talk to Leah after the town meeting. She offered to babysit when she could, but she thought she might need some kind of training. And of course Ms. Genevieve offered to watch them whenever I needed help."

"Leah's in school during the day, so Genevieve will probably be a better fit, but we'll cross that bridge when we get to it. I'll check on some training for Leah. I assume you want to begin as soon as possible? I know the ladies want you to."

"I do."

"See about the license, and we'll go from there."

Bernadine glanced around at the house. There were a few dishes on the counter and a few baby toys scattered around the floor, but other than that the place was as spotless as it had been the day they moved in. "Christmas will be here soon. You and Bobby need to get a tree."

"That isn't necessary. The babies don't know anything about the holidays."

"This is your first Christmas in your new place and in your new life. I'll send somebody over with a tree, and sometime this week I'll get Tamar or someone to take you shopping for ornaments."

"But—"

"Kelly. Just say yes."

She dropped her head. "Okay. Yes."

"And I'll have Lily order you a laptop."

Kelly opened her mouth as if to protest, but Bernadine shot her a look, and she closed it. "Crystal can come by after school and get you going on the computer. If you know how to work your phone, getting up to speed on the computer won't be that hard." She eyed the young woman. "Do you have any concerns, need anything else?"

"No, ma'am. We're all straight."

"Okay, then let me get going."

Kelly walked her to the door. "My mother said Bobby and I would never have a good life. I think we're going to prove her wrong."

"I think you're right. Call if you need anything."

"Will do."

Over at the school, Amari was trying to work up the courage to do what Brain had suggested and ask Kyra to sit with him at the movies Friday night. He'd snuck glances at her all morning and caught her sneaking looks at him a couple of times too, but still he worried. He didn't want to ask her and have her say no, but whatever was going on inside him seemed to have a mind of its own. It kept whispering *Ask her, ask her,* to the point where he wanted to yell, *Shut up!*

After lunch, as they were walking back to the classroom, he couldn't stand it any longer. He called out, "Hey, Kyra. Wait up. Need to talk to you a minute."

He watched Leah and Brain pass a look between them, but they kept walking, giving him the privacy and space he needed.

She stopped. "Yes?"

He almost bailed, but pressed on. Praying his voice didn't crack, he asked, "Do you want to sit together at the movies Friday night?"

She looked off for a moment, then back at him, and said more words than he'd ever heard her say before. "I like you, Amari—I really like you. You're cute and you're funny and nice, but boys are a distraction, and I can't be distracted if I want to grow up and be a thoracic surgeon. Okay? Thanks for asking, though."

Stunned, he stared. He didn't even know what a thoracic surgeon was. He looked down at his Timbs, drew in a breath, and cursed himself for being so damn stupid. "Sure, Kyra. You . . . um . . . stick to studying."

In the classroom, Brain met his eye expectantly. Amari responded with a quick negative shake of his head and took his seat. Leah must've seen it too. Looking shocked, she stared at Kyra, who had her head in her book.

"Let's open our math books," Mr. James announced, so Amari did.

Lying on his bed after school, solemnly tossing a Nerf football in the air, Amari felt stupid and, yeah, sad. He'd taken a chance and put himself out there, and Kyra Jones had chopped him off at the knees. He hated girls.

His mom stuck her head in the door. "Hey. How'd your day go?"

He shrugged. "It was okay."

"You look a little beat down, baby."

"I'm good," he lied.

She said nothing for a moment, and then came in and sat on the edge of the bed. "So how's your quest to win the hand of the fair Kyra going?"

He studied her for a moment. “Did Dad tell you?”

“No, I figured it out on my own. It’s one of my mom superpowers.”

He cracked a smile. “I don’t even know if it’s worth your time.”

“Helping you figure stuff out is always worth my time, so shoot.”

“Okay, so I know I’m not old enough to go out on like a real date, but Brain suggested I ask her to sit with me at the movies.”

“And?”

“She crushed me like a bug on the sidewalk. She was nice about it and everything. Said she liked me, thought I was cute, but basically boys were a distraction. She wants to be a thoracic surgeon, and I guess the two don’t go together.”

“Hurt your feelings, huh?”

He nodded.

“I’m sorry you got your feelings hurt.”

“Me, too.”

“I don’t think I’ve heard of a fourteen-year-old who didn’t have time for boys, but I suppose that’s better than being so boy-crazy she can’t think straight. There are enough of those in the world already. Tell you what, don’t be too down on yourself. Somewhere in your future is the girl you’ve been looking for. You’re cute, funny, and smart in ways that a lot of boys your age aren’t.”

“That’s what she said, except for the smart part.

I had to come home and Google what a thoracic surgeon was."

"And?"

"It's a medical doctor who operates on the heart, lungs, esophagus, and other organs of the chest."

"Thanks. I learned something today."

"You're welcome."

"Unfortunately this won't be the only heartache you'll have before that really special girl shows up; life always sends us more than one."

"Great."

She leaned over and placed a kiss on his forehead. "You'll be okay. Might take a minute or three. You never know, she might just change her mind."

"Thanks, Mom. You and Dad make an awesome parenting team."

"We're learning as we go."

"What's he cooking for dinner?"

"I believe catfish, sweet potatoes, and steamed broccoli. His favorites."

"Mine, too. Tell him to cook extra."

"Will do. Get your homework done, and I'll call you when dinner's ready."

Alone again, Amari didn't feel a whole lot better, but at least he knew he would live.

Downstairs, Trent looked up from the seasoned cornmeal he was dredging a filet in. "Amari okay?"

"Kyra stepped on his heart." She told him the story.

"A distraction?"

"Yes."

"Interesting."

"I thought so, too."

Devon came into the kitchen and asked, "When are we going to put up the Christmas tree?"

"Saturday," Trent told him.

"This Saturday?"

"Yes."

"Are we going Christmas shopping, too?"

"Yes. Christmas shopping, too."

"Yes!" he said, executing an exaggerated fist pump.

During their first Christmas as a blended family, they'd gone to the mall, done their shopping, had lunch, and then come home and put up their tree. Trent and Lily decided to make that a tradition. Having grown up in foster care, Amari had never experienced the excitement tied to the holiday. Devon said he and his grandmother used a small tabletop tree she'd found at the Goodwill. Trent assumed that was because money had been tight.

Trent and Lily had both grown up with all the excitement and holiness of the season, and they wanted to make memories for their sons, so the shopping and the tree had become the first of their family traditions.

"What do you want for Christmas, Mom?"

"I don't know, Devon, whatever you get me will be fine. But there is something special I want you to do."

"What?"

"After we put up the tree, I want you to read the Christmas story from Luke."

"In the Bible."

"Yes. I'm making it a July family tradition. That okay with you?"

Trent's heart swelled. His Lily Flower was so awesome.

"Yeah, Mom, that's way okay." Devon rushed over, gave her a big hug, and whispered, "Thank you."

"You're very welcome. Now go tell Amari it's time to eat. Then the two of you get the table set."

"Yes, ma'am." He looked to be the happiest boy on the planet when he hurried out of the kitchen.

"You rock, baby doll," Trent told her. "What a great idea."

"Thanks. My mama used to say, 'Jesus is the reason for the season,' and we need to be reminded of that. This way our kids always will be."

Chapter 12

Friday morning, Bernadine pulled into the lot of the Power Plant and wondered why there were so many vehicles there. Usually she was the first to arrive, but these cars and trucks were idling with their engines running, and their drivers were inside. Perplexed, she got out of her truck. The moment her boots made contact with the salted, snow-cleared pavement, vehicle doors swung open and men piled out and began to approach. Alarmed, she fumbled for her phone, intending to call for backup, but upon seeing Lyman Proctor, the grizzled president of the Franklin Chamber of Commerce, she relaxed. "Morning, Mr. Proctor. You scared me there for a minute."

"Morning, Ms. Brown. Sorry to alarm you, but we need to speak with you."

She glanced around at the stern faces of the group accompanying him and realized some were familiar. The temperature was twenty-five degrees, and the wind was blowing. Way too cold to discuss anything outside. "Okay. Come on in."

She unlocked the door. One of the men politely held it open to let her enter first, and she thanked him, all the while wondering if this meeting had anything to do with their crazy-as-a-bedbug mayor.

Inside, as the men removed their coats and took seats, she sent a text to Trent, asking that he come to the office immediately. She had a feeling he'd be needed. While she waited for her Keurig to do its thing so she could have coffee, she asked Mr. Proctor, "What's this about?"

"Astrid."

Her assumption had been correct. "She's your mayor, Mr. Proctor. I can't see how I can help."

"We want to move our businesses to Henry Adams."

Stunned by that, she took in the determination in their faces. That she was momentarily at a loss for words was an understatement.

Proctor said gently, "Let me make the introductions first, just in case there's someone here you don't know."

"Go right ahead. Anyone want coffee?"

As she handed out cups of brew, he began. In response to the names, she nodded at the town pharmacist, the grocery store manager, the owner of a gravel-hauling operation, and a short, smiling man who ran the coffee shop. She already knew Arnold Katzman, who, with his wife Emma, co-owned Franklin Flowers. He toasted her with his cup. "Great coffee, Ms. Brown."

"Thanks."

One guy owned the tire repair shop, another a sporting goods store. All in all, they represented a cross-section of the Franklin business community.

"Not everyone interested could make it here this morning, Ms. Brown," Mr. Proctor explained, "but there are more."

Just then, Trent, Lily, and Bobby arrived.

"Morning, Bernadine, Lyman," said Trent.

Proctor responded, "Trent, Ms. Lily. Good morning."

Trent introduced Bobby and then asked, "What have we missed?"

"We're just getting started," she assured them. "Go ahead, Mr. Proctor."

He began with a litany of complaints about services being cut, forced evictions, and just plain old meanness on Astrid's part. He informed her that every firefighter on the force had quit in response to the treatment of Luis Acosta, so there was no longer a department. The community was up in arms about the library being closed more hours than it was open. Businesses had been hit with a new surtax so outrageous, it threatened their meager profits and livelihood. Rents were going up, as were loan payments taken out on farm equipment, vehicles, and building improvements. "When Astrid gets done, there won't be a town, so we want to move here. She may own our buildings and the land beneath them, but we own our inventory."

Bernadine looked to Trent and received a shrug. She still had no idea how to deal with this aside from saying yes, but that would open the floodgates to problems that made her head hurt just thinking about them. "Astrid's been mayor less than a month—maybe she'll come to her senses. Is there someone advising her that you all can have a sit-down with?"

The men shared a look. Proctor said, "I don't want to tell tales out of school, but her closest adviser is her bed buddy, Meryl Wingo."

"The high school principal!" Bernadine squawked.

Proctor nodded. "The married-with-five-children high school principal."

"Wow!" Lily said softly.

The tire repair store owner, Ethan Wells, added, "They've been close for years."

Bernadine was blown away. After gathering herself, she said, "Gentlemen, we've talked about expanding Henry Adams, but we can't accommodate all of you so quickly. Am I to assume you'll all need a place to live, too?"

Proctor nodded. "She'll evict us first thing."

"We won't have anyplace to house you until maybe next fall. And how do you plan to pay for the move, get your buildings constructed, and all the rest?"

"We're offering to put up our inventories as collateral, and some of us have savings. We're hoping you can point us to a banker who'd consider lending to us."

Bernadine knew no bankers taking flowers,

tires, or coffee machines as collateral for business loans. She would give Tina Craig, her financial adviser, a call and ask, though. "Does Astrid know you're considering this?"

"As far as we know, no. At least not yet, but she will eventually."

"So if she finds out you met with me and why, and decides to evict you all at, say, noon today, what are you going to do?"

Proctor shrugged. "Do our best to survive until the spring. Somewhere. I own a lumberyard—things are pretty slow for me in the winter anyway."

Bernadine sighed. She really wanted to help them, but she faced a dilemma. Could she, and would it be wise? As she'd said, Henry Adams was looking to expand, but not overnight. Either way, Astrid was going to throw a fit, and Bernadine had no desire to spend the Christmas season battling the devil.

"So give me a rough estimate on how many businesses are looking to relocate," said Trent.

"Besides the people here, there are about five or six more." He glanced around at the people with him, and they nodded in agreement.

"Then we're talking fifteen to twenty, plus your families?"

"Yes."

"That's going to be quite a load. You'll have to pay taxes if you move here."

"Of course. Would we own the land?"

Bernadine replied, "No idea. That's something I'll have to add to the mix as I think this over, but I'd never hold the land over your heads the way Astrid is doing."

"Good."

The gravel hauler, Dick Slater, one of the two Black men in the group, spoke up. "I'd like to start my kids in your school, if that's possible."

"When?"

"Tomorrow."

Chuckles were heard.

"Astrid's been reviewing the teacher contracts, and she's cut a lot of the positions. The classrooms are overcrowded, and many of the teaching staff are threatening not to come back after the Christmas break. My kids' education is important, and I'm not the only one wanting to make a change."

Astrid hadn't wasted any time putting her stamp on things, Bernadine thought. "How many children do you have, and what ages?"

"Two boys. One five, one seven."

Little ones. They were going to have to hire another teacher, maybe two. Luckily they'd had the forethought to build the school with expansion in mind. "Nonresidents have to pay tuition, but if you'd like to enroll them, it would be better after the break."

"Understood."

"See me after we're done here for the forms

we'll need filled out," said Lily. "That goes for anyone else interested, too."

"Will do."

This was turning out to be more than a notion, Bernadine thought to herself. But the question nagging her was: Why? Why was Astrid doing this? So she asked.

The answer was unanimous: "She's broke."

"I've lived in Franklin all my life," said Proctor, "and since Astrid's daddy died and her grandmother Mabel moved to Florida, there's been no one with a brain in charge of the town. She's been using the town coffers as her personal checking account for years—especially the past few. She doesn't work at anything, so she has to have some way to pay for the new Caddy she buys every year and her trips to Europe and having the house redecorated whenever the mood hits her. Bleeding the town dry is the only way. There've been very few new residents in the last five years, and many of the houses are sitting empty, which is why she keeps raising rents and adding surtaxes on businesses. I wish I knew how to get in touch with Mabel. She never put up with Astrid's nastiness, and she'd be appalled to know the town her grandparents founded was on the rocks, and that the residents were being treated this way. Then again, she has to be in her nineties now. Maybe she does know, but is just too old to do anything about it."

Bernadine was glad to have all this new information. It gave her a great deal of insight into Astrid, but what to do with it was anyone's guess. "Gentlemen, is there anything else you need to say?"

There wasn't, so she said, "I'm going to talk to my lawyers, my finance people and have them offer me some advice, and get back to you after the holiday."

Proctor looked stricken.

"Mr. Proctor, surely you didn't expect me to answer you today? If you did, I'm truly sorry, but this is not something I can decide to do on the spot. There's a lot to take into consideration here."

"I understand, and you're right." Proctor still looked sad, though.

Bernadine felt bad for him and his group, but not enough to make a decision without input from her experts. "So let's meet again after the first of the year, and go from there."

They nodded and thanked her.

As they donned their coats and prepared to leave, Mr. Proctor said, "Thanks again for hearing us out, Ms. Brown."

"No problem. I'm going to keep my fingers crossed that we can work this out somehow."

Bernadine and her administrative crew spent the rest of the morning making phone calls in an effort to evaluate the feasibility of Mr. Proctor's proposal. Tina was on the case, as was Bernadine's legal team, who were investigating what type of contracts or documents might be needed to go forward. Three of the men in the group had children they wanted to transfer to Jefferson Academy. Their kids were all younger than the students presently enrolled. From where she sat, Jack had enough to do without having to incorporate first- and second-graders into his lesson plans, so she'd get with him after school to talk about expanding the teaching staff. With any luck they'd be able to have someone hired and in place by the time school started back up after the Christmas break. Thanks to Astrid and her machinations, the stress of turning the world had just upped itself a few more notches—and she hadn't even started her Christmas shopping.

Entering the school auditorium for movie night, Bobby and Kelly were surprised by the sheer number of people inside—Black, White, young, old, men, women, teens, little kids. The air was festive, buzzing with voices and laughter as people visited, staked out seats in the kiva-shaped room, and stood in line for hot dogs, popcorn, nachos, drinks, and small plastic bowls of Tamar's homemade ice cream. After all he'd experienced this week, Bobby didn't know why he continued to be surprised by the happenings in town, but guessed it was because he had to keep pinching himself to make sure it was real. They'd left the twins at home in the care of Ms. Genevieve. She'd come over a few times during the week to get to know them better, and both she and Kiki had enjoyed the visits. Tonight was the first time they'd ever left the babies with a sitter, though. They were admittedly apprehensive, but looked forward to a few child-free hours.

"Hey, you two. Good to see you." It was Mal July. "Get yourselves some eats and grab some seats before the place fills up. Going to get real crowded before the lights go out."

Kiki asked, "You do this every Friday night?"

"Without fail. Gives us something special to do and helps us stay in touch, especially during the winter. Do you like old movies?"

"I guess. Genevieve said tonight it's *Star Wars*."

"Yep, and for us real old folks, *The Bronze Buckaroo*."

"Who?" Bobby asked with a laugh.

"*The Bronze Buckaroo*. One of the movies Hollywood produced in the thirties and forties for folks who look like us. The Buckaroo was a singing cowboy. Guy named Herb Jeffries."

"Never heard of him."

"Most people your age haven't. But he died recently. We're showing the movie in his honor, and so the kids can check him out."

"I learned something," Kiki said.

"When you roll with us, you learn a lot," Mal pointed out with a smile. "Let me get going. Enjoy yourselves."

They nodded their thanks, and he moved on.

Kiki looked up at Bobby. "*The Bronze Buckaroo*."

"I know."

As Mal predicted, more and more people were filing in. Bobby spotted Trent's son Amari and his friend Brain down front, setting up a small podium onstage. "You want popcorn?"

"And a hot dog and a soda."

"Then let's go." In Dallas they would never have been able to waste money on something as frivolous as popcorn, but he'd been surprised by his first paycheck earlier. The amount wasn't large, but it was substantially more than he was accustomed to bringing home.

Moving through the crowd, they were greeted with smiles, words of welcome, and questions about the twins. People wanted to know how they were faring. Had they put up their Christmas tree, and were they getting used to the cold weather? "No!" Bobby and Kiki replied as one. That brought on laughs. Bobby felt as if they were in the midst of family, and he liked that.

After running a quick sound check and setting up the podium so Tamar could make her announcements, Amari and Brain went to the kitchen. The place was a hotbed of activity as Tamar, Rocky, OG, and their team of volunteers prepared the food. Because the boys were now members of the crew, they were allowed to grab their snacks without having to stand in line, so they loaded up and went to their seats. Most of their peers were already there. Wyatt and Zoey, Devon, Leah, and Tiffany, along with some Franklin kids, took up one row. Eli and Crystal were MIA because they were holding down the Dog along with Siz. Leah had saved a seat beside her for Brain, so he joined her. Amari took a seat in the row behind everybody and started in on his nachos. He still had the heartbreak blues but was determined not to let that keep him from enjoying *Star Wars*, one of his favorite movies.

"Hey, Amari. Can I sit next to you?"

He looked up to see Kyra Jones standing above him. He was so surprised, he stuttered. "Uh, uh, yeah. Sure." That she wanted to sit next to him sent the blues packing.

"Thanks."

"You're welcome."

Once she made herself comfortable, he feverishly searched his mind for something to say that wouldn't sound lame. That she'd actually sought him out had his brain shooting all over the place. "But I thought—"

"I know. My dad says I need more balance in my life. He sorta made me come."

Yay, Megatron. "Ah." She smelled so good. "Do you know everybody?"

Brain and the kids in his row had all turned around to look on.

"I think so. Hey, everybody."

They all responded with a greeting. Brain had a look on his face that said, *Whoa!*

Leah smiled. "Glad you came to sit with us."

Amari belatedly remembered that Kyra was in school with them. Of course she knew them all. *She's going to think you're an idiot!*

Rather than open his mouth again and prove it, he simply sat and stared ahead—but his heart was smiling.

Chapter 13

The following morning, when Rita Lynn saw the number on her caller ID, she smiled and picked up. "Morning, Trent. How are you?"

"Doing well, Mom. How about yourself?"

"Same here. And the family?"

"They're good, too. We're at the mall, doing our Christmas shopping. The kids and I want to know what's on your list."

She melted inside. "You guys don't have to get me anything."

"You're getting something anyway, so it may as well be something you like, as opposed to something you'll have to pretend to like."

"Okay." Amusement filled her. She enjoyed his wit. "Let me think. Okay. I'd like a picture of the family. Another of each of my grandsons, separate and together. And one with just you and Lily."

"Got it. What else?"

"That isn't enough?"

"No. Sorry."

She glanced at Paul, seated beside her on the deck. He grinned.

"Is Paul there?"

"Yes."

"May I speak to him, please?"

"Sure." She handed the phone over. Apparently to keep from being overheard, he took the cordless into the house.

He returned shortly and handed it back. "Trent?" Rita asked.

"Hey, Mom. Paul gave me everything I needed."

"Good," she said, chuckling. "Can't wait to see you and the family."

"Same here. Take care of yourself."

"Will do. You do the same."

She ended the call and sighed happily. "Am I supposed to be this giddy?"

"Yes."

"What did you tell him?"

"Not a thing."

She punched him playfully. "Terrible man."

"Did Val get our tickets?"

"Yes. We fly in on the twenty-seventh and out January second. I hope that won't be too long a stay. I'd hate to be an imposition."

"It'll be okay."

She looked into his face. "Are you sure you won't mind meeting Malachi?"

"Are you planning on having any more babies with him?"

"Of course not."

"Then I'll be fine."

She cuddled close to him on the bench. "I love you so."

He kissed the top of her head. "Ditto."

After the call ended, Trent related what he'd been told while he and the family ate lunch at one of the mall restaurants. "Paul said she's a big college basketball fan. Likes to read, has a Kindle and a Nook, and likes jigsaw puzzles. She also likes music."

Lily said, "All doable. Good."

"Did he say what kind of music?" asked Amari. "I don't want to get her Jay Z and she likes Aretha Franklin."

"I'm pretty sure you can pass on the Jay Z."

"How about hard rock?" Devon asked while dunking a fry in the small mound of ketchup on the edge of his plate.

"That's probably a no, too."

"If she has a Kindle and a Nook, how about we

get her a gift card?" Devon suggested. Like Lily, their youngest loved shopping online.

"And there's a KU Store here in the mall," Amari pointed out. "You think she'd like a Jayhawk hoodie? I looked up Monterey on Google. It can get kind of cold there—at least for California."

"Another great idea. You guys are the bomb-dot-com," said Lily.

Amari gave her the side-eye. "No one says that anymore, Mom."

"Except for old people," Devon drawled.

Trent and Lily shared an amused look. "I'm so sorry," Lily said. "I'll send out an e-blast when I get home and let my old friends know."

Both boys rolled their eyes.

Trent enjoying watching the boys act in concert. It showed they were moving toward the sibling closeness he and Lily were hoping for but had never personally experienced.

Devon said sadly, "I wish Davis was coming for Christmas."

"So do I," Lily replied.

Her son was in South Africa helping the government install software for a big data project. He'd be back in the States after New Year's.

"He's promised to try and Skype with us Christmas day."

"Not the same."

"I know, baby, but it's the best we can do."

Devon had a special bond with Davis, first formed when he became Lily's foster child. He got a real kick out of having a big brother, and the two loved each other very much. Trent liked him too, and looked forward to seeing him when he returned.

After lunch they finished the last of their shopping and returned home.

The first order of business was getting the boxed tree out of the garage and setting it up in the living room. It was seven feet tall and had hundreds of lights that glowed clear or in bright colors, depending on the settings on its small green remote. They'd bought the tree the year before via Lily's favorite television shopping channel, and Trent had to admit it was an awesome purchase. Ornaments came next, and the boys had a great time hanging their favorites. While at the mall, they'd been encouraged to pick out one or two new ones—yet another of Lily's family traditions. Devon found a guitar and a baby Jesus in a manger. Amari's choices were, of course, cars—a Ferrari, a classic T-Bird, and a replica of racer Danica Patrick's green GoDaddy.com car, which he'd be wrapping and presenting to Zoey.

Last year, after decorating the tree, Trent, the designated cook that week, had taken the easy way out after the long day and made pancakes for dinner. At the time, Amari said he thought the meal should be a tradition, so this year Lily whipped up pancakes again. Amari volunteered to man the skillet of bacon, and Trent and Devon handled the eggs.

They ate, laughed, talked about skating on the ice rink scheduled to open during the school break, and how they were all looking forward to the arrival of their newfound grandmother, grandfather, and Aunt Val.

"I never had a grampa," Devon said somberly. "I hope he's nice."

Amari assured him, "He will be. He's married to Gramma Rita. He's going to be awesome, right, Mom and Dad?"

"Absolutely."

Later, up in his room, Amari lay on the bed, thinking about Kyra. They'd been texting each other about stuff. He'd found out she liked old-school jazz like John Coltrane and Miles Davis, and wanted to be an architect if she changed her mind about being a thoracic surgeon. When he texted back and told her he was thinking about being a NASCAR driver, she replied that maybe she should stick to the thoracic surgeon plan, because he'd probably need one. He looked up from his phone to see Devon standing in the doorway. "You busy?" Devon asked.

"Nope. Come on in. What's up?"

He took a seat on the bed. "How do I get girls?"

"What?"

"How do I get girls? I saw the way Kyra was looking at you. How do you do that?"

Amari studied him. "I wasn't doing anything, Devon. She just came and sat down."

"Yeah, but she could've sat anywhere. Instead she sat with you."

"Who knows? I'm no expert on girls."

"Do you think I'm cute?"

"What?"

"Do you think I'm cute? Like the ways girls think guys are cute."

"Hell, I don't know. Ask Zoey or Crystal."

Devon gave him a level look.

"Well, maybe not Crystal—but Devon, I don't know. You need to go back to your room. You're starting to sound crazy. And lay off the liquor, okay?"

Devon grinned, and Amari grinned back, glad he'd gotten the joke. "Get out of my room," he said.

When Devon was gone, Amari shook his head. He was sorta liking this new and improved Devon. His little brother was growing up. He just wasn't sure into what.

A short while later, dressed in their pajamas and robes, they gathered in the dimly lit living room for Devon's reading of the Christmas story. The logs in the fireplace blazed, and the crackling of the wood played gently against the silence. The tree was on and twinkling, and the drapes were open to let in the light of the falling snow. Bible in hand, Devon sat on the carpet in front of the fireplace. Upon receiving a nod from his mom, he began reading aloud: *"And it came to pass in those days that there went out a decree from Caesar Augustus that all the world should be taxed . . ."*

After the boys went up to bed, Trent stood behind Lily, his arms around her, as they looked out at the snow. Soft jazz played through the speakers. "It's really coming down," she said.

There was a winter storm warning up until tomorrow morning. The howling wind could be distinctly heard even through the glass as it whipped the snow so ferociously, they could see nothing but white. "Probably no church in the morning."

"No. Lots of digging out, though."

There was silence for a few moments, and then Lily said quietly, "Devon read well."

"Yes, he did. We had a good day."

She nodded. "Our sons are going to be okay." She turned. "I have awesome sons because they have an awesome dad."

"Their mama's not bad, either."

They shared a kiss, and he held her tight against him. He was so thankful for her, for so many things and on so many levels, that he ached from the sweetness. "You ready for bed?"

"No, I want to stay up and watch the snow."

"Then dance with me."

She smiled, and they danced slowly in the darkness while the world filled up with snow.

The storm quit at about five in the morning, but not before dumping nine and a half inches on the area. Not a record by any means, but throw in the blustery winds and it was more than enough to shut everything down. Looking out their window, Bobby and Kiki were amazed at the sight. What amazed them more was Rocky. She had a plow attached to the front of her truck and was slowly clearing the drive that led out to the main road. "Do you think I should go out and help her?" Bobby asked.

"Girlfriend looks like she's handling her business pretty well, but you might want to give Tamar a call."

So he did. They spoke for a moment and after the call ended, he said, "She said she's good. Rocky already did her drive."

Still watching Rocky, Kiki said, "I can't believe people actually go out in that. In Dallas, the city would be shut down for weeks."

A text came through on his phone. He read it, and his eyes widened.

"What's the matter?"

"It's from Trent. Said he'll be here in half an hour to pick me up, and to dress warmly."

"For what?"

He shrugged. "Shoveling, maybe."

"Then you need to get moving. You should probably put on those long-john things."

"I'm not wearing those."

"Okay, Mr. Tough Guy. When Tamar brought them over, she said everyone here wears them."

"I'll be fine."

She said to the twins sitting in their high chairs, "Your hardheaded daddy's going to be a Popsicle when he gets back."

Bobby laughed and went to get dressed.

When Trent arrived, he spent a few minutes with his plow-equipped truck helping Rocky first. When he finally came in, he handed Bobby a shovel. "For your steps. Where's your hat?"

"I'm good."

"It's seventeen degrees, and the windchill is five below. You can get frostbite quicker than you can blink. First to go are ears, fingers, and toes. So unless you want the twins growing up with a daddy who looks like Vincent van Gogh, get your hat."

Kiki came out from the back with the knit hat, heavy gloves, a scarf, and the long johns Tamar had been kind enough to provide. "Here," she said.

Bobby eyed her and then checked out the way Trent was dressed. He took everything and went into the bedroom.

When he returned, Trent looked him up and down. "Now we can go."

"This is my first snowstorm," Kiki said. "Anything I need to do?"

Trent shook his head. "Nope. Just enjoy being inside."

"I can do that."

Bobby glared.

"Don't hate, baby. Have fun."

Trent chuckled, handed Bobby the shovel, and Bobby followed him out. As soon as he stepped outside, the frigid air took his breath away. "Oh god!" he yelled. "It's cold!"

"Yep. Let's get your steps cleared." Trent waded to his truck and pulled a shovel from the bed.

Bobby stared like he'd grown three heads. "I'm not about to be out here. I'm going back inside." He could see his breath, and it felt like his nose hair was freezing.

Trent said, "You sound like my kids their first winter. Stop whining. Shovel."

So he did. He didn't like it, though. At all.

"Put your back into it. Not trying to be out here all day. Here, like this."

Trent showed him how to maximize the amount of snow the shovel would handle. "Every time it snows, clear your steps and the path to your car."

Once that was done, they moved to Bobby's car. "Get in and start it up."

Trent used his arm to scrape down the thick

coat of snow covering the door. "We need to get you a scraper. I'll get mine."

Bobby couldn't believe this was happening. He got in, and it was like being in a cave. The snow made it impossible to see out. The engine turned over like clockwork, and he was thankful for that. He hit the button for the window to bring it down, but nothing happened. Trying again, he heard a knock on the partially cleared window. He opened the door, allowing a ton of snow to fall in, covering his thighs below his coat. "The windows won't go down."

"Frozen. Wipers too, probably. Just let the engine run. Come on out."

Kiki had been right about him turning into a Popsicle. The wind was blowing, and he was freezing and kicking himself for believing it was okay to be out in this with no socks in his Timbs. Trent gave him a quick lesson in unearthing his car, using an old broom he brought back from his truck and a long-handled scraper. The snow was piled high, so it took a while, but they finally cleared enough away that the car was recognizable again. The defroster was barely making a dent in the thick crust on the front and rear windshields, though. Bobby swore the car looked as miserable as he himself felt.

Once that was done, he joined Trent in his truck, and they drove off.

It was late afternoon by the time Trent dropped

Bobby back at the trailer again, so frozen and sore he could barely make it up the steps.

Kiki took one look at him and said, "Oh, my poor baby."

"We're moving back to Dallas just as soon as I can feel my feet and hands."

"That bad, huh?"

"I never want to see snow again." He didn't care that it was mid-December and that, according to Trent, it might still be snowing come early April. Being out there had been brutal.

"I'll start you a warm bath."

"Thank you," he whispered. Every muscle he owned hurt from all the shoveling, and he couldn't stop shivering. He was glad Trent made him wear the extra gear. If he ever thawed out, he planned to go shopping for more. They'd used the truck to clear the parking lots of the Power Plant, the school, the church, and the rec center, but the walks and steps had to be shoveled and salted by hand. Even with the help of Mal, the colonel, and the rest of the men, it had been a long, exhausting, freezing work detail.

Bobby finally managed to remove his wet clothes and eased into the warmth of the water in the tub. "Oh god, this feels good."

Standing beside him, Kiki gave him a smile. "You soak, I'll finish dinner."

"I think I'm too whipped to eat."

"I doubt that, but get yourself warm. I'll check

on you in a bit." Leaning in, she gave him a kiss.

After his soak, he ate the roasted chicken, potatoes, and greens she put on his plate. When he finished, he kissed his kids, fell across the bed, and slept like a dead man.

Chapter 14

On Monday morning Bernadine rode with Mal to the county courthouse for the sentencing phase of Odessa Stillwell's trial. Bernadine doubted she would ever forget the sight last spring of the people running in terror from the explosions and flames from the fire Odessa had set. That she had been in reality targeting Bernadine because of her opposition to a pipeline that a big oil company wanted to run across local land haunted her, as did the knowledge that two innocent people lost their lives. The jury in the case had found Odessa guilty of second-degree murder. "What do you think she'll get?"

"Life, probably," Mal said without looking away from the traffic.

The state of Kansas had the death penalty but hadn't exercised that option since 1995. The ongoing debate over the repeal of the measure was being played out in the legislature and editorial sections of the big newspapers. Bernadine didn't support the death penalty, but she did think

Odessa should be remanded to prison for the rest of her life.

When Bernadine and Mal entered the quiet courtroom, Odessa and her lawyer were seated up front. Directly behind them sat her son, Al. On the far side of the room were the Sanderson twins, Megan and Marie. It was their parents, Mike and Peggy, who'd died in the fire. They'd come to Henry Adams to see the Friday-night movie in celebration of their thirtieth wedding anniversary, not knowing it would be their last.

Bernadine walked over and greeted the twins with hugs and kind words. She hoped the sentencing would give the girls some measure of closure, even though nothing would bring Mike and Peggy back. Beside them sat their grandfather Joel, Mike's dad. She shared a hug with him also. No parent should have to bury their child.

As she and Mal took seats, Mal leaned over and said softly, "Freda just came in."

Freda was Odessa Stillwell's granddaughter. Her discovery of Odessa's gasoline-doused clothing in the family barn had given the prosecutor the evidence they needed to bring charges. She was also the recipient of the $250,000 reward Bernadine had posted for information leading to the then-unknown arsonist's arrest and conviction. According to the report from her financial people, the check had been sent and cashed. Freda was also friends with the Sanderson family, and she shared hugs with them before taking her seat.

"All rise."

Judge Amy Davis appeared and took her seat on the bench. "Please be seated."

From her dealings with the judge in the past, Bernadine knew her to be tough but fair. She also had a sense of humor, but there was no amusement in this case, and her face and manner projected that. She took a moment to flip through the documents before her and then invited the twins up to read their statements. In voices that shook with emotion, they spoke about the loss of their parents, their devastated lives, and how hard it was for them to get up each morning knowing neither of their parents were there. Bernadine found their words heartbreaking. Odessa for her part seemed to stare off unseeingly, and it was impossible to tell whether the words had any effect. Her son Al appeared moved, however. He kept dashing away his tears. Bernadine remembered the day he'd confronted her at the Dog, and how badly he'd scared her, but he'd played no part in the fire. That he too would be losing his parent underlined the painful ripples set in motion by that night's senseless actions.

In the end, Odessa Stillwell was sentenced to life in prison with no hope of parole, due to what Judge Davis called "reckless disregard for human life." It was justice, but Bernadine knew it was small consolation to Joel Sanderson and the twins. Nothing would bring Mike and Peggy back, but at least everyone had the satisfaction of knowing Odessa Stillwell would be taking each and every breath until she drew her last behind bars.

On the drive back, neither Bernadine nor Mal had much to say at first. She looked out at the snow-covered landscape and hoped Joel and the twins would find joy again someday. Finally, in an effort to beat back the dark cloud of feelings hovering over her, she asked, "What do you want for Christmas?"

"For us to get back to where we need to be."

She raised her eyes to his.

"You're right, the whole thing with Rita Lynn—stupid. Can't change the past, people's actions, thoughts, none of the above. I've missed you. And I'm sorry if I made you doubt how I feel about you."

And she'd missed him as well. His phone calls every morning and at night before bed, having lunch with him, and their dinner dates. She was in love with him, and she knew deep down inside that he loved her as well—even when she doubted it. "Anything else you want?"

"Besides your forgiveness?"

She nodded.

"A weekend with just you and me."

They'd taken a few day trips together, but nothing overnight. She'd been using having to set a good example for Crystal as an excuse, but that's all it was, an excuse to hide her insecurities behind.

"Where would you like to go?"

"Anyplace where I can wear shorts."

"Key West? I know a nice place where we can walk the beach. Watch the sunset. Relax."

"Sounds great. Especially the relaxing part. You need that."

And she did.

"And, baby?" he said quietly.

She glanced over.

"I just want us to get away. Nothing more. I don't want you to think I'm pressuring you."

"You've never pressured me. Well, maybe when we first met, but you still had a lot of snake oil in your blood back then."

His eyes mirrored his amusement. "True."

"No, I want to go. I think we're ready."

He looked away from the road for a moment. "I think we are, too."

"Then, to Key West. And Mal—I want us back the way we were, too. Let's go forward."

"Thanks. Now, what do I get for the woman who has everything? Remember, I'm on a fixed income now."

"You are so crazy."

"What do you want?"

"Something money can't buy."

"And that is?"

"Your company for a weekend in Key West. And who knows, we may even stay a few days longer."

"You got it."

The dark clouds melted away, and sunshine filled her spirit. Mal's company was all she needed to make her life right again. She just had to stop being afraid of committing fully.

Back at the Power Plant, Reverend Paula was sitting in the outer waiting room, flipping through a magazine. "Hey, Paula," Bernadine said. "How are you? How'd things go at home?"

"Too long and ugly to talk about. Let's just say I'm glad to be back where sane people reside."

Bernadine realized she knew next to nothing about Paula's family, other than they lived in Oklahoma, and she'd escaped there right out of high school. "Are you waiting for me?"

"Yes, ma'am."

"Then come on in."

"How'd the sentencing go?"

"Life with no parole."

Paula took a seat, and Bernadine stashed her purse in the bottom drawer of her desk.

"Sadness for everyone concerned," Paula said solemnly.

"I know. Are you just visiting, or do you need something?"

"Stopped by for two reasons. One, I'd like a bell for the church."

Bernadine was confused. "What kind of bell?"

"One we can put in the steeple. I want Trent and his elves to design and build it. I had a bell at my old church in Miami, and when it worked, it made it sound like Sunday morning."

Bernadine thought about that. It might be nice to have a bell. She remembered instances when cities and towns were called upon to ring their church bells in concert for national events of celebration and for mourning. It would be good for their little town to be a part of that. "Any idea how much it might cost?"

"No. I wanted to run it by you first."

"Okay, get with Lily and see what you can find, and then talk to Trent about the installation."

"Sounds good. Thanks. My second request: I'd like to take our kids on a mission trip."

Bernadine rested against her chair back. "Any idea where?"

"I'm thinking Jamaica. A friend heads up an orphanage there, and he's trying to get some housing built and a new well dug. I know most of our kids didn't grow up with privileged lives, but I think they'd benefit from going down and connecting with children in a country that's not as blessed economically."

Bernadine really liked the idea. Paula was a wonderful addition to their community. Her ability to counsel and relate to the kids was priceless. "So how much is this going to cost?"

"Let me find out how many kids want to go and talk to my friend there first. They might be able to stay on the grounds, which would cut costs, but airfare is probably going to be a big expense."

"My jet is set up for ten passengers."

Paula sat up in surprise. "I hadn't even thought about that. I was thinking commercial."

"Put that in the equation."

"I will. Thank you, Bernadine. I'll work up a plan and get it to you after the first of the year. I know your plate's groaning right now."

"A bit." She was really looking forward to some time away with nothing to do but enjoy Mal's company. "The Acostas doing good, as far as you know?" She owed them a personal visit.

"Far as I know. Great family. Too bad Astrid didn't appreciate Luis."

"I don't think she appreciates anyone not named Astrid Wiggins."

"It must be pretty tough being her."

"Paula, please."

"No, think about it. A person with that much anger inside has to be hurting. Your husband runs off with the runner-up in the Miss Heifer contest. The neighboring town is doing way better than your own, which adds to your feelings of inadequacy and insecurity, and now everyone in the county knows your parents had to pay a man to marry you. How awful that last one has to be."

Bernadine wasn't buying. "I know you're all

about love and forgiveness, and in many ways I am too, but those crazies she called down on us when Cephas left Zoey that gold could've done more damage than they did. They could've hurt Zoey. They could've—"

"But they didn't, Bernadine," Paula said, cutting her off gently. "You can't hold a could've against someone."

"Sure I can. I own this place," she said, humor in her tone. She studied Paula's always serene face, and her voice turned serious. "I get what you're saying. You want me to extend an olive branch, don't you?"

"Yes. It might make a difference."

"She's going to take a match to it. Guaranteed."

"So you keep trying. That's all we're asked to do. Keep trying."

Cletus would sprout wings and fly before Astrid accepted any kind of truce or sit-down. But who knew? As much as Bernadine disliked the woman, if there was a way to end the madness, she'd give it a shot. "Okay, Paula. I'll call her in a few and see if we can't open up a dialogue."

"Good for you."

"Anything else?"

Paula shook her head and stood. "No. That's it for now."

"I like the idea of the bell and the mission trip. Let's see if we can't make both happen."

"Okay." The reverend zipped up her long green

down-filled coat and headed for the door. “Stay warm.”

Bernadine was just about to pick up the phone and do her part for world peace by calling Astrid when her sister Diane, looking upset, walked into the office.

“You’re back.”

“Yes, and I just left the store. Did you know that Gary fired me?” Diane hung up her parka and sat.

“You didn’t call him the day after you and I talked?”

“No, I was busy, but I did call him a couple of days later.”

“A couple of days?” Bernadine echoed skeptically.

“Yes.”

“But I told you to call him immediately. Right then, Di.”

She blew out a breath and looked away. “Now what am I going to do?”

“Find another job,” Bernadine tossed back without hesitation.

“But he knew I was coming back. I need to get a lawyer. This is not right.”

Bernadine couldn’t believe this. “You have no grounds to sue. He gave you a chance to keep your job. You were fired because of you.”

Diane blew out another breath. Finally she said, “Okay, I’ll start looking right after Christmas.”

"No, you'll start looking today. Immediately."

"But Bernie, I haven't even started my Christmas shopping."

"Not my monkey, not my circus. You have rent and a car payment, remember?" One would think Diane was one of Crystal's peers, the way she approached life. She was too old to be so irresponsible. As Bernadine noted more than once, her recently divorced sister was easier to have around now than when she first arrived in town a few months back, but she still had a long way to go to become the serious, independent woman she needed to be to take charge of her own life.

"Well, I do have some good news."

"And that is?"

"I have a boyfriend," Diane said, smiling coquettishly.

"Really." Bernadine's Spidey sense started tingling.

"His name is Rance. I met him in Hawaii. He's a big-time venture capitalist, and he is rich, rich, rich."

She held on to her skepticism. "Where'd you meet Rance?"

"On the beach, my first day there. Told me I was the most beautiful woman he'd seen in his life, which of course I didn't believe, but he took me out on his boat that night, and the next day we went dancing and had a sunset picnic. He's so exciting."

"And did Marlon and Anthony meet Rance?"

"They did, but they didn't like him."

"Ah. Did they say why?"

"I think they were just mad because he was monopolizing my time. I was supposed to be down there hanging out with them."

"I see. Or was it because they thought Rance was trying to play you? Lots of men make their living preying on vulnerable women."

"I'm not vulnerable, and he's not that way. In fact, you can meet him. He came back with me. Rance, honey, come on in."

Bernadine stared at Diane and then up at the tall, handsome man who entered. He looked like a model. The coat draped casually over his arm was cashmere, his well-fitting charcoal suit top-of-the-line, his tie tasteful. His hair had just a touch of gray at the temples. He was elegant, refined, and camera-ready. All she could think was, What the hell was he doing with Diane?

"Hello. So you're my Diana's sister. She's told me all about you. I can't figure which one of you is more gorgeous. I'm Rance Gordon." The hand he extended had the perfect amount of shirt cuff peeking from beneath his jacket sleeve, the better to display the expensive Rolex on his wrist. If fake had a scent, he reeked so much she needed a gas mask.

She smiled and lied, "Pleased to meet you."

"Same here. May I call you Bernadine?"

"Please."

He sat down next to Diane, who was ogling him like a sixteen-year-old meeting Smokey Robinson back in the day. Bernadine wanted to grab her by her shoulders, shake her, and yell, "Snap out of it!" If he was a venture capitalist, she was a unicorn.

"So you're a venture capitalist?"

"I am. Offices in San Francisco and Boston."

"Ah."

"Your sister says you're a very wealthy woman."

She didn't respond, but Diane did. "She owns this whole town."

Bernadine kept her face unreadable.

He smiled like an elegant shark. "If you need investment advice, I'm at your disposal."

"So what brings you to Kansas?"

"Thought I'd see if there were any business opportunities to be had."

"You have offices in San Francisco?"

"I do."

"A friend of mine is considering investing in a start-up called Unicorn. They're working on a beta for digital wearables. Ever heard of them?"

"I have. In fact, we gave them their first two million to extend their R&D."

"I'm impressed." Mainly because she'd just made that up. There was no such start-up, and he was either a con man, a gigolo, or both. The designation didn't matter, though. She just needed him gone and out of her sister's life. Immediately. "So, Rance, how long will you be visiting, and where are you staying?"

"I invited him to stay with us," Diane piped up.

"Sorry. No." The way he tensed for just a split second was telling. She met his gaze, and the smile he sent back was again shark-like.

"Why not?" Diane asked.

"Not trying to offend, but I don't allow strangers in my home." Not only did she not trust him, there was no way she'd allow him near Crystal.

"That's mean," Diane protested.

"No, Di, it isn't. He is welcome to join us for dinner at the Dog tonight, though."

"It's okay, sweetheart," he told her reassuringly. "I can get a room nearby. And we'd love to join you for dinner. Is there a hotel in town?"

"No," Bernadine said. "Closest places are along the highway you took coming in."

He didn't like hearing that either, but he played it off. "Then I guess we need to get going."

"Yes, you should."

They got to their feet and put on their coats.

Bernadine had one last jab to throw. "And Diane, don't forget you're supposed to be looking for a job."

He startled. "A job?"

Diane's fury was plain. Bernadine didn't care. If telling him the truth sent him packing, so be it. Diane would be better off. "Yes, she was fired from her custodial position while she was in Hawaii."

He coughed. "Custodial? She told me she was your vice president."

Bernadine gave him a smile that didn't reach her eyes. "My sister is such a kidder."

He took Bernadine's measure. She didn't blink. He inclined his head politely. "Pleasure meeting you. We'll see you later."

As he turned to leave, Diane angrily flipped Bernadine the bird and followed him out.

Once they were gone, Bernadine placed her forehead on the desk and cried aloud, "Lord, what next!"

After a few minutes she picked up her phone and called Kyle Dalton to ask a favor. They talked for a short while about how best to implement what she wanted done. When they'd agreed upon a course of action, she thanked him, took a deep breath, and called Astrid.

The secretary put her through. "What do you want?" Astrid, always the professional, snapped.

Mindful of Paula's advice, Bernadine held on to her temper. "I was hoping we could get together for lunch one day this week and try to work out our differences."

"Are you going to stop the improvements over there?"

"No."

"Then go to hell!" The line went dead.

Bernadine tossed her phone on the desk. So much for world peace.

Tommy Stewart was on his knees, looking up at the U-shaped pipe beneath the small sink. He needed a weapon. He'd thought about using the lid of the toilet tank, but it was heavy and unwieldy, and he wasn't sure it would be maneuverable enough to do what he needed it to do—knock Astrid out, so he could escape. If he missed, he might not get a second chance. A pipe could be held in one hand, and if he had to hit her more than once he could. The only problem was how to free the pipe from the sink. It ran down from the bowl into a U joint with another pipe that ran into the wall. He had no tools, and there was nothing in the room he could use to knock it loose. Even if there were, the process would be noisy, and that might bring her and her shotgun down to investigate. He didn't need that.

Using two hands, he grabbed the pipe up high where it met the sink and pulled. Nothing. Putting his shoulder and back into it, he pulled again, this time harder. It wiggled just the tiniest bit, and his eyes lit up gleefully. The caulk was old and brittle. It might take a while to actually get it to detach, but he was encouraged. Keeping his eyes and ears open for her next visit, he anchored his feet flat against the wall and pulled.

Chapter 15

Walking into the rec center's auditorium, Trent smiled to himself watching Bobby moving around like an old man. Apparently he was still feeling the effects of yesterday's shoveling. At Bobby's age, nineteen, Trent had been able to knock out the snow at Tamar's, head over to Marie's to do hers, help Mal at the Dog, and still have the energy to spend a few hours cross-country skiing with Gary and his friends—but then again, he was a country boy born and raised. "Did you lift weights back in Dallas?"

"Yeah, but after the babies, there wasn't time or the money to be in the gym."

"I have a set of weights in my basement you're free to use. Build yourself up so the snow doesn't wear you out so badly next time. Long way to go before April."

"I feel like an old man."

"Noticed that."

Bobby shot him a grin.

They were there at the auditorium to do a final inspection of the work done by the hired repair crews. As a result of the riot, windows needed replacing, floors needed to be sanded and buffed, the components of the sound system had been ripped apart and stolen, thus needing to be replaced and installed. In addition, some of the kitchen appliances had been looted, along with all the town's emergency supplies stored there.

Trent scanned the place. It looked as good as it had before. The seats had been cleaned, the aisles swept. The gleam of the newly laid stage floor could be seen from Mars. A few workers were moving about, pushing vacuums and brooms, but overall the rec center was ready for the movies on Friday and any other event that might be held there.

"Let's check the kitchen."

It too was in great shape. Tamar and her ladies were there, putting the area back together. "Morning," he said.

Tamar looked up from her clipboard. "Morning, you two."

"How's it going?" Trent asked. With Tamar were Genevieve, Marie, and—to his delight—Anna Ruiz. He was glad Tamar had taken her under her wing.

"Well, all the emergency supplies are in that mountain of boxes over there, and they need to be stacked and put in the storage room."

He smiled. "Is that a hint?"

"You know I don't hint. Take your coats off and get going."

They did as ordered, moving and stacking boxes for the next hour. Some had to be opened so the contents could be checked, noted on Tamar's inventory sheets, and put away. First-aid items and cases of bottled water were put in one place; food, paper cups and plates, and plastic utensils in another. They stacked cots, pushed two popcorn machines into place, hooked up the new dishwasher and the huge fridge, while the ladies filled the three new freezers with everything from hot dogs and Popsicles to ice packs.

After they'd finished and been given permission to go on their way, Trent led Bobby down to the gym with its brand-new hoops, volleyball nets, and shuffleboard courts.

"You all don't need the outside world, do you?" Bobby asked as they made their way back outside to Trent's truck.

"Not really. This is how our communities functioned during segregation. Everything needed to be on-site because we weren't allowed access anywhere. But in truth we're no different from all small towns. The only thing we don't have anymore is our own post office. It used to operate out of a dugout."

"What's a dugout?"

"A place dug out of the ground on the side of a hill. The original Dusters lived in them the first few years, after founding Henry Adams."

"What?"

As they drove back to the Power Plant, Trent gave Bobby a quick history lesson. When he'd finished, Bobby shook his head. "I don't know if I could've lived in a place underground."

"Many of the Dusters said they preferred living underground in Kansas to dying above-ground in the places they moved from. It was pretty terrible in the South back then."

"Where's the post office now?"

"Franklin."

"Can I ask you something? If it's too personal you don't have to answer."

"Okay."

"What made you decide to marry your wife?"

That surprised him. "I wanted her to be with me for the rest of my life."

"You didn't have to marry her to do that, though, did you?"

"No, but for me it was about making that public statement. I wanted the world to know that she held my heart. So to do that we had the wedding, said the vows, signed the papers. Family and friends were there to bear witness. If I could've gotten a bullhorn and stood on top of the Empire State Building to let people know how much I love her, I would've." He glanced at Bobby. "Marrying her was also a way to ensure our sons' futures. If I drop dead tomorrow, I know my boys will get all the financial benefits they're entitled to because their mother and I are married in the eyes of the law."

He fell silent, giving Bobby time to process

his words before asking, “You thinking about marrying somebody?”

Bobby cracked a smile. “Yeah.”

“If I can help, let me know.”

“I will, but can you keep it to yourself for now? I want to think about it some more.”

“No problem.”

“Thanks.”

Trent was pleased that the young man was contemplating making the ultimate commitment. Watching the way he and Kelly interacted, he could see how much they cared for each other, and there was no doubt that Bobby truly loved the twins. The people of Henry Adams would love to bear witness at another wedding, especially one that wouldn’t involve Trent’s crazy relatives, the Oklahoma Julys.

For the rest of the day, Bobby thought about Trent’s response. There was no question that he loved Kiki and wanted to be with her forever, but would it change them? He knew couples back home whose relationships had changed in every way once they got married. Some of the guys chafed at the idea that they couldn’t play around anymore, so they did it on the down-low. Some of the girls got real bossy and started acting like they’d been magically changed into the guy’s mama, dictating who they could hang with, where they could go, and what time they had to be home. He didn't see Kiki turning crazy as a result of a ring, but it was something to consider. Or was it? She'd never cheated on him as far as he knew, and yeah, he'd slipped a couple of times—that's what guys did—but he hadn't since the pregnancy, and certainly not after the twins were born. He had no plans to go down that road again.

Trent's words echoed in his head. *If I could've gotten a bullhorn and stood on top of the Empire State Building to let people know how much I love her, I would've.* Truthfully, that was how Bobby felt.

He watched Kiki now as she sat on the couch, using a yellow legal pad to compile the list of supplies she'd be ordering to get her hair place up and running. Ms. Bernadine and the other ladies decided she could use one of the large metal storage units behind the rec center as her place of operation temporarily, until a permanent location could be built in the spring. She was ecstatic, and he was happy for her.

She'd hung with him through so much over the years: the gang, the struggle to make ends meet, the daily grind of being poor. Because of her love for him, she'd been kicked out of the house by her mother and stopped going to church, yet she'd never once complained—about anything. Something else Trent said right after they met came to mind: *A man is only as strong as the woman who holds him.* Because of Kiki, Bobby was the strongest man he knew. It was time to honor that by letting the world know.

Entering the Dog that evening, Bernadine spotted Diane and Rance at a booth. Before joining them, she took a moment to speak privately with Rocky and Mal in his office, letting them know of the plan she'd put together with Kyle Dalton.

"What time is Kyle coming?" Rocky asked, once Bernadine shared the details.

"He said no later than seven, and it's almost quarter of now."

Mal chuckled. "Never been part of a superspy mission before, Bernadine. Remind me to stay on your good side."

"Let's just hope it works."

Upon joining Diane and Rance, she asked him, "Did you find a place to stay?"

"I did," he replied. "Definitely not a five-star, but it'll work for the short time I'll be here."

Diane's jaw dropped. "Short? I thought you were staying until New Year's Day."

He shook his head. "No. I have to be in London the day after tomorrow. I'll be flying out tomorrow afternoon. I'm sorry, darling."

Never to be heard from again, Bernadine thought to herself. Learning Diane was an unemployed custodian and not Bernadine's vice president meant he'd be moving on.

Rocky approached the table. "Hi, Diane. Good

to see you." She nodded a greeting to Rance, who took one look at her beauty and stared with wide eyes.

He instantly thrust out his hand. "Rance Gordon."

She didn't offer hers. "Hi. Rocky. Nice to meet you. Take a moment to look over the menus, and I'll be right back."

Staring after her, Rance said, "This little place is filled with beautiful women."

Diane tittered.

Bernadine didn't.

Kyle Dalton entered the Dog a few minutes later and took a seat on the far side of the room. He met Bernadine's eyes briefly. He glanced at Rance as if in passing, but she saw him take a good look before greeting Mal, who'd come to his table to take his order.

"So, what's happening in London, Rance?" she asked casually, looking over the menu.

"My partners are meeting with some men from Helsinki about a hotel complex slated to be built in Dubai."

"Sounds exciting."

"More like routine, but they need my expertise, which is why I have to go."

Diane pouted prettily. "I was looking forward to you being with me for Christmas."

He leaned over and placed a kiss on her forehead. "I'll be back just as soon as I can. This meeting shouldn't take more than a day or two. I'll make sure I call."

"You'd better."

Rocky came back a few minutes later to take their order, and after she left again, he asked Bernadine, "How in the world did you wind up owning the town?" Bernadine saw no harm in telling the story.

"And you brought in at-risk kids?" he asked at one point.

"Yes."

"How noble. You must've had some divorce settlement. What business is your ex-husband in?"

"Oil," Diane volunteered.

Rocky returned with their plates, and they began their meal. While they ate, Diane asked Rance about his travels. To hear him tell it, he'd been all over the world, dispensing venture capital like Santa delivering toys. He regaled her with a list of the five-star hotels he'd supposedly stayed in: the Ritz-Carlton in Hong Kong, the Nam Hai in Vietnam, and the Amankora in Bhutan.

"You ever stayed at any of those places?" Diane asked Bernadine.

She had, but she shook her head. "No. Way too rich for my blood."

"I'm sure you can afford to stay wherever you want," Rance countered smoothly. "Are you involved with anyone? Gorgeous woman like yourself probably has to beat the men off with your Hermès bag."

Again it was Diane who answered. "She's hooked up with that guy over there." She pointed out Mal.

"Really?" The look on Rance's face said he found Mal lacking.

And so it went, him trying to find out just how much money she had, if she and Mal were serious so he could ascertain his chances of getting his hands on her wallet, and her politely changing the subject.

By the end of the meal she couldn't wait to be rid of them both. Finally Diane said, "Honey, we need to get you back to your hotel."

"I doubt it should be called that, but I agree. I need to make some calls to my office."

They stood and put on their coats.

"Have a good evening, Bernadine," Rance said.

"You, too."

Diane smiled. "Don't wait up."

Bernadine didn't reply, but inwardly wondered how her sister could be so incredibly clueless. She might not consider herself vulnerable—but Bernadine did and Rance certainly did, too.

Once they'd gone, she glanced out of the window beside the booth, watching them drive off. Satisfied they wouldn't be returning, she looked over at Kyle. He stood and, after grabbing his coat, walked to her table. In his hand was one of the Dog's large, clean linen napkins. Using the napkin, he carefully picked up Rance's silverware and glass, wrapped them in the napkin, and placed them in a brown paper bag he took from his pocket. After putting on his coat, he gave her a wink and made his way to the exit.

Mal came to the booth. "Do you really think that fancy-pants is wanted?"

"If not, I'll eat my hat."

"Great plan."

"I think so too, if I must say so myself. Now, I'm going to go home and wait for Kyle to call. With any luck it shouldn't be too long."

"Let me know as soon as you hear anything, Ms. Mastermind."

"Will do." She gave him a quick kiss and headed to her truck.

Driving home, she didn't feel guilty in the least for what she'd set in motion. Rance Gordon, for sure not his real name, was wanted for something, somewhere, and it wouldn't be for jaywalking. She knew she was right because after her divorce, she'd done a fair amount of traveling both domestically and abroad and no matter her destination there were men both young and old waiting to target her as prey. It got to the point where she could pick them out from across a room, along a stretch of beach, or in a hotel lobby. She'd never said anything to

Diane about it because there'd never been a need.

Now those experiences had come in handy. Rance was wanted, more than likely for fraud, and with the help of Kyle's FBI fingerprint databases, it would be proven. Diane was going to throw a fit when her so-called venture capitalist lover was picked up and hauled off to the pokey, but she'd get over it. And with him out of her life, she could concentrate on finding a damn job.

Two hours later, she got a text from Kyle. *THK U! Bringing yr sister home. B there shortly.*

"Yes!" She threw a fist pump and dashed off a short text to Mal. After putting her robe on over her pajamas, she hurried downstairs to wait.

She didn't have to wait long. When she opened the door, the crying Diane was hysterical. "Oh, Bernie. We have to get Rance a lawyer. He's been arrested!"

"Really? Hi, Kyle."

"Hi, Ms. Brown."

"They're taking him to jail. I need you to call somebody."

"I'm sure he and his partners can take care of it." She focused on Kyle again. "How many warrants?"

"Ten."

She froze. "That many?"

"Fraud, identity theft, larceny, bigamy—and that's just the tip of the iceberg. Real name's Gordon Macy, by the way. Got a couple of hits on Interpol's database, too. We're waiting for them to get back to us."

Diane stared between the two of them, and then, as if a lightbulb had switched on in her head, she yelled at Bernadine, "You did this!"

"Guilty, just like Macy is. I knew he was up to no good the minute he walked into my office."

"How could you!"

"Have you not been listening? The man's a criminal, girl!"

"It's a mistake!"

Kyle took that as his cue to leave. "I'm heading back to the office. Thanks for your help, Ms. Brown."

"Anytime, Kyle, and thanks for yours."

His next words were directed at Diane. "Ms. Willis, we'll likely need to interview you as Mr. Macy's case goes forward. I'd advise you not to leave town."

Eyes wide, she nodded.

He inclined his head and left.

Standing at the closed door, Bernadine eyed her sister's tears. Crystal stood on the stairs, looking confused, but Bernadine ignored her for the moment. "Di, I'm not going to apologize for trying to keep you safe."

"You just don't want me to be happy, do you!"

She didn't respond. With any luck, by morning Diane would realize she'd been bamboozled and step back into the real world with the rest of humanity. "You should go on to bed and try to get some sleep. Things will be clearer in the morning."

"I hate you!"

Bernadine sighed.

Sobbing, Diane rushed off to her room. Saddened by her attitude, Bernadine raised her gaze to Crystal, who asked, "What the heck is going on?"

After she'd filled Crystal in on all the sordid details, Bernadine turned out the lights and climbed the stairs to her room. Once there, she booted up her laptop, booked the trip to Key West for Mal and herself, and crawled into bed.

At breakfast the following morning, Diane entered the kitchen and sat down without a word. Her eyes were red and puffy, and the anger on her face was plain. Bernadine and Crystal were in the midst of the meal. They shared gazes, and Crystal rolled her eyes.

"Morning, Di," Bernadine said.

Diane cut her sister a nasty look but didn't speak. Instead she reached for the bowl of eggs.

"Whoa, whoa. You don't come to my table and eat my food and not speak. Who do you think you are?"

Crystal chose that moment to get to her feet. "I'm going to meet Eli for school." She gave

Bernadine a parting kiss on the cheek. "Bye, Mom."

"Bye, Crys. Have a good day."

"You, too." She didn't bother saying anything to Diane.

Once the door closed on Crystal's exit, Bernadine said, "Now, let's start over. Good morning, Di." She refused to call her sister Diana, the fanciful name she'd adopted for herself.

Seemingly cowed, she replied, "Good morning, Bernie."

"Better." She felt like she was raising the gold-weave version of Crystal all over again, except Crys had never been this out-and-out delusional.

"You had no right."

"Really? Did you see his reaction when I told him you were a custodian?"

"He was just surprised."

"Yes, he was, and after hearing the truth, had you driven him to the airport, you were never going to see him again."

"You don't know that!"

Bernadine wanted to smack her. "Do you think the FBI arrested him just for fun? He had ten warrants, Di. Ten! Stop trying to sugarcoat this. You're smarter than that."

Diane looked away with tear-filled eyes.

Bernadine drew in a calming breath and gentled her tone. "There's nothing wrong with wanting someone to love you. After a divorce, it's the first thing many women look for to soothe the hurt. But this man wasn't the one, sis."

The tears fell freely.

"And I wasn't trying to steal your joy. I was just looking out, like big sisters are supposed to do."

After a long silence, finally she whispered, "I know. God, I feel so stupid. Marlon and Anthony tried to warn me."

"You're not stupid. You're just trying to find your way, like everybody else. We all stumble sometimes. It's how we learn."

"Just like the last time we had one of these talks, you're a much better sister to me than I am to you."

Bernadine didn't respond to that.

"Thanks," Diane said meeting her eyes. "And I mean that."

"You're welcome. I need to get to work. Are you going to be okay?"

She nodded. "I'm going to look for a job this morning. It'll help take my mind off the fake Mr. Rance and get me back on track."

"Good idea. I'll see you later."

"What kind of schooling do you have to have, to be an engineer?"

Bobby and Trent were in the office, searching online for steeple designs for Reverend Paula's church.

"Depends on what kind of engineer you want to be."

"How many different kinds are there?"

"Maybe thirty."

Bobby stared. "That many? Really?"

"Yes. Everything from electrical and mechanical to marine and automotive."

"What kind are you?"

"I have a master's in architectural and a bachelor's in mechanical."

"And the difference?"

"Bachelor's is a four-year program. A master's takes two more. Why the questions?"

He shrugged. "I like doing the stuff you've been showing me, but I'm not wanting to be in school that long."

"Time's going to pass anyway."

Bobby scanned him. "Never thought about it like that."

"How's your math?"

"One of my best subjects, when I went to school—which in high school wasn't a lot. Dropped out in the tenth grade. But I do like making numbers do what they do."

"Then that's a plus. There's a ton of math requirements for any engineering program. How about physics?"

"No clue even what that is."

"No problem. We have two of the best young physics brains around in Preston and Leah."

Trent scanned him in turn. "Are you seriously considering this?"

He'd been considering a lot of stuff lately. "I don't know, man. I move here, and you all got me thinking so much crazy stuff, I don't know if I'm coming or going." He paused and said honestly, "Makes me want to shoot higher."

"Nothing wrong with that."

"But isn't college expensive? Who has that kind of cash? I sure don't."

"I do, and I'll make you a deal. If you really want to do this, I'll put up the money. I'll pay your tuition, spring for your books, and pay you a stipend every month so you and Kiki will have something to live on."

Bobby froze.

"More than likely you'll have to do two years in community college to get yourself up to speed, but nothing wrong with that."

"But why would you do that?"

"Because I can, and because I think it'll be a good investment."

"Investment? In what?"

"In you. In busting open the stereotype that men who look like us aren't smart enough. In the future, so your kids can grow up and bust open other stereotypes. In you looking at yourself in the mirror on the day you cross that stage with your degree in your hand and marveling at how far you've come. I'm willing to invest in all of that and more."

"But what if I don't make it?"

Trent shook his head. "Remember the last time you asked me that question? What did I say?"

Bobby smiled. "What if I can?"

"Yeah. So talk to Kiki. Think on it. Reverend Paula would say pray on it. After the holiday, let me know."

"Okay." He quieted. "I never knew my dad. Your sons are lucky to have you in their corner."

"Now I'm in yours, too. Welcome to the family."

Bobby dropped his head to hide the moisture in his eyes. When he got himself together, he raised his gaze to the most remarkable man he'd ever met. "Thanks," he whispered.

"No problem."

"One last thing."

"Shoot."

"Where can I buy a ring?"

Chapter 16

Trent drove home after work feeling pretty good about the day. That Bobby had been so affected by what Henry Adams and its citizens stood for that he was contemplating shelving his old dreams to pursue new ones that were both brighter and higher was moving. He had nothing but admiration for a young man willing to give an unknown path a try, and he'd support him in any way he could. Worries about the costs were negligible. The yearly royalties he received on the patents he'd filed back in his twenties were ongoing. He'd never be as wealthy as, say, Bernadine, but he was set enough financially to assist Bobby with tuition and books and still have plenty left over when it came time for Amari and Devon to journey toward their own dreams.

When he was growing up, his family had little extra money. Mal had used the GI Bill to get his degree in veterinary medicine, but after graduation, between the prejudice of some of the local farmers and the barely-getting-by status of the others, he was barely getting by himself. He and Tamar couldn't afford to send Trent to college. But he'd gotten excellent grades all his life and scored high on the SAT, and that earned him enough scholarship money to enroll. He covered the rest by working the entire six years it took him to get his master's. And he'd worked hard: pumping gas, mopping floors, cleaning restrooms and toilets, and spending his summers doing the grunt work at any construction site that would hire him. Back then he made a vow that if he ever had children, he'd find a way to pay for their entire education so they could devote themselves to their studies and not have to juggle school with employment in order to eat.

His sync sounded, and Jack's name came on the display. "Trent?"

"Yeah, Jack. What's up?"

"When you get home, I want you and Lily to take a look at the school's web page."

"Something wrong?"

"Nothing dangerous—just something to make you go *hmm*. It's tied to Zoey's band. Devon's got groupies."

"What!"

"Yeah, man. It's crazy. Check out the page and then get back to me and let me know if you two think we need to do something about it. Talk to you later. Bye." The call ended.

Groupies?

"Groupies?" Lily asked skeptically when Trent relayed the message.

"That's what Jack said. Groupies." He'd booted up his laptop as soon as he got home, and they were now at the kitchen table, waiting for the school website to load. Once it did, Trent clicked around until he found the band's page. The kids had named the band HA. There were a couple of videos loaded. They'd been edited to make the group look and sound much more polished than Amari claimed they were. One featured Devon crooning the old school standard "Stand by Me." He'd always been charismatic onstage, and although the video needed better lighting, the charisma came through loud and clear.

"The boy can sing," Lily remarked.

Trent agreed.

"There's a link to contact the band." Seeing it, Trent clicked, and when the link opened, they both stared. There had to be fifteen short videos—each only seconds long—from girls as young as eight and as old as fifteen, all saying "Hi" and "You are sooo cute!" and "Here's my number, call me!" and "E-mail me please, you're amazing!"

Trent scrolled through. "Jack wasn't kidding. Look at this, Lil." Three girls were posed in bikinis.

"I'm looking," she said disapprovingly.

"Here, wait. A video from Devon."

Their son's face appeared. Speaking in a voice several octaves lower than normal, he said smoothly, "Hi, ladies. Thanks for your awesome support. I'll respond to each and every one of you as soon as I can. Come see our first concert Friday night at the Henry Adams movies. Ciao." And he winked.

His parents blinked.

Trent looked at Lily.

She said, "Damned if the boy doesn't sound like a tween version of Barry White."

Trent laughed. She did too.

"So what do we do?" he asked.

"Lock him in his room until he's thirty-five."

"I think he found his swag."

"Jesus be a fence . . ."

Trent continued searching the page. "Does that say 'Book the Band'?"

Sure enough, HA was booked for two appearances over the Christmas break. One was a birthday party for a nine-year-old girl in Franklin, and the other—another birthday party—was in Topeka.

"Okay. Game over," Trent said. "How do they plan to get to Topeka?"

Lily shrugged. "You know Devon loves the Greyhound bus."

Trent read aloud: " 'Contact our manager: W. W. Dahl.' "

"I assume that's Wyatt. Lord have mercy."

"I think it's time to set some boundaries."

"Yep. I'll call Gemma."

"I'll call Reggie. Roni's underground at the studio. I don't mind them being in a band, but there'll be no traveling."

"Or little hotties throwing panties."

When he stopped laughing, he asked, "Do you think Tamar or Dad knows they're performing Friday night?"

She shrugged. "Send her a text."

Tamar texted back that she had given her approval for one song.

"At least they had the good sense not to just show up on Friday saying they wanted to play."

"You never know. She might have said okay. As tough as she can be on them sometimes, she really loves those kids."

He agreed, but having grown up with her,

he'd learned to never leave anything to chance.

After they talked to Jack and the parents involved, it was agreed they'd meet at the Julys' after dinner.

"Are we in trouble?" Devon asked worriedly when told about the meeting.

"No," Trent said. "We're just getting together to set some ground rules for the band. There are some things on the school website we need to talk about."

Amari cracked, "Sounds like trouble to me."

Trent shot him a look.

"Sorry."

Lily said, "We noticed all the girls sending you phone numbers and e-mails."

Devon grinned. "Pretty chilly, huh?"

"No."

"No?"

"No. You're too young to have groupies, baby. Sorry. There'll be no e-mails or phone calls coming in or going out. In fact, we're going to have Jack remove all those links."

He pouted. "I thought you said I wasn't in trouble."

"You're not. Your dad and I are just doing the responsible parent thing so that there won't be any trouble down the line."

He didn't look pleased with that explanation. His parents weren't concerned.

When the band members and their adults

arrived, they were ushered into the living room. Zoey was accompanied by Reggie, Roni, and her aunt Cassidy, who'd been helping them with their practices. Wyatt entered with his grandmother Gemma. Jack attended the meeting, too. The adults had all been given a heads-up earlier on the website, and were in agreement on to how to proceed.

Gemma said, "I've called the family of the girl in Topeka and talked to her dad. He had no idea she'd booked a band for her party. Turns out she'd snuck one of his checks to pay the twenty-five-dollar fee, which she mailed to Wyatt." Gemma eyed her grandson, who squirmed a bit. "I told the dad I'd shred the check. He thanked me and said he appreciated my calling."

Roni asked, "And the girl in Franklin?"

"Her parents didn't know she'd hired a band either, but no checks or cash had been sent, so they're fine. I've also let Mr. W. W. Dahl here know that from now on, any financial business tied to the band or anything else he's involved in goes through me first. Right, Wyatt?"

"Yes."

"I removed the contact links," said Jack. "When they asked me to add them I thought it was a good idea, but didn't know it had bloomed the way it did. My apology to the parents for not being as diligent as I probably should have been. I'll also talk to the parents of the band's sax man."

Lily asked, "Who shot the videos of the band and uploaded them?"

Wyatt reluctantly raised his hand.

"You did a great job. The editing was awesome. You made HA look very professional."

His eyes widened with surprise.

Trent took in the kids and said gently, "This meeting isn't about punishing you guys. We just need some rules of conduct in place."

"And we're very proud of your initiative and enthusiasm," Cass added. "It just needs guidance."

"So we can still have the band and play Friday night?" Zoey asked.

"Of course. In fact, we're all looking forward to it."

The kids grinned.

Reggie said, "But no more web presence without approval, and definitely no more bookings, okay?"

They nodded.

After a few more minutes of talk about Friday's upcoming performance, they all shared parting hugs and thank-yous and left the Julys to return home.

"I think that went well," Trent said to Lily when Devon had gone to his room.

"I agree. Now let's just hope they play by the rules. Be awfully tough having to paint Marie's fence in this kind of weather."

"As a kid who's been there, done that: Not fun. At all."

• • •

Bernadine was just preparing to leave the office for the day and meet Mal for dinner when a man and a woman appeared in her doorway. The man was Steve Tuller, who'd been Tommy Stewart's lawyer when Tommy tried to shake her down for his bogus roach-in-a-sandwich debacle. She didn't know the nondescript woman with him, who was of average height and had short brown hair.

"Mr. Tuller," Bernadine said, "what brings you here?"

"Hello, Ms. Brown. Something we'd like to discuss if you have the time. This is Sandra Langster."

"Hello, Ms. Langster."

"Hi, Ms. Brown. Call me Sandy."

"Okay."

Tuller said, "I know you and I didn't meet under the best of circumstances the last time, but I'm hoping we can look past that for now."

She remembered how embarrassed and apologetic he'd been upon learning he'd been duped into taking Stewart on as a client, so she gave him the benefit of the doubt. "I was on my way home, but I have a few minutes. Please. Come on in and have a seat."

After they'd made themselves comfortable, she asked, "Now what can I do for you?"

"I'm a PI," Sandy said. "I've been hired by Tommy Stewart's mother to find him."

A private investigator? That certainly got her attention. "And what have you turned up?"

"Truthfully, a bit of this and a bit of that. His mom's a distant cousin of mine, and she initially thought you might have had a hand in his disappearance."

Bernadine eyed her. "Really."

"Yes, but I've been watching you for the past few weeks, and I'm pretty sure you didn't."

"I could've told you that," she said, trying to decide if she was offended or not. She was, she decided.

"I never apologize for doing my job, ma'am. Tommy caused you and the people here a lot of grief, and in my line of work that's the folks you always look at first in a case like this. Nothing personal."

"I understand." Bernadine actually did. "So having scratched me off your list, who's at the top now?"

"Astrid Wiggins."

"I could've told you that, too. Mr. Tuller, how are you involved?"

"I'm representing an interested third party."

"Whose name you aren't going to reveal, again. Am I correct?"

He turned red for a moment. "Yes."

She shook her head, hoping he wasn't being led down the garden path again. "So, how can I help, other than agreeing that Astrid is your prime suspect?"

"How much do you know about her?" Sandy asked.

"Not enough to get her out of my hair."

Sandy smiled. "I've talked to a few people in town, and they all feel the same way. Does she impress you as a woman who eats fast-food burgers every day?"

Bernadine paused. "I don't know anything about her eating habits, but she's one of those skinny Minnies. I don't see her doing burgers."

"Neither do I. I've been watching her for the past two weeks, and every day she buys a sack of burgers. Even on the nights she meets Mr. Wingo at the motel up on 183, she gets a bag, takes it into the house, and then drives off."

Mr. Wingo was the high school principal with the wife and five kids. "And your conclusion?"

"Maybe I'm clutching at straws, but my gut says, either willingly or unwillingly, Tommy's in her house."

"So do you think she's right?" Mal asked as they ate dinner in their booth at the Dog, an hour after Sandy and Tuller left her office. They were keeping their voices down so as not to be overheard.

"Since this is Astrid we're talking about, I wouldn't be surprised if she has him tied up and gagged in a closet."

"Is the PI going to talk to Will?"

"No idea, but my guess is, she doesn't have enough solid evidence yet. Law enforcement can't ask for a search warrant just because Astrid's been seen buying burgers. She did say she wished the mom would've contacted her earlier, so maybe she could have found out who torched his car and what happened to his phone. Apparently none of the towers can pinpoint it, and no calls have been made on it since he disappeared."

"Any record of him calling Astrid?"

"Sandy said no."

"This is pretty interesting."

"It is. I'm also wondering who Tuller's client might be. Last time he wouldn't confirm it, but I'm pretty sure Astrid hired him for Tommy. We know she's crazy like a fox, so I doubt she'd hire him to look into the disappearance. Or would she?"

"Tuller would be a fool to work for her again."

So many unanswered questions and no real answers—unless one counted fast-food burgers as one, and at this point she couldn't see how.

"How's Diane? She come to her senses yet?"

"She had this morning. Now, whether she's still on Planet Reality with the rest of us is the question. She said she was going to look for a job, but I haven't heard anything from her today."

"Anything else from Kyle on Don Juan?"

"No, but I booked our getaway. I'm really

looking forward to not turning the world for a while. My arm's tired from all this spinning."

They spent a few moments talking about the trip, and she added, "The sunsets are amazing. Just wait until you see them."

"More interested in seeing you relaxed and enjoying yourself. Have you told Crystal about the trip?"

"No, but I will this evening. I know she's not going to want to be in the house with Diane, so I'll let her decide who she wants to stay with while we're gone." Crystal would probably choose her friends Kelly and Bobby, but then again, maybe Diane needed to be the one to leave. Bernadine wouldn't be happy to return home and find her sister had taken it upon herself to redecorate the place.

When Bernadine got home, she knocked on her sister's closed door.

"Come in."

She entered and found Diane packing a suitcase. "What're you doing?"

She smiled. "What's it look like? I found a job."

"Where?"

"Topeka." She walked to the closet, took down a hanger holding a pair of slacks, and added them to the few other pieces of clothing on the bed.

"Topeka?"

"Yep. Did a Skype interview this morning, and I start on Monday. It's a manager position for a dental office. I called Harmon, and he actually sent them a really nice recommendation."

"Whoa. Wait. Where are you going to live, how are you going to get there, all that?"

Diane began emptying the dresser drawers of the few items they held. "I'll figure it out once I'm there."

"Di . . ."

She held up a hand. "Bernadine. Please. I'm going to do this. I have to do this."

"But—"

"After you left this morning, I looked at myself and finally admitted what a mess I am. All my life I've waited on people to make things easy for me—Mama, Harmon, and now you. Remember the wake-up call I got about my kids while working the night shift at Gary's store?"

"I do." Listening to some women talk about the joy their children and grandchild brought to their lives pushed Diane to reconcile with her own.

"This mess with Rance—or whatever his real name is—was a wake-up call too, only a different kind. I need to grow up. Period. I need to stop acting like the world should bow down and kiss my feet and start handling my business. I don't want to be who I've been anymore."

Bernadine was taken aback.

Diane folded the slacks and placed them in the suitcase. "I'm going to drop the whole stupid Diana persona and be Diane. You and Lily and the rest of your friends here have so much confidence. I envy that, and I want some too, but the only way to get it is to find my own."

Bernadine didn't know what to say.

"All I ask is that you let me take the car so I can drive to Topeka, and I'll figure it out from there. If I have to sleep in it until I can find a place I can afford, I'm prepared to do that, too. Soon as I get my first check, I'll send you next month's car payment. I promise."

Bernadine was still trying to figure out who this woman was and what she'd done with her sister. "Are you sure about this?"

She nodded. "Yes. It's time, Bernadine."

"Okay." Diane even looked different. Was confidence already taking root? "You know I'm not going to let you sleep in a car. I'll—"

She stopped her. "I don't want your money."

"Di, consider it a loan."

"No. I need to do this my way, please. All I need is the car. I drove down to Hays earlier this afternoon and sold a bunch of my clothes and jewelry to a resale shop. Of course I got less than half of what I paid, but I have enough cash for gas and to put toward rent if I'm careful with my spending."

She was impressed.

"I got this," Diane told her, smiling. "All I need besides the car are your prayers and good wishes."

"You have those. Come here."

They shared a teary hug. "So damn proud of you, girl."

"Thanks. And thanks for being the best big sister a silly bitch like me doesn't deserve."

Bernadine chuckled. "When are you leaving?"

"First thing in the morning."

"Do you need help packing?"

"No. I'm fine. I don't have many clothes left. Just my coat and a few things for the job. I'll have to make do with what I have for now."

"Okay. I'll come back later and check on you."

Bernadine walked to the door and met her sister's gaze. The gospel tune by Mary Mary came to mind. "Go get your blessings, girl."

"Going to try my best."

Upstairs, Bernadine wiped at the tears in her eyes as she walked into Crystal's room.

"You okay?" Crys asked, glancing up from the homework spread out on her desk. "What's the matter?"

Bernadine sat in a chair and explained.

"Wow. Are you sure that's her down there? Did you see any pods?"

She laughed. "As in *Invasion of the Body Snatchers*?" They'd shown the original version a few weeks back at the Friday-night movies. "No pods. Just Diane."

"If she's talking about sleeping in a car, there have to be pods in her room somewhere."

"She says it's time for her to grow up."

Crystal still looked skeptical. "I guess. When's she leaving?"

"First thing in the morning."

"Not trying to be mean, but good. She's not my favorite person."

"I know. She's been tap-dancing on my last nerve too, but I'm wishing her well and hoping everything works out the way she wants. We all deserve happiness."

"True, and as long as she's happy somewhere else, I'm happy."

Bernadine loved Crystal and her point-blank way of expressing herself. "Speaking of happy, Mal and I are going to fly down to Key West for a few days after Christmas."

"It's about time."

That surprised her. "What do you mean?"

"Just what I said. I don't know why you two haven't taken off before."

"I've been trying to set a good example for you."

"What kind of example? How to deny your own happiness? Since we're talking about that."

Bernadine blinked with surprise.

"I'm almost grown, Mom. You and OG having a good time together is not going to make me run out and sleep with the first guy I see, or think you're a bad mother. In fact, between what you've been teaching me about respecting myself and what I learned in Dallas, a guy is really going to have to have his stuff together before I let anybody sample this crystal."

Bernadine snorted.

"I'm just saying." She grinned.

"You are a mess."

"So, go to Key West and be happy like a room without a roof. You've made everybody we know happy, Mom, even Diane. Now it's your turn. Do I need to play Pharrell for you?"

"No." What a remarkable young woman Crystal was growing up to be. "I initially came up here to ask who you wanted to stay with while I'm gone because I figured you wouldn't want to be here with Diane. But since she's leaving, I guess that won't be necessary now."

"No, I'll be good here by myself, and the Julys are next door if I need anything. Go. You don't have to worry about me."

"I don't, do I? I'm loving this new and improved Crystal a lot."

"It's all because of you."

"Some of it, yes, but most of it has been you."

"Thanks. Have you heard about Devon and his groupies?"

"What?"

"Oh, Mom. You're not going to believe this . . ."

Chapter 17

The following morning Bernadine rose earlier than usual to see her sister off. When she got downstairs, Diane had her one suitcase by the door—she'd sold the others—and her coat on, ready to go.

"Are you sure this is what you want to do, Di? You know you're welcome to stay if you want."

"I know, but I have to do this."

They hugged. "Thanks for everything, Bernadine."

"You're welcome. Make sure you text me every couple of hours so I'll know you're okay."

"I will. Tell Crystal good-bye for me."

Bernadine nodded solemnly.

Diane picked up her suitcase. Bernadine stood in the door and watched as she backed the little brown car down the drive. With a toot of the horn, she drove away, and a sad yet hopeful Bernadine closed the door.

True to her word, Diane sent short texts along the way. After taking 183 south, she picked up I-70 and headed east. Hayes to Topeka was about two hundred miles. Barring any problems, Bernadine figured she'd be there before noon. Sure enough, by late morning she received a text. *Here. Heading to dentist office. Found the money you hid in the glove box. U don't listen well do you??? ☺ Love you!*

Bernadine responded: ☺ *Love you more.*

Tommy Stewart had no way of determining night from day, so he spent the waking hours telling himself stories, drawing pictures in the dirt, and when he got really hungry, she'd arrive with his food. By the clock in his stomach, he guessed she delivered his burgers around the same time each day. On this day, when his stomach began to growl, he figured she'd arrive soon. But instead of sitting and waiting like he had been doing since being locked in the little room for who knew how many days now, he lay down on the poor excuse for a mattress, and with the now-freed pipe hidden beside him, wrapped himself in the thin quilts and waited. It had taken him what seemed like hours to work the pipe loose. His shoulders ached from all the pulling, and his hands did too, but if things went according to plan, he'd be free soon. Hearing the key in the lock he began to moan as if he was in pain. When she stepped in, he increased the volume.

"What's the matter with you?" she barked.

"I need a doctor. My stomach's killing me."

She stepped farther into the room. "You'll be fine."

"No!" he cried. "I'm hurting really, really bad." He brought his knees up to his chest and began rolling back and forth. "I've been throwing up, too. It's like somebody's poking me in my side with a hot poker." He kept moving, moaning. "Please take me to a doctor, urgent care, something. Once they figure out what's wrong, you can even bring me back here. I promise I won't tell the doctors anything about you. Please! I don't want to die in here. Please!" Out of the corner of his eye he saw her put down the bag of burgers and come closer. "Please, Ms. Wiggins, get a doctor!"

She came closer. "Oh, for heaven's sake."

Cradling the shotgun, she bent down to get a look at him, and that's when he rose up and crashed the pipe across her shoulder. She cried out and fell to her knees, dropping the gun. While she slumped, moaned in pain, and clutched the injured arm, he scrambled to his feet and tossed the gun out of her reach. "Stay down," he warned, breathing hard, filled with adrenaline and fear.

She raised her angry gaze and snarled, "You little bastard! I'll kill you!" She latched on to the leg of his jeans, and he didn't know if she was trying to yank him down or pull herself up. Panicked, he brought the pipe down again. Hard. Her scream filled the room. Not knowing what else to do, Tommy stood frozen for a few seconds, then tossed the pipe and ran.

Bernadine was gathering her coat and purse in anticipation of driving to the Dog for lunch when

Tommy Stewart stumbled into the office, looking wild-eyed and crazy.

"Ms. Brown! Hide me, please! Don't let her find me!" He was coatless, filthy, and shivering with cold. His hair was matted, and the smell! He fell to his knees, put his face in his grimy hands, and began to cry. "Oh god! I had to hit her! I had to."

After recovering from being scared half to death, Bernadine picked up her phone and speed-dialed Will Dalton.

The county EMTs arrived with Will. After they took the smelly and sobbing young man away in their unit, Will drove to Astrid's. No one answered the door. After hearing Tommy's story, Will and his deputy thought she must still be lying injured in the basement room, so they broke out the glass in the door and let themselves in, but there was no one in the house and no gold Caddy in the garage. They didn't find a pipe or a gun, either. Will called in an APB and went back to the hospital to talk to Tommy.

Later, he returned to Bernadine's office.

"Why in the world did he come here?" she asked.

"He said he went to his mom's first, but she wasn't home. He didn't have a key and didn't want to break in because he figured that would be the first place Astrid would look. He was also afraid that if he ran into any of the businesses in Franklin, asking for help, they'd call Astrid. He didn't know who to trust, but he knew you wouldn't call her."

"So he ran all this way in the freezing cold."

"He was pretty scared. The docs are giving him fluids. Has a touch of frostbite on his fingers and ears, but they think he'll be okay."

"And his mother?"

"She drives a big rig. She's out in Idaho somewhere, delivering a load. Talked to her on the phone a little bit ago. She'll be back tomorrow."

"And the PI, Sandy Langster?"

Confusion furrowed his brow. "What PI?"

She related the details of her meeting with the woman and Steve Tuller.

"First I've heard of this. Wasn't Tuller the one involved with the roaches?"

She nodded and passed him the business cards the two left with her when they visited. He wrote down their phone numbers. "If she contacts you before I can get hold of her, have her call me stat. Same goes for Tuller. They may have information we can use in the investigation."

"I will. Where do you think Astrid is?"

He shrugged. "All the hospitals in the area have been alerted. If she's as injured as Tommy says she is, she'll probably turn up."

And she did, later that evening at a hospital in Topeka. She told the police Tommy Stewart broke into her home, assaulted her, and she wanted him arrested.

• • •

When Devon entered the kitchen, Amari took one look at his brother's swag attire and cracked, "Does Captain Hook know you've been in his closet?"

Trent hid his laugh, barely. He glanced Lily's way. Her shoulders were shaking with suppressed laughter, and there were tears of mirth in her eyes.

"I think I look pretty chilly," Devon said confidently.

Amari looked between his parents, shook his head, and said, "Mrs. Payne's going to give me and Brain a ride to the rec so we can get the sound system ready. I'll see you there."

He got his coat and left. Trent dearly wished he could go with him so he could step outside and laugh. He really thought he might burst if he didn't get relief soon.

"How do you think I look, Dad?"

Trent coughed and cleared his throat. "I don't think I've ever seen anything quite so swagalicious before, Devon."

Lily was crying. "I think I hear my phone. Be right back."

Trent swore he'd find a way to pay her back for not telling him about this in advance, but then again, no verbal description would have been sufficient. One had to see this to believe it, and even now Trent was having a hard time. The long-sleeved red velvet coat with its black belt and large faux gold buckle did indeed resemble something Captain Hook would wear. The hem hit Devon low on his thighs and showed the black jeans tucked into his black knee-high boots. He had a long black scarf tied around his neck, and on his head a black beret cocked to the side. In a way he looked quite swaggish, but also very strange. Trent couldn't wait to see what Zoey and the other band members were wearing—or maybe he could.

Lily returned with her coat. "You guys ready to go?"

While Devon hurried to get his coat, Trent said to her, "I owe you for this, Fontaine."

She mimicked a kiss.

Laughing, they walked out to join Devon.

Extra excitement was in the air at the rec center. This would be the auditorium's first hosting of movie night since the riot, and everyone was anxious to see the renovations. There was more seating available than at the school's auditorium, which meant more people could attend. The place began filling up fast. It was also the last day of school before the break. In four days it would be Christmas, and that added to the excitement as well. Tamar and her crew had the place decorated with Styrofoam snowmen, wooden sleighs filled with brightly decorated packages, and trees sporting ornaments and garnished with popcorn garlands. The music for the evening was seasonal R&B classics like Eartha Kitt's "Santa Baby," "Rudolph the Red-Nosed Reindeer" by the Temptations, and "I Saw Mommy Kissing Santa Claus" sung by the very young Michael Jackson and the Jackson Five. The regular movie-night snack menu was supplemented with candy canes, hot chocolate with marshmallows, and Marie's famous gingerbread, made from a recipe passed down through the generations via her many-greats-grandmother Cara Lee Jefferson, one of the town's first schoolteachers.

As Trent handed Lily her cup of hot chocolate and took his seat, he watched the smiling Devon, clad in his swag clothes, being fawned over by a bevy of lined-up little girls. "Lil, he's signing autographs."

"I see that," she said as she sipped. "He'll have to walk home tonight because that little pea head's going to be too swollen to fit in the car."

He snorted. "I'm still trying to get over the outfit."

"You should've seen my face when he showed me what he wanted to buy. At least he paid for it on his own."

"Amazing."

"Truly," she added. "We have Captain Hook, and there's Zoey. Looks like she's been in Tina Turner's closet."

She had on a long purple wig, a sparkly white

shirt, a white skirt, and a pair of white patent boots. Both W. W. Dahl and Freddy, the sax player, were wearing black suits over black turtlenecks and Blues Brothers sunglasses.

Trent chuckled. "I hope they play well enough to back up all that swag."

"If Amari's to be believed, probably not."

Seeing the Acostas enter, Trent waved them over. When they arrived, he said, "Sit with us."

Anna said, "We'd love to."

Luis sat down next to his mother-in-law. Alfonso and Maria asked permission to join the other kids down front and, after getting the okay, left the adults.

"So many people," Anna said.

Lily said, "I know. Are you all ready for the holidays?"

"We are," Luis said. "In fact, Tamar wants us to host Henry Adams's first *posada*."

He explained that *las posadas* was a Mexican tradition that reenacted Mary and Joseph's search for shelter right before the birth of the Christ child.

Anna said, "Like Joseph and Mary, we go house to house, except we sing carols. In Mexico everyone is then invited to a home for pozole, and there's a piñata for the children. It's a wonderful way to bring the community together."

Trent said, "What a great idea."

"Our trailer isn't large enough to host everyone for the pozole and the piñata," Luis said, "so

Tamar suggested we use one of the rooms here at the rec."

"Sounds like fun. I can't wait."

Lily asked, "So what is pozole?"

Anna explained, "It's like a soup . . ."

After they'd entered the noise-filled auditorium, Bobby and Kiki scanned the place for two free seats. The twins were with their Henry Adams grandmother, Genevieve. "There're two over there," Bobby said, pointing. "You grab them, and I'll get us something to eat."

"Okay. Hot chocolate too, please."

"Gotcha."

Kiki went to claim the seats, and Bobby made his way over to the food line. He couldn't believe how many people there were, and wondered why there were so many little girls mobbing Devon, and why he was dressed so wack. He also couldn't believe how nervous he was. The ring he'd gotten for Kiki had been burning a hole in his pocket since he'd picked it up earlier that day from the jeweler over in Franklin. The owner was nice enough to let him buy it on credit—after Trent cosigned the application—but the most important thing was that he had it. He was going to propose to her onstage right before the movie. He'd already cleared it with Tamar. He'd asked that she not tell anyone, so he was pretty sure no one else knew. Kiki didn't, for sure.

• • •

Down on the stage, Amari and Brain were going about their duties. Watching Devon holding court in the side aisle, Amari said, "Tell me he is not signing autographs."

Brain paused, looked over, and said, "If I did, I'd be lying. Who's he think he is, Usher?"

"Not wearing those clothes."

Amari spotted Kyra Jones walking down the center aisle, carrying a box of popcorn and a drink. When she saw him, she waved. Her braces were gone, and she had a new haircut. She didn't look like Jaws anymore. In fact, she looked like a babe. He was so surprised, he stood frozen.

Brain said, "Don't just stand there like a dumbass, wave back! Thought you were from Detroit."

That snapped Amari into motion, and he waved in return. "Aw, man, here she comes." He busied himself with the mic.

"Hi, Amari." Her smile showed pretty white teeth.

"Hey, Kyra. What's up?"

"I'm free of the metal!"

"I like the haircut."

"Do you?"

"I do."

"Is it okay if I sit with you again?"

"Sure. Leah's over there. Brain and I'll be done in a few minutes."

"Okay."

He watched her leave and cracked, "As the OG would say, 'That girl is fine.' "

"Don't tell Leah, but I totally agree."

Their jobs done, they went to the kitchen for snacks and made their way to their seats.

The night got underway when Tamar stepped out onstage. Everyone quieted. The evening's movies were the animated *Rudolph the Red-Nosed Reindeer* and *A Christmas Story*. Ralphie's quest for a BB gun was a Henry Adams favorite.

"Welcome, everybody. Doesn't our auditorium look grand?" Applause sounded. "We give thanks for the great job done by the repair crews. First up is a new band. They started out calling themselves HA, but they've changed their name. Ladies and gentlemen, Exodus!"

The applause rang out, as did the screams of joy from Devon's groupies. The lights, under the direction of Siz in the booth, hit the stage, and there they stood: Zoey in her Tina wig, holding a red guitar that looked twice her size; Devon decked out like Hook and holding a pair of rhythm sticks; and Freddy in his suit and dark glasses, his sax hanging from a strap around his neck. Zoey counted them down, and Freddy started wailing on the sax. The kids in attendance greeted the first few familiar notes with screams, and by the time Zoey sang "Hey baby, even though I hate ya I wanna love ya," even Amari and the teens were on their feet dancing to Exodus covering Ariana Grande's "Problem." Freddy was strong on the sax, and although Zoey still wasn't very good on the guitar, it was loud, and her pure-as-gold voice made up for her lack of playing skill. When the band reached the chorus, Devon snatched the mic free and moved to the apron of the stage. Leaning down, he began whispering the refrain, and the little girls lost their minds. They charged to the front of the stage and began singing back. Zoey sang the band into the second verse, and then into the short rap, accompanied by the voices of everyone in the house under the age of eighteen. The energy was so high that when the song should've ended, Zoey kept it going, and for another five minutes Exodus rocked the house.

They finally took their bows to a tremendous ovation. Siz shut down the spotlights, and the waving band hurried offstage.

Tamar stepped up to the microphone. "Wow! Let's give them another hand."

Applause shook the building again. The band came back out onstage, linked hands like a cast on Broadway, and bowed.

After their departure, Tamar said, "Even had me dancing. Mal, I want that song on the box in the Dog ASAP!"

"You got it!" he called back, and everyone laughed and cheered.

"Now, before we start the movie, there's one

more thing to do. Bobby and Kelly, where are you?"

Bobby stood up.

"Come on up. Kelly, you too."

They walked down the aisle together. Kelly had confusion all over her face. Once they got to the stage, Tamar stepped out of sight, and Bobby walked to the mic. "First off, I want to thank everyone for all you've given to me, Kelly, and the babies. When we first got here, I wasn't sure this was the place for us to be, but you've changed my mind and our lives. So thank you, very much."

He waited for the applause that greeted that to end before saying, "Kelly and I have been together since middle school, and no matter what I was doing, right or wrong, she was there. I love her a lot."

A chorus of *Awws* sounded from the crowd.

"And because I do love her, I want the world to know . . ." He walked over to where she stood and got down on one knee. Her eyes went wide as plates. He took the white velvet ring box out of his pocket and opened it.

"Oh my god!" she whispered. "Oh my god, Bobby?"

"Will you marry me?"

She started jumping up and down. Her hands flew to her mouth, and tears rolled down her cheeks.

People in the audience started yelling, "Say yes!"

She was so moved initially, all she seemed capable of doing was—nothing. Finally finding her voice, she said, "Yes."

The audience cheered, and many of the ladies wiped at their own tears. As he placed the ring on her finger, took her in his arms, and kissed her, more cheers and applause went up.

When they returned to their seats, the house lights dimmed, the large screen lowered into view, and the animated *Rudolph the Red-Nosed Reindeer* began.

That night, as they lay together in bed, Kelly looked at the small sparkler on her finger. "I love this, Bobby."

"One day I'll get you a bigger one."

"No, this one is perfect." Turning his way, she said in a serious voice, "We've never talked about getting married. Can I ask what's changed?"

"Me. Being here. Seeing life in a different way. Trent's helped a lot."

"You two have gotten pretty close."

"Yeah. He's a great man. If I had a father, I'd want him to be like Trent. Being around him is going to make me a better dad to the twins."

She cuddled close. "I think you're pretty awesome now."

He kissed her on the forehead. "Do you think Reverend Paula can marry us on New Year's Day?

I'd like for us to start the year out as officially husband and wife."

"You are so sweet. That's kind of soon, but we can ask her. Even if we can't get all the paper-work done, we can still have a little ceremony and do all the legal stuff later."

He thought that was a great idea. "One more thing to tell you."

"What?"

"I think I want to go to college and be an engineer like Trent."

She rose up and looked into his face. "You're serious," she said.

"Very. And he said he's willing to make an investment in our future, so he's offering to pay tuition, books, the whole deal."

"Oh my god!" She fell flat again.

He saw her tears and eased her close. "Aww, baby, you have to quit all this crying."

"I'm just so happy. Last Christmas we didn't even have enough money to buy each other a piece of gum, and now . . ."

"I love you, Kiki."

"You've never said that before."

He chuckled. "I know. Not something guys do where we come from, but for your love, I'm going to tell you that every day. Every day." As he held her tight, Trent's words floated across his mind again: *A man is only as strong as the woman who holds him.*

Chapter 18

In the days leading up to Christmas, Rita Lynn could hardly contain her excitement. In less than a week's time she and Paul and Val would be winging their way to Kansas. Her phone was filled with the photos Trent had been sending, of Lily and Devon and Amari. That he'd taken the time out of what she knew had to be a busy period for him to do something so nice was further evidence of his big heart. Earlier she and Paul watched the video he'd sent of last night's performance by the band Devon was in. Now, meeting Val for lunch, she shared it.

"What in the world is Devon wearing?" Val asked, laughing.

"According to Trent, Devon calls them his swag clothes."

She chuckled. "Oh, my, look at all the girls. Devon can sing. They're really jamming."

"Yes, they are. I like the song."

Val watched the rest of the performance and handed the phone back. "I'm looking forward to seeing them."

"Me, too. You sent my packages?"

Val nodded. "They should be arriving in the morning. Did you tell Trent to expect them?"

"No. Christmas gifts are supposed to be a

surprise. I'm assuming they'll pay attention to the 'Do not open until Christmas' sticker I put on the box."

"I'm sure they will."

They concentrated on their meals for a moment. Then Val said, "Have something I want to talk to you about."

"And it is?"

"I'm going to look into in vitro fertilization after the new year."

Rita paused. She knew the challenges women of Val's age, class, and status faced in finding someone compatible to share their hearts and lives with.

"I'm tired of waiting for Mr. Right."

"So you'll have a baby alone?"

"Yes. I have the donor picked out. You know my friend Manny Diaz?"

"Yes, and I always thought you two made a stunning couple. I never understood why you never became more than friends."

"He's gay, Mama."

"Oh." Rita felt ridiculous.

Val reached over and patted her hand. "It's okay. Manny's smart, has a great personality. We've talked about it pretty seriously."

"Is he going to sign off on paternity?"

"Yes. He and his partner, Kevin, have a baby on the way with a surrogate."

Rita shook her head. "Lord, it's a whole new

world. So what do you need from me and your dad?"

"Just love and support."

"You got it. You're going to be a great mom."

"Going to try my best."

They spent the rest of the meal talking about the particulars, and Val answered as many of Rita's questions as she could. As Rita Lynn drove home, thinking about Val, she smiled at the thought of a potential new grandbaby and thanked God for yet another awesome blessing. Life was good.

Life was also good for the folks of Henry Adams as they prepped for Christmas. The last trips for shopping were done, packages wrapped and tucked away. The snow continued to fall, which meant more shoveling for Trent and Bobby and their crew but lots of cross-country skiing and snowman making for those who enjoyed being outside. The kids basked in the freedom from school and spent their days playing video games and basketball at the rec, and doing their best to avoid Tamar and her never-ending tasks. The Dog was decked out in wreaths, garlands, and a tree decorated with miniature animals, CDs, and candy canes.

On the evening of the twenty-third, Trent answered a knock on the door. Outside were the Acostas, singing. Because they were singing in Spanish, he had no idea what the words were, but Anna's lovely soprano voice mixed wonderfully with Luis's baritone. At the end of the song, the Julys got their coats and joined the Acostas as they sang their way over to Bernadine's. They sang at each of the houses in the subdivision, adding the Paynes, Garlands, Dahls, and Jameses to the procession, switching from Spanish to traditional American carols and back again as they made their way.

They then got in their cars, drove out to Tamar's, and sang there. She added her alto to the chorus, and then the Douglas family and Reverend Paula joined in. The caravan made its way to Marie's house, where she and Genevieve bolstered the caroling with their voices. After making a final stop at the farm where Clay and Bing Shepard lived, the procession drove to the rec.

They spent a few minutes listening to Anna give the history behind the *posada*, explaining that it was celebrated in Spain, Mexico, and many places in America, particularly in the Southwest. She went on to say that in some countries the *posada* lasted nine days—one day for each month of Mary's pregnancy.

Luis added, "*Posada* is a lot more involved and richer than what we did this evening, but we wanted you all to have a taste of our traditions. Speaking of tastes, that delicious smell filling the building is the pozole. It's a soup that families traditionally eat following the *posada*. It's made with pork and chilies and lots of hominy corn."

"But pozole is all about the garnishes," Anna added.

Everyone lined up for their first encounter with pozole. The garnishes on the table included thin slices of cabbage, radish, and avocado, along with cilantro and small wedges of lime. For those who wanted to add more heat and spice, there were chilies and hot sauce. The idea was to add what-ever garnishes you wanted to the base soup, grab a few tostadas, and enjoy.

Whereas Devon and Brain were a bit skeptical, Amari, who'd always been an adventurous eater, dove right in, and after his first few spoonfuls declared, "Mrs. Ruiz. This—every year, every Christmas for the rest of my life."

"Do you like it?" she asked, laughing.

"Yes, ma'am."

Gemma and Wyatt, who'd had Spanish neighbors in Chicago, were familiar with the soup, and Wyatt almost beat Amari back to the main table for a second helping.

After dinner the piñatas were raised, yet another *posada* tradition. The kids had a donkey at their end of the gym, and although the game was usually for children, the adults, who'd settled their differences over the debacle with Rita Lynn, had a pig on their end. Given short, fat T-ball bats and blindfolded, the batters were spun around a few times and sent to find their stuffed papier-mâché prey. Much hilarity ensued as swings were taken that met only air, some that met with people not quick enough to get out of the way and in Genevieve's case a bull's-eye that split the pig in half and sent the contents of pennies, wrapped peppermints, nuts, and other low-cost, fun items all over the floor. She said later she imagined it being Cletus.

When it came time to go home, everyone thanked the Acostas for adding their rich traditions to the cultural quilt of Henry Adams, and they all looked forward to participating again next year.

On Christmas Eve the Dog closed at noon. It would stay closed until the day after Christmas to allow the staff time with their families. The Julys drove to the church for the 5:00 p.m. service, at which Amari and Devon were serving as acolytes. The boys took the stairs down to the lower level to put on their vestments, while Lily and Trent went up to the sanctuary to take their seats. Gold-foil-wrapped pots of red poinsettia framed the altar, and the traditional Nativity crèche anchored a small table in the back. The service was always a beautiful affair, from the short opening chorale concert in which Roni sang, to Reverend Paula's traditional white vestments, to the candlelit singing of "Silent Night" that marked the end, but this Christmas Eve would be even more special: the Douglas twins were being baptized, and Trent had been asked to be their godfather.

Lily said quietly, "I think you'll be an awesome godfather."

Trent nodded at Marie and Genevieve as they took their seats across the aisle. The sanctuary was filling up around them. "I'm going to do my best. Have to admit I'm pretty honored to be asked."

They watched Amari, now in his robe, walk solemnly up to the altar to light the candles as a prelude to the beginning of the service. As he lit each one, Lily said, "He's come such a long way."

Trent agreed. "Couldn't ask for a better son."

The sanctuary was packed as Roni stepped up to the microphone and raised her gifted voice in praise. When she was done, she transitioned to the role of organist and began the processional. As the cross bearer, Amari led the way down the aisle, flanked by torchbearers Devon and Kyra. Behind them walked Bobby, all decked out in a new suit, carrying his daughter, and Kelly in a lovely dress and heels, carrying Bobby Jr. Resplendent in her gold-accented white robe, Reverend Paula brought up the rear.

The baptism was held at the service's midpoint, and Trent and godmother Genevieve joined the Douglas family at the altar. The vows were spoken and the godparents read their promises. Then Reverend Paula took each twin in turn and, cradling the baby in her arm, slowly poured a bit of holy water over the crown of their little head.

Tiara laughed, but Bobby Jr. wailed loudly in protest. At the end, the congregation welcomed the two new Christians with rousing applause.

The service continued with communion and ended with the lights being dimmed in the sanctuary. The small white candles everyone had been given upon entering the church were lit. The sea of flames flickered in the shadows as the congregation sang "Silent Night." Their combined voices rose and filled the sanctuary. For Trent it was always the most moving experience of the church year, and yet another of the many reasons he loved living in Henry Adams.

That evening after church, Trent and Lily sat on the couch and watched their sons walking around the tree, trying to make their decision. They were allowed to open one gift on Christmas Eve. Devon finally settled on a small one from Amari. He tore off the paper, and his eyes popped. "Sick! Thank you, Amari!"

"What is it?" Lily asked.

He held it up. "A CD of James Brown's greatest hits!"

While both parents displayed their amusement, Devon said, "You know he died on Christmas Day, so can I play this in the morning while we open the rest of our gifts?"

Lily looked to Trent, who shrugged. "Sure, Dev. Why not? That'll be fun."

Amari's choice was a flat, medium-size gift from his parents. He pulled the paper off, and his eyes widened. "Oh, wow!" It was a framed print of *The March* by Jacob Lawrence. "Thank you!"

"Now you don't have to wait until you're grown and have your own place," Trent told him.

Amari studied it with a seriousness that reflected his growing maturity. "This is awesome." He raised his gaze to theirs. "Thank you, guys."

They rounded out the evening by starting a fire and roasting marshmallows, before being treated to Amari's rousing reading of *The Grinch Who Stole Christmas*.

Christmas morning, the residents awakened to two inches of freshly fallen snow. Kiki thought it was quite beautiful. Bobby, not so much, because he was anticipating having to go out and shovel later. In the meantime, they enjoyed a leisurely breakfast before turning their attention to the unbelievable amount of gifts the babies received from the community. Last night after church, people gave them package after gift-wrapped package. There'd been so many, Rocky had to help them get some of them home, putting a few of the larger items in the bed of her truck—most notably the two rocking horses from Grandma/ Godmother Genevieve. Now, as they opened the trove—while keeping an eye on the babies to make sure they didn't eat the wrappings—they found diapers, bedding, clothing, toys and more toys, and two huge plastic saucer things that, from the manufacturer's tag, turned out to be sleds. There were new snowsuits and mittens and hats and tons of little kids' learning CDs. Tamar gave them a box filled with baby-proofing items for the house that included locks for the cupboards, inserts to fit into the electrical outlets, and two sturdy baby gates. Kiki loved her. The Garlands gifted the twins with a CD player for their room and a bunch of music CDs to enjoy. There were storybooks and recorded books from Crystal, and enough stuffed animals to start their own zoo.

Once everything was unwrapped, they took it all in and Bobby cracked, "These people are way out of control."

"I know—but it's because they haven't had any babies here for a long time."

"I can see that, but we'd need like five more kids to use all this stuff." He glanced over and grinned.

"Don't look at me. Maybe in a few years, but right now these two are all a girl can handle."

"If it were up to me, we'd have at least three more."

"Good thing it's not, so get a grip."

When Mal knocked on Bernadine's door, what she saw left her speechless. A horse and sleigh were outside in front of her house.

“Would my lady like to go for a ride?”

She stood there so long, looking out in amazement, that Mal chuckled. “Baby?”

Crystal, in her pajamas and her new leather boots, looked around her mom. “Wow! Now that’s the shizzle. Looks just like a Christmas card.” The sleigh was brown, and the huge draft horse was decked out in ribbons and bells.

Bernadine finally regained the power of speech. “Where on earth did you get them?”

“Santa. He’s off the clock now, so he’s in Miami knocking back nonalcoholic mai tais.”

She laughed. “Give me ten minutes to throw on some clothes.”

“Make sure they’re warm. One of your furs would be best.”

Ten minutes later, with everyone on their porches watching and smiling, Bernadine, wearing her best full-length faux fur coat over a ton of layered clothing, was helped into the big sleigh by her personal Santa, wearing a red Santa hat. He climbed in beside her, and with a slap of the reins the horse pulled forward, the runners caught the thin coating of snow, and the neighborhood residents cheered until Santa and his lady were out of sight.

As they glided over the open snow, Bernadine thought that if she hadn’t loved this man before, she sure loved him now. He’d taught her to fly a kite, treated her to her first picnic in a pickup truck, taken her on her first high-speed chase, and now a sleigh ride. "This is wonderful, Mal."

"You like it?"

"I do. I really do."

"Wanted to give you something money can't buy."

"You did." Her ex-husband, Leo, had had all the money in the world, and by comparison Mal would be considered a pauper, but Malachi July was wealthy in ways Leo knew nothing about. She looked forward to priceless moments like this until death did them part.

"Are you nervous about meeting your sister?" Lily asked Trent.

They were standing in the baggage-claim area of the airport, waiting for his mother and her family to arrive. Devon was holding up a sign he'd made, "Grandma Rita" written on it. He said he wanted her to feel like a celebrity. "In a way, yes. The last time I had a lawyer in the family, I needed another lawyer to get rid of her."

"You are so crazy."

And then there they were: his mother, her husband, and his half sister. Trent hurried to meet them.

"Trent!" Rita cried.

He swept her up.

"I'm so glad to see you!"

She embraced Lily and her grandsons next. She then introduced Paul and Val.

Trent shared a shake and a quick hug with Paul, and then with Val, who eyed him affectionately. “Glad to finally meet you, big brother.”

Any unspoken worries he might have harbored about how she’d react to him were instantly swept away. “Hey, sis. Same here.”

“So, you’re Devon,” Val said.

“Yes, ma’am.”

“Your dad sent me the video clip of your band. You all were pretty good.”

He dropped his head shyly.

“I can’t wait for you to grow up and be famous, so I can have front-row seats.” She turned to Amari. “Hello, Amari. I’m pleased to meet my nephew.”

“Glad to meet you, too. How was your flight?”

“Way too long. I was so anxious to get here and meet you. Your dad says you’re into cars.”

“I am.”

“So is your grandfather, Paul. Maybe next summer you can fly out and see a NASCAR race with him.”

Trent thought Amari was going to fall over. The stunned kid looked from his aunt to his grandfather and asked, “NASCAR? As in, *NASCAR*?”

Paul chuckled. “I can’t get your grandmother or your aunt Val to roll with me, so I’m looking forward to having a buddy.”

Amari turned to Trent, and then back to Paul. He appeared speechless.

Lily asked, "Shall we keep your grandfather, Amari?"

"Hell—I mean heck, yeah!"

As they all laughed, Trent said, "Let's find your luggage and move this love fest to the house."

They'd just loaded the bags and themselves into Lily's SUV when Trent's phone sounded. It was a text from his cousin Griffin: *Call me later when you get a minute*. Trent paused, feeling a sense of foreboding, but told himself it was just his imagination. He made a mental note to touch base with Griff that evening. At the moment, he wanted nothing more than to celebrate being reunited with his mother. Everything else would have to wait.

The two families spent the afternoon eating, opening gifts, and having a good time. Trent knew he was grinning like an idiot, but he didn't care. Each time he glanced Rita Lynn's way, he found her watching him as if to make sure he hadn't disappeared, and he felt the same way.

Mal stopped by to meet Paul and Val. He only stayed a short while, after which he left with a wave on his way next door to Bernadine's.

That evening they had dinner at Tamar's, and after returning home, Trent remembered he was supposed to call Griffin. His cousin picked up right away. They spoke of general things first, like how Thad and the Oklahoma July clan were faring and how much Amari loved the bow-and-arrow set Griff sent him for Christmas. "So were you just checking in, or is something on your mind?" Trent asked, finally.

"Yes on both, but the latter involves you and our son."

Trent tensed. "Meaning?"

"I've been contacted by Melody's husband. He wants to meet Amari."

Trent didn't know what to say. Melody was Amari's biological mother.

"You still there, cousin?"

"I am. Just trying to figure out my response."

"I had the same reaction, especially when he admitted that he was the one initiating contact, not his wife."

"What?"

"Yeah. I asked him if she knew he was reaching out. He said yes."

"Do you think he's telling the truth?"

"The man's a congressman. They always lie, especially to those of us with Native blood."

Trent reacted with a smile.

"But he's a former reverend—which may or may not be any better, considering the church's history with our people, but he sounded legit."

"So how do you want to play this? Do you want to talk to Amari about it?"

"No. Leaving this up to you. In fact, if Amari agrees to meet with him, you should be the one to go with him. You're his dad in the eyes of the law, and I'm afraid that if I go, and Melody does decide to get involved, it'll be the Thrilla in Manila revisited. Our history's pretty toxic. Amari doesn't need to be in the middle of that."

Trent agreed. He knew Griffin to be one of the saner members of the Oklahoma clan, but he'd been a habitual heartbreaker his entire life. "What's the congressman's name?"

"Ernest Carlyle."

"*The* Ernest Carlyle?"

"The one and only. How he wound up married to Melody is anyone's guess."

Carlyle had been representing his Detroit constituency for decades and was one of the higher-profile members of Congress. "Text me his number, and I'll put it in my phone. I want to talk to Amari first."

"Sounds good. And Trent, sorry to be passing the ball to you in this, but you'll be better at it than I'd be."

"Thanks . . . I think."

"Let me know what you decide to do. And if Amari wants to talk to me, he knows he's always welcome to call."

"Okay, Griff. I'll keep you in the loop."

"Appreciate it. Later."

And the connection ended.

Amari was spending the night over at the Paynes', and Devon was at the Garlands', so only the adults were in the house when he stepped back into the living room after the call. Apparently, Lily could see something wasn't quite right.

"What's wrong?" she asked.

He told her.

"Amari's been dreaming of meeting her, but this doesn't sound like a dream come true," Lily said.

"I know. I'm not sure *what* this sounds like." He was still wondering about Carlyle's motive for wanting to meet Amari.

"What kind of mother would refuse contact with her own child?" Rita asked.

Val said, "Not everyone is like you, Mom. She may have legitimate reasons for putting him up for adoption, and that has to be respected, no matter what. We don't get to pass judgment."

"I agree," Trent said, "but when that child is your own, you take a more personal view. He's hurting inside. Just like I was before you contacted me, Mom. When there are no answers, you get filled up with all kinds of doubts about your self-worth, and I hate that he's having to deal with it."

"So what do we do?" Lily asked.

"I'll talk to him when he comes home in the morning, and see how he feels."

"He's going to want to go."

"I know, Lil. I just don't want him to be hurt any more than he already has. We know he's a survivor, but he's been through so much in his life. It would be nice if he could get some type of closure."

The room quieted for a moment as they all mulled over the situation. Finally Paul said, "All we can do is hope for the best. He's blessed to have the love and strength of you and Lily behind him."

Trent said, "Thanks, Paul. I just hope it's enough."

Chapter 19

Just as Lily predicted, Amari wanted to go see Ernest Carlyle. "I want this to be over," the boy said. So now, with the aid of his phone's GPS, Trent navigated the Detroit highways, and the intricacies of them brought to mind the years he'd lived in LA. There was of course snow on the ground, like back home, but apparently there'd been no recent snowfall because the piles lining the streets were pocked with oil, dirt, and grit, reminiscent of the national media's portrayal of the once-vibrant city. Amari had grown increasingly quiet since they picked up the rental car. Trent wondered if he was thinking back to his old life, and the differences in his world now. "Anything familiar, son?"

"Not really. I know this is the west side. I lived east. Still looks the same, though. People waiting on the bus, cars rusted out from the salt. Liquor stores. Little grocery stores. Looks bleak now. Never noticed that when I lived here. Winter was always the worst time for me. No gloves. Paper coat. Always cold. Always hungry."

When Amari glanced over, his eyes held muted sadness. "I'm glad I'm not that kid anymore."

For the rest of the ride he observed the passing landscape but remained silent.

The Carlyle home was in an affluent neighborhood, with large homes and spacious snow-covered yards. The cars parked out front sparkled in the bright winter sun. Trent pulled into the driveway, as he'd been instructed to do, and cut the engine. They sat in the silence for a minute or two. "We can still turn around and go back to the airport," Trent said.

"No, we're here now. Might as well go in and see what happens."

"I got your back."

"I got yours."

They were ushered in by a woman wearing the black-and-white uniform of a maid. She led them into a quiet, book-lined room with floor-to-ceiling drapes framing the single window, in front of which stood a large, ornate desk. Carlyle entered a few minutes later. "Welcome to my home, Mr. July, Amari. I'm Congressman Ernest Carlyle."

Trent had seen Carlyle more than a few times on television. He was always dressed impeccably, and today was no exception. The hand Trent shook was firm and solid. "Pleased to meet you, Congressman."

"Call me Ernie."

"Trent."

Amari shook his hand. "Nice to meet you, sir."

Trent noted Carlyle's small show of surprise and wondered if the man hadn't expected Amari to have manners. Deciding to give him the benefit of the doubt, Trent vowed to reserve judgment until he saw how this played out.

"Please sit. Are you two hungry? Can I offer you some refreshments?"

"No thanks," Trent said, and looked to his son. "Amari?"

He shook his head. "No, thanks."

At Carlyle's invitation, Trent and Amari sat on the soft brown leather couch, but their host remained standing, leaning back against the big desk. "Thanks for coming. I know you didn't have to."

"Why are we here?"

"I wanted to meet my wife's son. I've been wondering about him for some time now."

"You aren't going to challenge my adoption, are you?" Amari asked pointedly. "Because if you do, you'll have to chain me down to keep me here. I already have a mom and dad."

Carlyle seemed amused, and said to Trent, "You and your wife must be great parents to bring out such passion."

"We do our best."

"He's a fine young man."

Trent sensed sadness in Carlyle but wondered if it was real, or if he was just imagining it.

"No, Amari," Carlyle said finally. "This visit isn't about changing your life in any way. I've been a congressman for thirty years now, but before that I was a reverend. And although I no longer have a congregation, I am still a man of God. My wife owes you the gift of seeing her face. She also owes you an explanation as to why she made the decision that she did. You must have wondered about it."

"I have, but I figured she didn't want me, so hey," he offered dismissively.

Trent's heart broke because he knew beneath that swagger was a tremendous amount of pain, having lived with the same until he and Rita Lynn found each other again.

"I have to tell you that Melody's agreed to see you only because I asked her to."

Amari shook his head. "Then I don't want to see her, if you're making her do it."

"Nobody's making me."

Trent and Amari turned at the sound of the female voice.

Melody was a beautiful woman. Tall. Skin the color of dark coffee. The snug yet tasteful fit of the charcoal-gray wool dress showed off her opulent curves. Dark hair brushed her shoulders and the makeup was perfectly applied.

"Hello, Amari."

"Uh, hi," he stammered.

Trent now knew where Amari got the curve of his lips and the cut of his nose. His son bore a strong resemblance to Griffin, but he bore an equally strong resemblance to Melody.

"I didn't want to do this meet with you, mainly because I don't like having to deal with how selfish I was back then, or to hear that I did the wrong thing in giving you up. But"—she turned to her husband—"Ernie's asked me to, and no woman should deny her husband something so simple."

Her icy cycs caused Trent to wonder if theirs was a troubled marriage, and if that might be the sourcc of Carlylc's air of sadness.

She took up a position by the drapes and looked out at the snow. "So here's the deal," she began. "I was a strippcr at a little club outside the city." She glanced back over her shoulder at Amari. "Yes, I danced around naked for money."

"I know," he replied.

"Really?"

He nodded. "Griffin told me."

"Ah, Griffin. Real stand-up guy, that one. Did he tell you we were only together about two weeks?"

"No."

"We were. I thought we were working on something permanent and good, but I woke up one morning and he was packing his things. Said he was getting restless and needed to get back on the road." She went silent, as if thinking back. Trent sensed she was harboring pain, too.

"And so he left. No forwarding address. No number. Didn't say if he was coming back. Gave me a kiss good-bye. Jumped on his bike. Gone. I was nineteen. A month later, I found out I was pregnant."

There was another silent moment. "I kept dancing, hoping no one would notice, but after a while, they did, of course. I was fired." She added sarcastically, "Nobody wants to see a pregnant stripper. Had no job, so I couldn't pay rent. Got evicted. Parents had kicked me out years before for being fast and stupid—couldn't go there. Went to stay with a girlfriend. Her man started hitting on me. She put me out. I had no place else to go. So I went home to my parents."

She chuckled bitterly. "Have to give it to them, though. They took me in even after all I'd put them through in high school. But even pregnant I was trying to run the streets. Still partied, drank, got high. Did all the things a mother-to-be shouldn't." She turned to Amari. "No health issues because of that?"

He answered softly, "No."

"Good. I didn't want a baby. I saw the awful lives some of my friends had because they'd gotten pregnant too early, and I didn't want to be them. They all looked tired, unhappy. Only a couple of their boyfriends stayed around after the babies were born. They were struggling. Living on welfare. Houses filled with roaches. I wanted to be able to go to the club when I wanted to and not have to worry about babysitters or any of the other stuff tied to kids. Shots, diapers, ear infections."

"So you gave me to the state."

"I did. You would've had a real bad time had I kept you. I went back to dancing. Living here and there. Always broke. Taking the bus. Hoping to find a man to take care of me. Kissed a lot of frogs back then."

"And I went into foster care, living here and there with people who got paid to beat me up, starve me, and treat me like shit. I slept on pissy mattresses and lived with crackheads. Never went to the same school twice, which meant I couldn't read. Teachers didn't care. Most of the foster parents didn't, either. So to give myself something to do, I started stealing cars."

She turned, surprise on her face. "Wait. When were you adopted?"

"Two years ago. I was in the system until I was eleven."

Her mouth dropped. Her eyes swung to Trent, who nodded to corroborate Amari's story.

Amari continued, "So, in the words of Langston Hughes, my life ain't been no crystal stair, either."

His words were flippant, defiant, and so on

point, Trent wanted to give him a high five. He saw Ernie's lips curve with a small, satisfied-looking smile.

She looked him up and down. "When Griffin showed up at my door, asking if I'd had his child, I assumed you'd been adopted as a baby."

"No."

"Wow," she uttered softly, and turned back to the view outside. "But you're doing okay now."

"I am."

"Good." She turned to her husband. "Anything else?"

His jaw tightened, and he shook his head.

"Nice meeting you, Amari. Have a good life."

And she walked out of the room.

In the silence following her exit, Carlyle said, "Amari, I'd like to stay in touch with you. Melody and I don't have any children. If you'd care to come and spend some time with us during the summers, I'm sure she'll relent at some point."

Amari didn't even pause to consider the offer. "No. I'm sorry you don't have any kids, sir, but she doesn't want me around and I spent the whole first part of my life with people who didn't. I'm not doing that again. It was nice meeting you."

Riding in the car back to the airport, Trent didn't press him to talk but let him have his peace. It had to have been difficult for him because the way Melody sauntered out of the room had been difficult for Trent.

When Amari finally did speak, he asked, "Do you think he wanted me to be his kid?"

"Maybe."

"Neither one of them looked happy."

"No, they didn't."

"Was it okay for me to tell him what I did?"

"The truth is always right, no matter what."

"Good. If had to visit him, I'd go back to stealing cars."

The light went red, so he stopped and asked, "Is there anyone here you'd like to see?"

"No, Dad. I just want to go home."

"Okay."

When the light turned green, he drove on.

It was late when they finally got home. Everyone was gathered in the living room watching the television and apparently waiting for their return, but Amari just said good night and went up to his room, leaving his dad to give them the details of the awful trip. Up in his room, he wiped at his tears he'd refused to let flow until then and put on his pajamas. A soft knock on the door made him hastily dash away the water. "Just a minute." Seeing his red eyes in his mirror made him wish he could make the traces of tears somehow disappear, but since he couldn't, he called out, "Come in."

It was his mom. "Hey, baby."

"Hey, Mom."

"Just came up to check on you. Dad said it was pretty rough."

"She was a bitch."

"I'm sorry."

He could feel the emotions rising, and he didn't want to cry, but he really did. And because Ms. Lily was so awesome, she already knew what was going on inside of him and just opened her arms.

He practically ran to her, and she held him tight and he held her tight and sobbed out his heartache. "I love you so," she whispered. "So much."

"It was terrible."

"I know, baby. I know."

"I wanted her to like me. I wanted . . ." He heard his pain echoing in the room, and he didn't care because he was safe with this woman whom his dad loved. Since the day they met, she'd been in his corner, offering unconditional solace, care, and understanding. Melody might have brought him into the world, but Lily Fontaine July was his mom, and as her tears mingled with his, he was so glad she loved him, too.

He finally eased back and ran his palms over his wet cheeks. A silly thought came to him. When had he grown taller than her? "Since when did you get so short?"

She brushed the tears from her own cheeks. "Smartass."

He grew serious, and their gazes held. "Thank you."

She whispered, "You're welcome. Dads are good for some stuff, but sometimes a boy just needs his mom."

The truth in that curved his lips into a small smile.

"I'm always here for you, Amari. Always. Okay?"

He nodded and gave her another fierce hug. The hurt of the visit was still raw, but his true mom, this mom of his heart, had dulled it a great deal.

"Are you going to be okay?"

"Eventually, yeah."

She cupped his cheek lovingly. "Then I'll see you in the morning. Don't stay up too late."

"I won't. Good night, Mom. Thanks again."

She shot him a wink, and he watched her go. His door closed quietly.

The next morning, Rita approached Trent for a favor. Lily, Val, and the boys were at the ice rink, taking advantage of the new skates Rita had given them all as gifts. Paul had gone along to drink hot chocolate. Having been born and raised on the island of Kauai in Hawaii, he didn't know how to skate, and had no interest in learning.

"I want to talk to Marie," Rita told her son.

Trent paused. "Are you sure?"

She nodded. "We need to get past this and move on."

So they drove there. Trent saw Marie's truck parked outside. "Looks like she's home."

Rita climbed the stairs. Marie opened the door to her knock, took one look at her, sneered, and closed the door in her face.

Back in the car, Rita said, "Well, that was fun."

But Trent saw how deflated she looked. And at that moment, his respect for Marie was gone, and his feelings for her were forever changed.

Chapter 20

Instead of being at home, packing for her getaway to Key West with Mal, Bernadine sat fuming in Judge Amy Davis's courtroom. Judge Davis didn't appear any happier, but Bernadine considered that small consolation. The matter before the bench had to do with Astrid wanting Tommy Stewart to be charged with breaking and entering and assault, but Steve Tuller—who she was surprised to see representing Tommy—wanted Astrid charged with false imprisonment and a laundry list of other charges tied to her allegedly drugging the young man and holding him hostage in a basement room of her house for almost a month. And since the local prosecutor had her hands full trying to figure out who should rightly be on trial, Judge Davis was trying to sort it out. It was a mess.

Astrid, who had more hubris than anyone

around, was representing herself. She seemed to believe the law should be what she said it was. According to Bernadine's lawyer, James Edison, who was seated beside her now, Astrid had tried to get the case tried in Topeka, which had of course been nixed by the judge on the grounds that the alleged crimes happened locally and thus would be tried in her court. Astrid was still mad, and to prove it, she continued to argue with Judge Davis about the jurisdiction issue.

"I still think that if I filed the charges in Topeka, we should be in Topeka."

"Ms. Wiggins, the matter is settled. Let's move on."

Bernadine saw Steve Tuller shake his head at Astrid's continued cluelessness.

"Ms. Wiggins," said Judge Davis, "please present whatever evidence you may have so I can make an intelligent determination on who's being charged with what here."

Jim Edison, seated next to Bernadine, said, "I have never seen anything like this. I don't even know what you'd call this. It's certainly not a pre-trial hearing. I don't even know if this proceeding is legal."

Bernadine didn't care what it was called, as long as someone threw Astrid in jail and she could hop on her jet and fly to Key West.

"Mr. Stewart broke into my home and assaulted me."

"Was anything stolen?"

"Yes, some jewelry."

Tommy jumped up. "She's lying! I didn't steal anything from you, and you know it!"

The judge banged her gavel. "Mr. Stewart. Your attorney will have a turn in a moment. Please continue, Ms. Wiggins."

"He took my watch, which was on the wrist that he broke with the bat he used in the assault." She held up the cast on her arm.

Tommy would've jumped to his feet again were it not for the firm hand Steve Tuller placed on his shoulders.

"Did you know Mr. Stewart prior to the break-in?"

"He worked at the gas station my family owns, but I've only seen him in passing. We've never had any significant interactions."

Bernadine's jaw dropped at the woman's ballsy lie.

Judge Davis eyed Astrid silently for a moment. "Ms. Wiggins, I strongly encourage you to rethink your position on representing yourself."

"I know what I'm doing," Astrid snapped.

"Okay. Do you have any more evidence to put Mr. Stewart at the scene of this alleged crime?"

"No, just my side of the story. Which, with my family's standing in the community, has much more weight than the story of someone who grew up in a trailer park." Her contempt was plain.

"We're all equal under the law in this country, Ms. Wiggins."

"Whatever. I want him charged."

Judge Davis showed a small, cold smile and looked to Steve Tuller. "What do you have for me, Mr. Tuller?"

"Affidavits from the police, saying they found no evidence of a break-in."

"Because I was foolish enough to answer the door when he knocked, and he pushed his way in," Astrid broke in. "That's why there's no evidence."

Steve Tuller kept talking. "Affidavits from the doctors on Mr. Stewart's condition after his escape. Toxicology reports showing traces of a drug in his system consistent with Mr. Stewart's claims of being rendered unconscious. I've also asked Ms. Brown to offer her testimony on Mr. Stewart's appearance when he showed up in her office on the day of his escape."

"And I object to her even being here," snapped Astrid. "Everyone knows she lies."

Judge Davis employed her gavel, snarling, "That's enough, Ms. Wiggins."

Astrid didn't looked cowed.

"Anything else?"

"You have Mr. Stewart's account in your packet," Tuller informed the judge.

"Thank you. Now, what about this pipe he mentions? Did the police find it?"

"No, Your Honor, but—"

Astrid cut him off. "Because there wasn't one. He took the bat with him when he ran out. Probably tossed it somewhere."

"—but, as I was saying," Tuller went on, "we do have it."

Astrid stared with wide eyes.

"And we have Ms. Wiggins on video, tossing the bag it was found in out of the window of her Cadillac while being driven by Mr. Meryl Wingo to Topeka. Inside were also about twenty-five bags from one of the nearby fast food places. The police are testing the pipe for prints, and the fast food remnants for DNA."

"And you obtained this how?"

"Mr. Stewart's mother hired a private investigator, Sandra Langster, to look into his disappearance. Ms. Langster had Ms. Wiggins under surveillance at her home when she noticed Mr. Stewart coming out through the front door and running toward town. Mr. Wingo arrived at the home shortly after Mr. Stewart's departure. Also on video."

"I object!"

"To what?"

"All of it!"

Judge Davis ignored Astrid. "Do you have anything to say about all this?" she asked the county prosecutor.

The prosecutor stood. "Yes. Based on what we've just heard, my office will be looking at the evidence with the intent of seeking a warrant for Ms. Wiggins's arrest."

"No, you will not!" Astrid screamed angrily. "Do you know who my family is?"

A frail female voice said loud and clear, "Yes, I do, and on behalf of that family, once the prosecutor files her charges, I'll be suing you for embezzlement, forgery, and anything else I can make stick!"

Everyone turned to see an elderly lady wearing a silver mink coat enter the courtroom with the aid of a walker, escorted by three well-dressed young men who looked like high-powered lawyers.

"Who are you?" asked a confused Judge Davis.

"Mabel Franklin Lane. Astrid's grandmother."

Later in her office, having said good-bye to Jim Edison, Bernadine was on the phone with her pilot, Katie Sky, nailing down their flight itinerary for the next day, when Mabel Lane appeared in the doorway.

"Katie. I'll call you back." Bernadine put down her phone. "Come in, Ms. Lane. How might I help you?"

"Do you have a minute for an old lady?" The twinkle in her pale blue eyes filled Bernadine with amusement.

"Yes, ma'am. For you, I have all day." Bernadine would never forget the look on

Astrid's face when Mabel announced what she had in store. Now she watched as the old lady made herself comfortable, her team of lawyers helping her with her coat and walker.

"I'm so pleased to finally meet you," Mabel said. "Tamar has had nothing but great things to say about you and what you've done for Henry Adams."

She saw the surprise on Bernadine's face. "Tammy and I grew up together. Not many people have a friendship that goes back over eighty years. Of course, the world was segregated back then, but her parents didn't care, and neither did mine. In those days we were all just trying to survive out here on the plains."

"Tamar never mentioned knowing you."

"She always was one to keep her own counsel. It's one of the things I like most about her, but she's been keeping me abreast of the madness Astrid's been causing. On behalf of what's left of the family, my sincerest apologies. I have other grandchildren in Franklin, but of course none of them have wanted to stand up to her because she's a bitch. But I'm a bigger bitch, as she will soon learn."

Bernadine decided she really liked this lady.

"Unfortunately, Astrid is very much like my late husband. He too was filled with greed and hate. Met him at a barn dance. Handsomest man this little country girl had ever seen. Called myself falling in love, and didn't know who he really was until two days before the wedding, when he bragged about burning a cross in front of Cephas Patterson's place."

Bernadine went still.

"Yes, *that* Cephas Patterson. Tammy told me about the gold. Heard he left it to a little girl in your town."

"Yes, he did."

"Also heard Astrid was so fit to be tied, she wound up being the source of a lot of damage here. My apologies on that, too. Now, where was I? Oh, yes, my husband, Walter. No way was I calling off the wedding, not after all the money my parents spent. I give a high five to the young women of today who have the balls to call off their weddings because the guy is an asshat or a philanderer. We didn't do that back in my time. We bit the bullet, walked down the aisle, and cried ourselves to sleep on our wedding night. Society said you had to have a husband, even if he was a cheating, cross-burning, money-grubbing one like mine. Be glad you weren't alive back then."

"I am."

"But"—Mabel pointed a gnarled finger tipped with navy blue polish—"I was the balance for all his hate. Every time he and his yahoo friends burned a cross or harassed a colored family, I wrote a check to Tammy's church or to the

NAACP in Washington. Made him furious. There was nothing he could do to stop me, though. The money in his pockets came out of my trust fund, and my daddy had been wise enough to leave everything in my name so the Franklin family wouldn't lose control of the land."

"Smart man."

"Not smart enough to tell me not to marry Walter, though."

Mabel and Tamar together had to be something to behold, thought Bernadine. "So are you really going to sue your granddaughter?"

"You bet. Do you know she tried to have me declared incompetent this past summer? Talk about fit to be tied. Lawyers took care of that, though. She was trying to get her hands on the Franklin trust so she could keep buying Cadillacs and playing footsie with Meryl Wingo. The other grandkids had been complaining about how she was treating them. I knew Astrid could be a pain in the butt—she'd been that way all her life—but I figured the kids would work it out. But when Austin ran away with his little chippy and outed her the way he did, I believe she went around the bend for real."

Bernadine told Mabel about the meeting with Mr. Proctor and the businessmen.

"I heard about that, too. I'll be meeting with them later to get things stabilized as much as we can. Pump a bit of the trust's funds into the city treasury, and maybe appoint Lyman as the city manager."

"I think that would be a great idea."

Mabel smiled. "I've taken up enough of your time. Going to head over to Franklin now. You know things are bad when a ninety-two-year-old lady has to fly in and sweep up. Been real nice meeting you, Ms. Brown."

"It's been an honor and a privilege to meet you as well."

"Thank you. Now you go on home and get packed, so you can fly to Key West and have a good time with my godson."

Bernadine blinked.

"Who said there are no secrets in a small town?"

And with that, Mabel, her walker, and her minions left the still stunned and laughing Bernadine to return to her afternoon.

She wasn't alone for long, though. Her next visitor was Sheila Payne. "I heard there were quite the fireworks at Judge Amy's courtroom," she said upon entering and taking a seat.

"You heard right. I think Astrid's going to be too busy trying to stay out of jail to give anyone any more trouble."

"We can only hope."

"What can I help our VP of social affairs with today, or are you here as Sheila?"

"I am here in my official capacity. It's about Kelly and Bobby's wedding. I know you'll be funning and sunning in Key West and won't be here, but do you think we can spring for bus tickets for their moms to attend the ceremony?"

"Sure. Just talk to Lily."

"Okay. Are we giving them a gift from the town?"

"I think we've given them everything but seahorses already, Sheila. Did you have something specific in mind?"

"Not really. I just want to make sure I have everything tied up before you and Mal take off. I don't want to be bothering you while you're away."

"Thanks for that—I'd appreciate it if no one bothered us while we're away. If anything comes up that needs official attention, bug Trent."

"Gotcha. When are you leaving?"

"First thing in the morning."

"Have fun, get some rest, and enjoy."

"That's the plan."

"The world will be here when you get back."

"Thanks, Sheila."

As Sheila left, she passed the attorney Steve Tuller coming in. Bernadine sighed inwardly at the seemingly revolving door. *Tomorrow morning can't get here fast enough.* "Mr. Tuller. How may I help you?"

"Just stopped in to say thank you for making yourself available this morning, even though we didn't need you in the end."

"No problem. I was surprised to see you representing Tommy after the mess last time."

"Last time, between you and me, Astrid did indeed hire my firm to represent him. We'd done work for her grandmother, Ms. Mabel, in the past, and were under the impression that he had a legitimate claim against your store."

"Only to learn . . ."

He nodded tersely. "My partners and I weren't pleased, and neither was Ms. Mabel. She was furious to find out we'd been so ill used, as she put it. When Tommy's mom contacted me to let me know he was missing, I called Ms. Mabel. She was convinced Astrid was involved, and asked that I keep her in the loop—if and when he turned up, she wanted him to add his story about the roaches to the case she was building against Astrid."

"So you're representing her interests by being Tommy's lawyer."

"Yes."

Bernadine had a question. "Let's say Astrid is found guilty in Tommy's case against her. Will she do any time?"

"Probably not. More than likely it'll be a slap on the wrist and probation. However, the civil suit being brought against her by the family is another matter. Ms. Mabel has cut her out of the trust, which means she no longer has access to any of the town's funds—which she was helping herself to illegally—and she'll have to find somewhere else to stay. The house belongs to Ms. Mabel, and eviction proceedings have already begun. Astrid's going to need a lawyer to deal with all this. I hope she figures out a way to pay one."

Bernadine thought about the nasty way she'd evicted the Acostas. Karma's only a bitch if you are.

"Are you going forward with your civil suit?" Tuller asked.

"I'll get with my legal people and see what they advise, but sounds to me like there won't be anything left but the bones once the family gets done with her."

"Who knows, maybe she'll have to live in a trailer park. As a person who lived with my mother in a park as a child, I was pretty offended by her remarks in court today."

"I didn't grow up in one, but I was offended with you."

Tuller inclined his head. "Great doing business with you, Ms. Brown."

"Same here."

"Enjoy Key West."

"Thanks."

He made his exit, and she wondered if there was anyone on the planet that didn't know her plans for Key West. Oh, the joys of small-town living.

Chapter 21

When Bobby came home from work, Kiki was on the phone. From the sound of her side of the conversation, she had to be talking to her mother.

"Mama, if you don't want to come to our wedding, then don't. I was just trying to see if you wanted the bus ticket so you'd have a way to get here if you did." She glanced Bobby's way and rolled her eyes.

Bobby didn't like the judgmental, holier-than-thou Estelle Page, and the feeling was mutual. She'd never forgive him for what she termed "filling her daughter with the devil," and she'd never forgiven Kiki for being with him. As far as he knew, she hadn't seen the twins since the day they were born. She'd pledged never to allow Kiki in her home again as long as she stayed with him. He hoped she was ready to remain on her high horse for the rest of her life.

"No, Mama, we're not living in the van. The babies are fine, and no, the people here aren't running a cult. Yes. I understand you want to see them, but you can see them when you come to the wedding. No, I'm not moving back to Dallas without Bobby. How many times— Mama?" Kiki looked at the phone. "She hung up on me!"

"Your mama is crazy."

"She thinks we're living in a cult."

"Crazy."

Kiki dropped down onto the couch. "I really wish she'd lighten up. The twins are her grandbabies. She should be in their lives."

Bobby thought his kids could do very well without someone who saw the devil everywhere, but he kept that thought to himself. Crazy or not, she was still Kiki's mom.

"The babies are penned up, watching a video."

"I'm going to go say hi. Be right back."

"Leave them in jail, Bobby. They wore me out today. Baby Bob has been throwing up all day. He's settled down now, and I just want to catch my breath."

He found them inside the large playpen. At the sight of him they started chattering and crawled to the edge. Tiara pulled herself up along the side. Holding on with one hand, she raised the other one to be picked up. "You two been whipping on your mom today?"

He picked Tiara up and gave her a kiss. Bobby Jr. began crying, so he leaned down and picked him up, too. "I hear you're not feeling so hot, buddy." He kissed him and then set them both down. Bobby Jr. began wailing instantly, and that set off his sister.

"Bobby!" Kiki yelled from the front room.

"I just picked them up to say hello," he shot back.

She appeared in the doorway. "What part of leave them in jail did you not get?"

He turned, studied her, and stopped short at the sight of the tears in her eyes. Instead of snapping back in reply, he walked over and took her in his arms. "Rough day?"

"Yes," she whispered. "They didn't want to eat, or take a nap. If Bobby Jr.'s got the crud, that means his sister will have it too, soon, and they'll both be throwing up and crying and cranky."

He kissed her forehead. "Did you call Doc Reg?"

"Yes. He's on the road. He said he'd stop by this evening. I don't feel good, either. We're getting married in three days. My mama is Looney Tunes and thinks these wonderful people here are a cult."

Behind him the babies were screaming. For the moment he did his best to ignore them.

"Tell you what," he said softly. "What do you want to do this evening?"

"Run away."

"Not on the menu."

"You sure?"

"Positive."

"Okay, then how about a nice long soak in the tub and then read for a couple of hours."

"That's allowed. I'll take the evening shift with Monsters Inc., and you just chill."

"I haven't had a chance to cook dinner."

"I'll take care of dinner."

"You can't cook, Bobby."

"So me and the kids will eat Wheaties. Don't worry about that. Just go and get in the tub. Grab a book and consider yourself off duty."

She raised her eyes to his. "I love you."

"I love you too, my soon-to-be wifey. Now scat." He kissed her, and once she was gone, he turned to his screaming children. "All right. Daddy's here. Who wants to play poker?"

As he'd promised, Reggie Garland came by later that evening and checked out Baby Bob, as he was now being called. Reg thought he had a touch of a twenty-four-hour stomach virus and offered the parents some suggestions on how to make their son comfortable while the bug ran its course. He agreed that Tiara would probably come down with the same thing shortly, so they should be ready. They thanked him, and when he left, Kiki said, "You have to love a town where your neighbor is also your pediatrician, and he makes house calls."

Bobby cracked, "That's how cults roll."

The Douglases were awakened by a pounding on their door. Bobby, who'd been up all night with his sick son, stumbled to the door and opened it to find Estelle Page standing on the steps.

"Where's my daughter?" she demanded.

"Good morning to you, too, Ms. Page. Do you want to come in?"

She pushed past him and, once inside, stopped and stared around at the place. Bobby cracked, "Nice place, huh? While you pick your mouth up off the floor, I'll get Kiki."

He didn't need to, though. She came out of the back, carrying Tiara. "Mama! What are you doing here?"

"I came to try and talk some sense into you one last time."

"How'd you get here?"

"Pastor Garner drove."

Kiki sighed audibly. "Where's he now?"

"Out in the car."

"Go get him, and you can join us for breakfast. Bobby has to leave for work in about an hour."

Bobby could see Estelle eyeing the baby but pretending not to be interested. "I'm going to get washed up," he said. "Will you be okay?"

"Yes. You go and get together. Breakfast will be up in a few."

He raced through his morning routine so as not to leave Kiki alone too long. When he returned, a short older man wearing glasses was seated in the living room. "You must be Bobby," he said.

"I am. And are you Pastor Garner?"

"I am."

"Nice to meet you."

"Same here."

Bobby thought the man seemed pleasant enough.

"Nice place you have here."

"We like it."

"How much is the rent?" asked Estelle.

Kiki said, "We have the place for free right now."

Her mother stared. "Free?"

"Yes. Bobby, food's ready, baby. Pastor Garner, do you want to join us?"

"Yes. I'd like that. Thank you." He sat and said, "Let's say grace."

After the short prayer, Estelle said smugly, "I'll bet this is the first time that's been said here."

Bobby raised his gaze to Kiki.

"No, Mama, it's not. Reverend Paula lives in one of the other trailers, and when she comes over to have lunch with me, we always say grace."

"Who's Reverend Paula?" Estelle asked.

"The priest who baptized the kids on Christmas Eve."

That appeared to catch both visitors by surprise, but only Pastor Garner said, "My congratulations."

"Thank you."

But Estelle was not to be denied. "So tell me about this cult."

A knock on the door interrupted them. Bobby went to answer it. It was Tamar.

"Saw a strange car outside. Just wanted to stop by and make sure you kids were okay."

"We are. Kiki's mom is here."

"Wonderful. May I meet her?"

"Yes, ma'am." Bobby was pretty sure Tamar would take care of the cult nonsense once and for all.

She entered the kitchen, and Kiki made the introductions.

"Welcome to Henry Adams," Tamar said. "I'm Tamar July."

Estelle looked her up and down disapprovingly. "I'm Estelle Page. Are you one of the cult members?"

Tamar stopped. She looked at Kiki, then at Bobby, and lastly at Pastor Garner. "I'm assuming you're her doctor, and she's under your care?"

Bobby snorted. Kiki kept her head down to hide her smile.

Garner was smiling as well as he stood. "I'm Pastor William Garner. I'm very pleased to meet you."

"Same here. Did she really ask if I was a cult member, Bobby?"

"Yes, ma'am."

"Olivia and I were on the way to the rec, but I think I need to take off my coat and sit for a few."

"You know you're welcome, Tamar," Kiki said. "Would you like some coffee?"

"Please."

Kiki returned with a mug of the brew, black. "Here you go."

"Thanks, doll. Now, Ms. Page, let's begin again. Explain the cult remark, please."

"My daughter has obviously been brainwashed by the people who live here. She said she was given this place for free. No one does that without wanting something in return. Running drugs is my guess, since *he* knows all about that."

Tamar glanced Bobby's way. "Is she talking about you?"

"Yes, ma'am."

She offered him a pat on his hand before settling her fierce hawklike gaze on Estelle again. "How do you brainwash someone? Is there a special soap or detergent that you use?"

Garner was viewing the interplay with muted amusement. Bobby wondered just what role the man had come to play.

"How dare you patronize me."

"Be glad that's all I'm doing. My shotgun's in the truck. My ancestors gave their lives to found this town. How dare you demean the blood they shed and the sacrifices they made with your narrow-mindedness? Do you know anything about what the race endured to escape the butchery in the south after Reconstruction failed? Do you?"

Estelle jumped. She looked terrified, and Bobby wanted to cheer.

"There are no cults here. Just a town filled with people who heard how hard Bobby and Kelly were struggling and extended a hand. Yes, they live here, rent-free. They have a nice car, too. When was the last time you went out of your way to help someone change their life?"

Estelle looked decidedly uncomfortable.

"How long has the town existed, Ms. July?" asked the pastor.

"Since its founding in 1879."

He sat back with surprise. "My lord. That's remarkable. Where is it?"

Tamar supplied the answer.

"May Estelle and I accompany you into town, if it's not too much to ask?"

"I'd love to show you around."

Bobby Jr.'s cries announced he was awake, so Bobby went to get him. After changing his diaper, he brought him out and gently handed him to Estelle. "Say good morning to your grand-mother."

Estelle's eyes rounded, and she looked up at him in shock. He ignored her and leaned down to place a kiss on Kiki's cheek. "Going to work. I'll call you later."

Tiara threw her arms up. He lifted her and held her up over his head. Her giggles warmed his heart. He gave her a kiss, too. "Be nice to your mama today, missy, or we won't play poker tonight."

Handing her back, he nodded at the visitors and at Tamar. "You all have a good day."

A short while later, Estelle and Pastor Garner squeezed into Olivia with Tamar. When they returned two hours later, Estelle said to Kiki, "I need to ask your forgiveness."

Kiki glanced at Tamar. Pastor Garner looked pleased.

Estelle continued, "Pastor Garner came with me because he said he knew God had blessed you via the people here, but I didn't believe him. In truth, I chose not to believe him because I didn't want to admit I was wrong. But I *was* wrong. Everyone I talked to spoke so highly of Bobby."

"He's a good man, Mama. Yes, he got off track there for a while, but he's always had a good heart. Otherwise I wouldn't have had his babies, or still be with him."

Estelle began to cry. "I so want to be in the lives of my grandchildren."

"There's nothing stopping you. In fact, Tamar, can my mama stay with you until after the wedding?"

Estelle looked up, surprised.

"Sure," Tamar replied.

"The whole town is invited, so do you want

to be the mother of the bride and give me away?"

Estelle dropped onto the sofa and wept.

Kiki said to Baby Bob, "I think that's a yes."

On New Year's Day, Bobby watched his mother-in-law escort his bride down the aisle while Roni played Mendelssohn's "Wedding March." The church was packed. Much to his delight, his mother had come too, and was seated in the front pew, holding the nattily dressed twins on her lap. He doubted he and Estelle would ever be best buds, but she would always be welcome in his home. Beside him stood his best man and, yes, friend, Trent July. No other man meant as much as the mayor to him. With his guidance and support, Bobby was looking forward to having an awe-some life. In the last month he'd gone from a lowly valet who mattered to no one to a well-thought-of and respected member of a community he hadn't even known existed until Crystal showed up at their door last fall. Crystal stood across from him with tears in her eyes while she waited on her BFF to reach them. She too had been changed by this place, and he couldn't wait to see what the future held.

When Kiki reached him, the love in her eyes made him weak. They joined hands, and Reverend Paula began reading the words that would bind them together until death did them part.

• • •

The next day, Trent, Lily, and their sons took his mother and her family back to the airport. They'd had a fabulous time, and now it was time to part. He shared a strong hug with Paul and Val and then his mother. He looked down into Rita Lynn's eyes. "Thank you again for your courage."

She smiled. "We have a lot of years ahead of us, Trenton, Lord willing. You're stuck with me, whether you like it or not."

"And you're stuck with me."

She kissed Lily and then her grandsons. "Don't forget you're coming out for Easter."

"Can't wait," Amari told her. "Aunt Val's going to teach me how to surf."

Val nodded.

Devon asked, "Is it okay if I Skype you, Gramma Rita?"

"Of course."

He grinned.

She gave Trent one final hug. "Take care, my son, and take care of your wonderful family."

"You, take care of yourself, too," he whispered. And with a full heart, he watched her walk away and head to the gate.

Amari asked, "You okay, Dad?"

"Yeah, son. Your old man is okay. Let's go home." He took Lily's hand and they all headed to the doors.

And on the drive back, he thought about all that had happened in the last two weeks, and how incredibly grateful and blessed he was.

Down on the beach in Key West, Malachi and Bernadine clinked their glasses in a toast. "To love," she said.

"And happiness. Sounds like a segue to Al Green. Do we have to go back?"

She chuckled. "Eventually. Somebody has to turn the world, I suppose."

Mal sipped his drink and watched the sunset. "I suppose. Can't be me, though. I'd get fed up, the world would stop, and we'd all be thrown into space."

She laughed. "Can't have that, but how about we stay another week?"

"I vote yes."

So they stayed another week to continue enjoying each other, the sunrises and sunsets, and being in love.

Acknowledgments

Dear Readers,

This has to be the most emotional trip to Henry Adams so far. We have my editor, Erika Tsang, to thank for her excellent suggestions on improving the first draft, which led to this excellent installment—and the use of many tissues to staunch the tears. Also, thanks to you, my readers, for the continuous outpouring of love for our favorite small town via your e-mails, letters, and posts to my Facebook page. You've told your family, friends, neighbors, church members, and every-one else on the planet about the Blessings series– or so it seems—and I'm extremely grateful. May you all be Blessed.

Until next time.

B

Center Point Large Print
600 Brooks Road / PO Box 1
Thorndike, ME 04986-0001 USA

(207) 568-3717

US & Canada:
1 800 929-9108
www.centerpointlargeprint.com